Breath of Life

Also by Faith Baldwin
in Large Print:

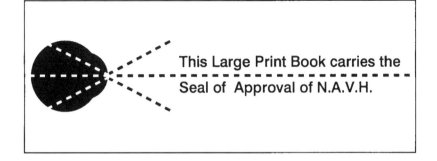

Breath of Life

FAITH BALDWIN

G.K. Hall & Co.
Thorndike, Maine

Published in 1997 by arrangement with
Harold Ober Associates Incorporated.

G.K. Hall Large Print Romance Collection.

The text of this Large Print edition is unabridged.
Other aspects of the book may vary from the original edition.

Set in 16 pt. Plantin by Minnie B. Raven.

Printed in the United States on permanent paper.

Library of Congress Cataloging in Publication Data.

Baldwin, Faith, 1893–
    Breath of life / by Faith Baldwin.
        p.   cm.
    ISBN 0-7838-8258-0 (lg. print : hc : alk. paper)
    1. Large type books.   I. Title.
[PS3505.U97B7   1997]
    813′.52—dc21   97-24790

The Breath of Life

The Breath of Life is Love; the new born flesh
Is animate and sentient, grows aware
Of hunger and of pain, of cold and heat,
Of light and dark, and, very soon, of fear;
Primal and groping, growing into strength
And equal weakness; never once to lose
The first compulsions, ancient as the stars.
How less predictable the spirit is,
Rooted in flesh yet aspirant to heaven,
Breathed into being by love's very breath,
The final gift, the naked, lonely soul,
Tragic and dual, huntsman and pursued.
The body weeps, hot tears are shed; they dry,
Laughter's forgotten, bones are brittle stuff,
The swift pulse lags, and, hourly, the heart
Grows quieter, and, ultimately, still.
Eased of its burden of delight and pain,
Once so intolerable.
                              The womb is dark,
A harboring place, for such a little while,
The earth's dark harbor too; it is forever —
So we are born, so die and so it ends,
The sweat and blood, the harsh deliverance,
The end as the beginning:
                              But the soul
The Breath of Life goes free, superbly one
With love, by love created and possessed
Five times forever and invulnerable.

Chapter 1

The old car rattled along the winding country road which followed the wide blue ribbon of the river. Summer lay like a drowsy enchantment over the north country, the car jerked and jarred in the ruts, bending branches whipped against the windows, dust rose like smoke. Now and then a restless bird flew across the road, a robin, his bright breast beginning to fade, an oriole, like a flame with wings.

On the right, farmhouses dreamed in the sun, old dogs lay supine under the shadow of trees or slept uneasily on doorsteps. In the fields the cows stood idle or lay in the shade, switching their tails, their large eyes, innocent of wisdom, contemplating the universe without rancor or delight. Young men, stripped to the waist, brown and lean, worked in the fields, children played, calling to one another, hens clucked uneasily, and the bright, burning sun beat down from a flawless sky, piled on the horizon with great, white, woolly clouds.

There were boats on the river, men fishing offshore, imaged in the still water, young people swimming, shouting at one another.

The two men in the old car had not spoken for almost a mile. Now the younger roused to comment briefly.

"It doesn't change," he said.

"Nope," agreed the other, "it don't. Same story, year in, year out. Hard long winters — this year the ice didn't start to go out till late April — and hot summers. We need rain." He spat out the window onto the road. "Your father used to say that no farmer ever lived that was content. Too much rain, or too little. How long since you been here, Ron? I don't remember."

Dr. Theron Lewis frowned, his dark brows drawn over his bright blue eyes. He answered, after a moment:

"Three — no, two years ago — right after I finished interning — just for a few days, when Mamie had pneumonia, remember?"

"That's right," said the man at the wheel. "Never thought she'd pull through. She was sickly all that year after your dad died. But Doc Barton was on the job night and day . . . You'll be seein' him, I expect . . . I met him in town last week and he asked me when you was expected, said he couldn't hardly wait."

"Good old Doc," said Lewis, smiling. He thought, I owe him so damned much.

Unpardonable, how life caught up with you, how you neglected people to whom you owed both your past and your future. I don't take the time to write Doc twice a year, he thought uncomfortably, and I'm not much better when it comes to writing Mamie.

"Doc's getting along," said his companion, "must be over seventy . . . let's see, seventy-one perhaps. He's a year or so older than me. You remember Jenny, don't you, Ron?"

"Jenny?"

"Doc's granddaughter. No, I don't suppose you do, she's a lot younger. How old are you anyway?"

"Thirty-two."

"Don't seem possible. Well, Jenny's twenty-one or -two, I guess. Her father was Doc's oldest son — Pete Barton . . . he married Ellie Norris. Lord, Ron, you went to school with her, didn't you? And they moved downstate. Pete wasn't never much good. Kept the old man hopping, keeping him out of trouble. While you was away Pete moved back here, and got himself killed in an auto smash. Ellie keeps house for Doc, and Jenny went downstate to train for a nurse. She's back now. Good girl, everyone sets a lot of store by her. She'd like to get the district nurse job here, I think, but it's filled, and likely to be for the next hundred years if I know anything about the girl who holds it. Anyway, Jenny nurses, private, in homes and in town at the hospital. Between jobs, she sort of runs Doc's office and goes out with him on calls. He's aged, these last couple of years, Ron, you won't know him. He don't say much but it's my opinion he ain't well. He was saying just the other day that he wished to God you'd come back and take over his practice. We could do with a younger man . . . not that there ain't some young doctors come into the district lately but people change slow, up here, and they like someone who belongs to the country, someone they've known since he was a kid, like you."

Ron Lewis shook his head. He said:

"I wish I could see it that way too. I did think of it for a time. But —"

A rural section, a poor section . . . the nearest hospital some twenty-five miles away, and not much of a hospital at that when you compared it to the hospital Ron knew as he knew the palm of his hand and which, after two years of interning and two as Resident in Obstetrics, he was leaving, to enter private practice with the man whom above all others he most admired.

They were nearing the crossroads that would take them away from the river and along the bisecting road that ran straight inland, past rocky field, and deep woods, little undulating hills, and cleared land, to the Lewis farm.

"How long you planning to stay, Ron?"

"A week or so, I hope." Ron Lewis stretched his long legs and sighed, "I'm pretty tired."

"Mamie hoped you'd stay a month. If you was her own flesh and blood she couldn't love you more," said Mamie Lewis's brother thoughtfully; "she thinks the sun rises and sets in you, Ron. It's too bad she never had none of her own — she always wanted a flock of kids. I suppose that come from teaching them before she married your dad, although sometimes it seems to me it ought to work the other way, and that after being shut up with a parcel of kids five days a week from fall to summer a

10

woman wouldn't ever want to see one again."

"Mamie," said her stepson sincerely, "is a swell person."

"She's all right." Mat Young cleared his throat and spat again. "Funny," he said slowly, "just her and me left. There were five kids between us, all dead now. I wish I could be more use to her."

"She couldn't have gone along without you, Mat," Ron told him gently.

"I can't do a decent day's work," Mat said fretfully; "just tend to the errands, drive to town now and then, help around the house. Doc Barton says I'll last my time. Well, maybe. But my grandfather lived to be ninety and died in the fields with his boots on." He turned his dark eyes, still bright and eager, on Ron. The flesh was drawn tight over his cheekbones, and the bright flush of the chronic cardiac was apparent through the dry brown weather-beaten skin. "*He* never took no care of himself," said Mat resentfully, "and all I do is take care. It about burns me up. I never thought I'd outlive your dad. He was as strong as an ox . . . he could work rings around me even when I was up to it. When I got back here from the West, thinner than a rake and sick as a pup, he took me right in. 'This is your home,' he says, 'and you'll stay in it. You'll get well, now you're back, and we'll run the farm together.' I won't forget that in a hurry." He coughed sharply. "Mamie," he added, "wasn't too pleased them days. She'd never forgiven me for running off, when she was half grown, and not writing home and not bothering about education and stuff like that. She set a lot of store on education, still does. But after your dad died — well, it was lonesome for her, you bein' away and all. So we sort of shook down together, you might say."

"She wrote me," Ron said, "that the new tenant was getting along very well."

"Who? Oh, him. He's all right," said Mat; "got a lot of newfangled ideas, went to agricultural school and all. But he's a good boy, hard working, never spares himself. New married when he come to us. Mamie had the small cottage fixed up for him. It hadn't been lived in since you and your mother and dad lived there before your grandfather died; then your dad moved into the big house. Anyway, they're happy there now; new wallpaper and a coat of paint does wonders. I fixed up the storeroom for them just last week. She's expecting a baby. Any day now, Doc Barton says."

"She?" Ron had forgotten old Mat's digressive style of conversation.

"Lily. That's Bill's wife. Bill Treat, the tenant," Mat explained, a little irritated by Ron's slowness. "I just told you!"

These were the Lewis pastures, the Lewis cows, Holsteins and Jerseys, the Lewis barns, red mellowed to a dark rose, the round silos rising beside them. There was the Lewis house, half stone, half frame, the original stone house, a hundred years old, the newer lean-tos of wood painted white, the red-brick chimneys. Here was Mamie's garden, mostly glads now, pink and white, salmon and purple . . . in neat symmetrical beds beside the house. And the apple orchard, old and gnarled, the bending whimsical shapes of the trees, loaded with unripe fruit. The well was there and the well sweep, and an old pump stood at the left of the house. But it was years since they'd had to pump their water.

They drove up and stopped and Ron got out and lifted his bag from the back of the car. The front door stood open and Mamie Lewis came running out. She was a little woman, with the figure of an undeveloped girl, and short curling pepper-and-salt hair. Her face was no bigger than a child's, thin and lined, dominated by enormous gray eyes.

"Well, Mamie," he said inadequately, feeling her bony arms about him, aware that her eyes were full of tears, that her lean throat worked, and that she could not speak for a moment.

She had been very good to him. He had resented her greatly, he had made things unhappy for her, and uncomfortable, but she had been patient, understanding how much he had loved his mother, whose place she had taken in his father's house. So, long before he went away to college she had won him over.

She had never let him call her mother . . . not that he had wanted to, ever. "I'm not your mother," she had said firmly. "You had your mother, your only one. And aunt is pretty silly. Suppose you call me Mamie?"

She had been the district schoolteacher, her home in another town. She had boarded at the Lewis's and had become his mother's best friend. She was there in the house when Harriet Lewis died in childbirth, leaving one rebellious, desperately unhappy son, twelve years of age.

Mat said, "I'll put the car away."

Mamie Lewis led her stepson into the house. It was cool there, and dark, with the shades down. The furniture, a mixture of fine old pieces and shoddy, modern, overstuffed, was polished until you could see your face in it. You entered directly into a square hall and on one side was the best parlor, open only for funerals, weddings and special company. It was open now and Ron, stopping to glance in, saw that it had not changed since his last visit. The hair wreaths of another generation hung on the walls, the haircloth sofa stood stiffly under them, and the round table was still in the middle of the room.

On the other side of the hall was the sitting room, cheerful with geraniums in full bloom, a comfortable huddle of furniture, books in an old secretary, a darning basket, a sleeping cocker spaniel on the fireplace hearth. The fireplace had been bricked up during Ron's boyhood. It was only on his last visit that he had persuaded Mamie to open it again.

What had once been a downstairs spare bedroom had been, as long as Ron could remember, a dining room, with a bay window, running in behind the sitting room. The kitchen was beyond and the big storeroom. The kitchen was enormous. It had served his grandparents as sitting room and dining room in the old days and served them well.

Mamie was talking. She held Ron's arm and her light, rapid voice ran on:

"It's so good to have you back . . . you'll stay the rest of the summer?"

"I can't" — he smiled down on her from his great height — "much as I'd like to . . . but I wrote you that I'm going to be Dr. Allen's assistant. A great stroke of luck for me; he's the best there is, you know."

"Yes, so you did. I was delighted for you, of course. But I'd hoped . . ." She added softly, "You grow more like him every day. The way you walk, the way you use your hands."

Once upon a time a much smaller and younger Ron Lewis had deeply resented the fact that everyone knew that Mamie Young had been in love with his father and no one else long before he met and married Ron's mother. But twenty years had gone by and Ron no longer resented that fact. It touched him deeply whenever he remembered it, as now.

She cried, "Whatever am I thinking about, standing here! Come on upstairs to your room, Ron."

She had put him in the big spare room, overlooking the orchard and the brook. It had been his father and mother's. He had been born in this room and in this bed, in agony, in sweat and blood, his mother had died. From this room the sound of her desperate screaming — yet she was a very brave woman — had reached a little boy sitting on the stairs, his hands over his ears, his heart frozen with terror, and his physical being sick to its depths. This door had opened and Doc Barton had come out, walking like an old man. But he hadn't been old then.

When Fred Lewis remarried he had what was then the spare room done over for himself and his second wife. He had never again slept in the room overlooking the orchard and the brook, never again slept in the bed which had been his father's before him.

Ron stood by the windows now, looking out. Pigeons were circling over the barn and the sun was declining toward the west. From an apple tree near by a robin spoke querulously and he could see over toward the woodlot a flight of birds like smoke, rising . . . red-winged blackbirds perhaps, and against the sky the restless wings of barn swallows, dipping and rising, rising and falling. . . .

Mamie was settling things on the massive bureau. She said, "You can't get a decent hired girl in these parts any more. They all want to go to town and work in Woolworth's, or at the factory, or somewhere. Look at that bureau . . . I dusted it myself this morning."

"You're not doing all the work, Mamie?"

"There isn't much," she said, "just for me and Mat. Lily Treat feeds the hands . . . there's two of them now. Of course lately, since she hasn't been well, I took them over, it was too hard on her. Bill, her husband, comes up for meals — only, of course, until the baby's born — or didn't Mat tell you?"

"He told me . . . their first baby, he said."

"They can't wait for it to come," said Mamie, a little flushed with excitement, "and I can't either. Well, as I said, Bill and the hands get their meals here now and Mrs. Roberts — you remember the Robertses, don't you? . . . She's a widow now and has a hard time to make ends meet — Mrs. Roberts has been helping me. After Lily's on her feet again I won't need her, except for the heavy cleaning. Not that I'm not strong enough but Mat fusses so — and he can't lift, he mustn't. He's always overdoing."

"And who feeds Lily?" asked Ron lazily, not caring. He was tired, pleasantly so. He had gone from New York to Syracuse to spend a weekend with one of his medical school classmates, now married and established in general practice, and had come by bus to the town nearest to the farm.

"We send things over," said Mamie. She went to the door and lingered there looking at him. She commented, "You're thin. Been working hard?"

"I'm all right," said her stepson, "and as for work, well, there are always babies and they get

17

themselves born at the damnedest hours." He smiled at her affectionately. "Have I time for a bath and a shave before supper?" he asked.

"All the time you want. Mrs. Roberts is feeding Bill and the hands early, to get them out of the way. We want to have you alone, your first night. By tomorrow dozens of people will be stopping by to see you. It was in the paper that you were coming."

"Bet you put it in," said Ron, laughing.

"It was Mat," said Mamie defiantly; "he's as proud of you as if you were his own." She smiled at him. "I'm so glad you're here," she said again. "But it hurts me so to think Fred — isn't. He was so proud of you, too . . . he wanted you to have the best."

"I have had it," said Ron, "thanks to him."

Thanks to the insurance policy. God knows how Fred Lewis had managed, with times as they'd been and through the uncertainty of a farmer's life. But the annuity had matured and it was all for Ron, for his academic education, and medical school. Of course he had worked to supplement it . . . In college first and then summers. The first two summers in medical school he'd come home and worked for Doc Barton, driving his car and helping him in the office, doing odd jobs about the house. The next two he had tutored, worked as counselor in summer camps, done odd jobs in a resort place. Because by that time Barton's son had come to live with him.

When Mamie had gone he unpacked his bag and went into the bathroom at the end of the hall. He stood there looking around. This had once been a small bedroom and was now a large bathroom, old-fashioned, cluttered, and sunny. He remembered how he had resented this too, put in since his father's second marriage. He hadn't even wanted to use it. Why should that woman, he had thought, have everything? The outhouse and the big tin tub in the kitchen had been good enough for his mother!

How unjust he had been to his father and to Mamie, what a brat of a boy, how patient and forbearing they'd been, he thought, as the artesian water, clear and blue, ran slowly in the old chipped tub. He remembered how, once, when he had refused his supper, when he had kicked and scuffed and called Mamie an evil name, his father had taken him out, over her protests, down by the barn and administered a very thorough hiding.

"She isn't your mother," Fred Lewis had said, "but she is my wife. And as long as you are under my roof and sleep in my bed and eat my food you'll respect her."

The whipping hadn't taught him respect but it had taught him caution. Mamie herself had taught him the respect, without apparently a conscious effort. It had been Mamie who saw to it that his natural growing-boy laziness did not interfere with his integral aptitude for hard work. She had kept him at it, had studied with him,

19

had heard his lessons, had even made him review during the summers before he went to high school when every instinct in him had rebelled and the blue river beckoned.

Learning wasn't easy to come by. An able-bodied boy worked on his father's farm, spring evenings after the long drive in from high school. Summers he worked on the farm, and had his own chores to do and executed them faithfully — or as faithfully as possible.

He remembered walking to grade school through the crisp autumn days, and the snow-bound winters. He remembered berrying parties in the summer. "What you pick and sell is yours, to put in the bank for your education," Mamie had said. He'd peddled the berries around at the summer camps along the river. Mamie sold chickens and eggs there too, sent him down with his basket full. Chicken and egg and butter money was hers, to keep.

When he started going to high school there weren't any buses and his father had risen very early to drive him in, and a neighbor brought him back. That was the way things were ar-ranged, in their district. Everyone lent a hand where he could.

Shaving, Ron frowned at himself in the wavy, obscure mirror. What a mug! he thought distaste-fully. Yet it was his father's face, and he had loved that very much. But his father's straight nose hadn't been broken in football and his fa-ther, even at the time of his death, had not had the triangular frown mark between the deep-set eyes.

He grinned suddenly. Well, it was his face and there was nothing he could do about it. Thin and brown, the cheekbones rather high, the chin very square, broken by a cleft. The cleft chin, and the blue eyes, were all he had from his mother.

Lydia Allen was amused by his cleft chin. "It gives you away," she had said more than once. He could see her saying it, a slight blond girl, with cool strange eyes, more green than blue, and a pert, tip-tilted nose. She was such a little thing, he thought, his breath quickening, he seemed enormous beside her, a veritable hunk of a man, all hands and feet, awkward and uncertain. Curious thing that a twenty-seven-year-old girl could do that to you. She seemed, he reflected, nearer seventeen than twenty-seven . . . save for her cool voice and cooler eyes, her latent light mockery. Yet in the wards, in the clinic, making his rounds there or in the private pavilion, he had never felt awkward. And his hands served him with deft sureness in the operating room.

He wasn't here to think of Lydia. Or was he? Had he come up here to ask himself whether or not she loved him, or might come to love him? During the past two years he had seen her with as much frequency as was compatible with his exacting job. She had broken a dozen engagements with him and then made a dozen more. She had encouraged him, openly; she had discouraged him, flatly. Her father had said once, smiling:

"Don't take Lydia too seriously, Ron, she doesn't know what she wants — yet. When she does, I hope it will be good for her."

When he returned to the city it would be to take up his work as Dr. Allen's assistant. He would be thrown more and more into contact with Dr. Allen's daughter. He said to himself, wiping the lather from his face, He knows I'm in love with her . . . somehow I think he's pleased.

But was Lydia pleased?

He hadn't had time for falling in love with anything except his work. And he had known what that work must be ever since the night he sat, sick and tortured, on the stairs and listened to his mother screaming. He had known it even before, when he had been banished from the house to a neighbor's — three times that had happened and three times he had been cheated of the companionship of a brother or sister. But on the night his mother died he knew for certain. He was twelve years old and that was old enough to ask himself why women must die in childbirth, why he must be deprived of the love and the care and the tenderness of a woman who had not failed him since he had drawn his first rebellious breath. He had said to himself afterwards, through the sick tears and the tearing sobs, lying alone across his bed, hearing the subdued clatter and rustle through the house which meant that the neighbors were taking over and doing what they could for the bewildered man who had lost his wife and child, he had said, "When I'm grown up I'll be a doctor and I won't let *anyone* die."

Well, he was grown and a doctor and he fought death daily with all the skill at his command, and women had died despite all he could do. Not many. But he remembered every one. And went on fighting.

Dressing, he looked from the windows again, lost in dreams of long ago and the dreams of the future. The sunlight lay thick and golden, across the apple trees, and dust danced in the light, shimmering. The birds called and the cows, released of their burden of milk, went back to the business of feeding and ruminating. He saw across the fields a stocky gray mare coming up by a split-rail fence, her long-legged colt running stiffly beside her. This was a far cry from the wards and the clinic, the hot streets melting in the sun, the loud-speaker calling with the monotony of a metronome . . . Dr. Lewis . . . Dr. Lewis. . . .

A far cry from the Allen apartment on upper Fifth Avenue and Lydia at the head of her father's table, her small blond head, her white shoulders, her interminable cigarettes.

She smokes too much, he thought.

Mamie called him and he turned guiltily to his dressing. He could smell supper. It smelled good. Ham, fried potatoes, curly lettuce, one of Mamie's superb chocolate cakes, and hot steaming tea, and perhaps a baked custard.

"Ron," called Mat from the foot of the stairs, "get a move on you . . . I'm starved."

"I'm coming," he said, and ran down the narrow stairs to where they waited for him.

Chapter 2

Doc Barton came out to see him the next day. They sat on the veranda that ran across the long wooden ell and talked and talked. Mamie brought out a pitcher of lemonade and a plate of cookies and stayed just long enough to smile at them and then went away again. She said, "You'll have a lot to say to each other."

Barton was a big man, heavy through the shoulders, thick through the neck. But he was losing weight, Ron saw with apprehension, his neck looked hung in folds. And his hand shook a little as he lifted the glass to his lips.

He said, at the end of two hours, "Well, you got what you always wanted, didn't you?"

"That's right. I've been lucky."

"Nonsense," said the old man; "you've worked for it." He sighed, stretched, and winced as if his joints troubled him. "I got what I wanted too," he said: "folks around me, neighbors, dependent on me. It's a satisfaction. Bring a kid into the world and then, twenty years later, *her* kid maybe. I've never had any money. But there's been a living in it, and my own roof over my head and enough to eat and to share. I was telling Jenny just the other day, if I had to do it over again, I'd do just what I've done. I wouldn't change. You don't remember Jenny, do you?"

"No."

"Guess you never saw her," said Barton thoughtfully. "She came to live with me after you went away. She's a fine girl, you'll like her. A fine nurse too. People think she's wasted, up here. I don't. They need what she has to give them. Not just what she's learned — and she passed highest in her class, both theory and practice — but what's in her, deep down. Understanding, sympathy. Not sloppy, you understand, but the practical kind. But she gives a damned sight too much of herself. She'll have to get over that if she wants to keep on nursing and live."

"I've known girls like that," said Ron.

"Salt of the earth but they never spare themselves." Barton grunted, reaching for a cookie. He said, between bites, "You couldn't work with a finer man than Allen."

"I know it," said Ron.

"I looked him up," said Barton, "and I've read some of his books. He's top-notch, all right."

"He's been very kind to me," Ron said, "right from the beginning. Told me when he suggested this arrangement that he'd had his eye on me from the first day he had anything to do with me in the hospital. That set me up," he admitted, "made me feel like a million dollars."

"Must be pretty near what he's worth," said Barton without envy. "Man like him comes high, in New York City."

"And deserves it," said Ron, on the defensive. "He does plenty of charity work. And there are dozens of cases he takes for as little as the most modest G.P."

"I know," said Barton; "I wasn't criticizing him. How old a man is he, by the way?"

"Sixty-odd," Ron answered, "but he has to slow up. He's worked too hard most of his life. Didn't let up, even when he could."

"Married?"

"A widower," Ron said, "one daughter."

He would have sworn that his voice didn't change but the sharp old eyes looked at him keenly and Barton smiled.

"Like her, don't you? Well, that's all right too."

"She's very attractive," Ron said cautiously.

"Make a good doctor's wife?"

"Even a bad doctor's," said Ron, laughing.

"Don't quibble with me," said Barton testily, "you know what I meant."

"Well, she's a doctor's daughter."

"It doesn't add up to the same thing," said Barton sagely, "except maybe in a small town. Wish you luck anyway." He lumbered to his feet and Ron rose with him.

"Where you going? Thought you were staying for supper."

"I am. I'll take a look at Lily Treat first . . . she's due most any time now."

"Taking her to the hospital?" Ron asked.

Barton shook his head.

"Her mother's coming on tomorrow. She won't hear of it, doesn't believe in hospitals. Everything's arranged, and I've delivered more

27

babies in farmhouses than in hospitals anyway," he said. "When they call me, I'll bring Jenny over — like as not it will take quite a spell as it's her first — and Jenny can stay with her till I'm needed. You haven't seen Lily yet?"

Ron shook his head. "Just the husband. Seems to be a competent young fellow, I like him."

"Nice kids. They want a family. Well, they're on the way to having one," said Barton, walking heavily across the porch and down the steps. "See you later, Ron," he said.

Ron watched him go down the path to the small gray tenant cottage. He thought, Mat's right, he's aged a lot. He ought to quit work. But he won't. He'll work till he drops.

Mamie came out and sat down beside him, smoothing the white apron over her print dress. She asked, "How'd you find him, Ron?"

"Doc? Old, and tired," Ron said, "he ought to quit."

"Who'll take his place," asked Mamie, "with the people around here?"

"God knows."

"We'd hoped it would be you," she said, "Mat and Doc Barton and I."

"I know. I wish it might have been. But I couldn't see my way to it."

"We understand," she said.

"I know you do, and you haven't reproached me," he told her, "not once. None of you . . . I feel like a heel."

"You needn't," she said. "You're doing what

you were meant to do, what you've always wanted to do, you haven't wavered from that by a hairsbreadth, Ron. We respect it in you. We wouldn't want you to be any different."

"Thanks," he said awkwardly, disturbed as always by praise and by any answering emotion within himself.

She asked, after a moment, "Remember Herb Andrews?"

"Of course. What's happened to him?"

"Nothing . . . which is what happens to a lot of people around here. He works in town winters and guides summers. There are more and more people building river camps all the time. He called up while you were out with Mat this morning, said he'd like to take you fishing to-morrow . . . along about five. He has a river shack beyond the crossroads. I said you'd be there, if it was a good day."

"How'd you know?"

"I know how you like to fish. You need to sit in a boat and not think of anything," she said; "it will do you good."

"Most relaxing thing in the world," he agreed. "I'll bring back a string for breakfast."

"See that you do," she cautioned him, smiling.

Toward five the next day Ron took the car and drove to the crossroads and Herb's shack on the river. Herb came out to greet him, unshaven and brown, a pipe in the corner of his mouth. They had gone to school together, they had lived near each other. "Like old times," said Herb, grinning. "Remember when we used to sneak off and go fishing and the chores not finished? Boy, did I used to get hell!"

Ron followed him down the shaky little dock and into the sturdy outboard motorboat and they chugged happily across the river.

"Bass hole's just the same," said Herb, busy with his lines, "they're still there, in the lee of the island, under the rocks, rising to the bait when they feel like. Minnow or spinner?"

"Let's try minnows first. Are we going to troll?"

"For a spell, till we see how things are. It's good to see you, Ron — you don't get up much, do you? Seems as if you've moved a million miles away, to another part of the country instead of just downstate. I haven't been to New York City in years," said Herb. "Last time I was there I got as drunk as an owl . . . that was after Gladys left me. You knew I was married, didn't you? Gladys Horton."

Ron remembered her, the redhead, in his class. All the kids had been crazy about Gladys.

"I'd forgotten," he said. "I'm sorry, Herb."

"She's married again," said Herb, "and that's all right by me. I was born lazy, I guess. I couldn't stand nagging. I couldn't stand an office. I didn't want meals on time. She's happier and I am too. I'm content, I go uptown in the winter and get me a job, but as soon as the ice goes out I come down here and loaf on the river. Gives me my living, that's all I ask. Well, here we are."

Shortly before nine o'clock Ron drove back to the farm. He had his string of black bass and a few fat perch. He was sleepy, happy and sunburned. He'd had a good four hours on the river, just water and sky, the small green islands and the sharp tug at the end of his line.

The sun had set in glory and wonder, and even now in the darkening sky there were rosy clouds, mauve and raspberry. A new moon was a silver sliver, the first star looked out . . . but it was still light on the river where color yet lay, thick as oil on the quiet water. But it was darker here and the Lewis house blazed with light, the tenant cottage was bright, and Doc Barton's car was parked outside the house.

Mamie met him at the door. She said breathlessly, "It's Lily — things started just after you left. Dr. Barton brought Jenny . . . I haven't been over, I'd just be in the way, Lily's mother got here two hours ago, thank goodness."

He patted her shoulder.

"Don't look so worried," he advised. "Doc's one of the best and she's young and healthy. First babies take their time about coming, you know."

She asked anxiously, "Couldn't you just step over in case Doc needs you?"

Ron smiled at her, and shook his head.

"He won't need me," he said cheerfully; "besides, this is his show — I've no business butting in."

"As if he'd think that!" she began indignantly. Then she stopped. "My land," she said, "and

31

you standing there and those fish dripping all over my carpet. Here, give 'em to me. You like them pan fried, don't you, for your breakfast? And you haven't had any supper!"

"I love 'em," he said fervently. "How about frying me one right now?"

He went upstairs whistling, to wash. He was tired and relaxed. When he came down he went into the kitchen, where his fish was snapping merrily in the pan. Mamie was there alone.

"Where's Mrs. What's-her-name?"

"I told her to go along home," said Mamie. "How about a few fried potatoes, a tomato salad, and some milk and cake?"

"Sounds wonderful. But you shouldn't go to all the trouble . . . I can get along with a sandwich, I didn't know Mrs. Roberts had gone."

"I'd rather be doing something," she said: "and it isn't any trouble, anyway. I keep listening for word . . . I mean . . ."

He said soothingly, "Doc will go and come back again. Bet you a nickel you won't see hair nor hide of the Treat heir apparent until tomorrow sometime."

"I'm glad I didn't have a daughter," said Mamie, "because if I had had and she was having a baby I declare I wouldn't know which way to turn."

"You would," he said, "and you'd spoil the life out of the kid — just as you did me."

"I never!"

"You always —" he began and then stopped.

"What's that?" he said sharply and rose from the old rocker by the window into which he had flung his lean length and went out, along the hall, to the steps, Mamie just behind him, making small worried sounds.

It was Bill Treat. His face was ghastly. He was running, his mouth half open, a distraught man.

Ron ran to meet him. "What is it?" he asked.

"Lily . . ." Bill looked as if he was running away . . . escaping from some horror too great to be borne. He did not look as if he was coming for help, but as if he had blindly run out of his little house, as if he would keep on running until he dropped. Ron's question was an interruption. He gasped, "She's — gone," he said.

"Hell and damnation," said Dr. Theron Lewis and covered the short distance to the tenant cottage as fast as his long legs would take him, and flung open the door on utter confusion.

A living room, neat as a pin. But beyond, a bedroom, the door wide. An elderly woman on her knees, weeping. A tall, slender girl in white. And Doc Barton, the sweat pouring from him, straightening up from bending over the bed.

He turned and saw Ron. He said heavily, with heartbreaking simplicity, "She's dead."

"When?"

"Just now . . . a minute, two . . ."

Ron pushed the kneeling woman aside. He said, "Take the baby!"

Dr. Barton looked at him, his old eyes filmed with the tears of defeat. He said helplessly, "I haven't anything . . . I — Good God," he said and held out his shaking hands, "I can't."

This was a dead woman on the bed. A young woman, with fair, plaited hair and a still pale face. Her eyes were still open. Her face had a look of frozen agony, which had not yet been effaced by the longer sleep.

"Get me a jackknife," Ron said.

A jackknife was sharp. A bread knife, a butcher knife, too clumsy, too dull . . . and every second counted.

Doc's jackknife was in his hand. It was sharp. A good knife, one which would cut life free from death.

The woman who was Lily's mother stood against the wall and screamed.

"Take her out," Ron ordered Jenny Barton. "Hurry!"

Jenny put her arm around the older woman, who wept and stormed and prayed, and took her from the room. Mamie was there, coming up the steps. Jenny left Lily's mother with her and went back. There might be something she could do.

The long swift incision; the short cut through the uterine wall, so that two skillful fingers could be inserted . . .

"Scissors," he said.

Jenny had them in her hand. Ordinary scissors, Lily's.

The two inserted fingers protected the baby. With the scissors Ron prolonged his intra-uterine cut, and lifted from the dark, the riven safety of the womb, the living child.

Doc Barton spoke. He said, "Here's a piece of string, Ron."

Ron tied the string around the cord an inch or two away from the baby, and cut the cord just beyond the ligature.

Jenny Barton, watching, felt the slow tears on her cheeks. She had not known that she was crying.

For half an hour she stood there, waiting, watching, holding her grandfather's heavy, trembling hand in her own while Ron Lewis worked over the baby . . . and then, suddenly, the long, thin, rebellious wail.

Jenny spoke, almost in a whisper. *"The breath of life —"*

"That's it," said Ron. He looked at her and smiled. "You can take over," he said.

Oil, blankets, agarol . . . This was Jenny's job. It seemed to Ron that somehow the agony had gone from Lily's little face. Not all in vain —

Later she would be cared for, her mutilated, life-giving body. Now there was the baby to think about, the grandmother weeping in Mamie's thin arms to be comforted.

He went out of that room of life and death and the older man followed. He kept saying humbly, "I hadn't a thing . . . I couldn't — I'm getting too old. She just — died, Ron. She was in labor, and she died."

"Weak spot in cerebral artery," said Ron, "giving way under strain. Cerebral hemorrhage.

Nothing to the rest, doc . . . a sharp knife, scissors, a piece of string. Everything at hand, and the whole business greatly simplified of course by that poor girl's death." He sighed deeply, sudden lines of strain around his mouth. "There's something you can do now."

"What?"

"Find Bill Treat and tell him he has a son. He won't have gone far, I think."

"I said, 'She's gone, Bill,' and he ran out of the house," Doc Barton said slowly. "Well, I'll find him."

"Mamie'll look after the grandmother," said Ron soothingly, "and Jenny will take care of the baby. You can help about the arrangements . . ." He thought, Barbaric, desolate, but it will give him something to do.

A little later Bill Treat came back walking like a man in a nightmare. He said, as he came up the steps, "I don't want to see — it."

"You don't have to," said Ron promptly, "but I would if I were you. Husky little devil, weighs eight pounds if my guess is anywhere near right. He's yours, you know."

Dr. Barton was back at the big house, calling the undertaker. Lily's mother — Ron never knew her name — had been put to bed in Mat's room. Barton, having himself once more in hand, had given her a sedative. Over in the cottage Jenny had oiled and dressed the baby . . . and Bill sat in the next room beside the sheeted form which was his wife.

Ron went in and through to the little room and looked down at the child, wrinkled and red, with a fierce, protesting scowl on almost nonexistent eyebrows. And Jenny, settling things, boiling up bottles and nipples in the kitchen, went back and forth quietly. She was, he realized, an extraordinarily lovely girl. Dark hair, heavy and uncut. Dark quiet eyes, and a still oval face, colorless except for the rose red of a sensitive full mouth.

"So you're Jenny," he said; "I'm Ron Lewis. Your grandfather's bad boy — years before your time. We haven't had time for a proper introduction."

She smiled at him. "I know," she said. She spoke softly as he did, because of the baby. "It was lucky that I persuaded her" — her voice broke a little — "to get some bottles and nipples. She laughed, I remember, and said, 'I'll nurse my baby.' And I said, 'Well, you never know. Sometimes supplementary feedings are indicated.'"

He asked, "You'll stay here?"

"Until we get the right formula," she answered, "and things are organized. I imagine Lily's mother will stay on. But meantime I can help — until she can take over and Bill's adjusted himself." She added, "He's taking this terribly hard; they were in love from the time they were in high school."

"I know." He looked at her consideringly. He added, "You're a very competent young woman, Jenny."

Jenny flushed faintly. She said, "Thank you — but I did nothing. It was you — and it was wonderful."

He felt awkward again, boyish, absurd. He said, "Nonsense!"

"I've seen dozens of Caesareans," she told him, "but always in the hospital . . . with everything to work with . . . I've seen mothers die on the table and — But this was different . . . this was almost like a miracle."

"It was nothing," he told her.

But it wasn't true. It was something. It was life out of death. It was his job. His heart swelled with it. He said, "I heard you say something a while ago . . . 'The breath of life,' you said. Well, it's like that, always."

"To you?" she asked.

"To me."

He had never said it before, not to anyone, just how he felt about his job . . . which was bringing the breath of life and which was just that to him.

He said, after a minute, "I'll have to get back to the house . . . Mamie will be wondering." He looked at her and smiled. "If ever you want to work in New York, let me know. I've just finished my residency at Lister Memorial. I'm going into practice with a very great man . . . perhaps your grandfather told you. So, if you want a job, in my end of things at my hospital, write me, will you? I'd like to work with you," he said, "again."

She would always remember that. She had done nothing, but he said *again*.

Jenny said, "Thank you," and her voice shook a little. Her voice was shaken by her heart. Yet what had her heart to do with a man she did not know? She thought, with a sudden surging of passionate loyalty, a loyalty she was to feel as long as she lived, *But I do know him.*

He had come into this house, he had brought life into it. He was a man utterly to be trusted . . . a man in whom you could believe with every ounce of faith that was in you . . . human, compassionate, and fine.

He was going now. He said, "Good-bye — you'll take over, won't you?" and smiled at her, a transforming smile, which made him seem younger, more vulnerable. Watching him go, her heart beat in warning drums and she could have laughed or wept with the new strange rhythm of excitement and expectation.

He went out of the little house, walking lightly. The baby, lost, forlorn, between this world and the one it had forever left, stirred and whimpered in sudden desolation, looking wizened and wise and unhappy. Jenny spoke to it, gently, touching it with her clever and practiced hand.

She had never met a man with eyes like that . . . with a face which changed so abruptly to a mask of concentration, with such sure, deft hands.

She thought, I can't leave Grandfather, but perhaps, someday —

Ron went back to the house and Mamie came to meet him. She said, "She's asleep . . . Lily's mother. Doc and Mat are going over to stay with Bill awhile."

"Good." He was tired again and, as suddenly, famished. He asked plaintively, "When do I eat?"

"Good land," said Mamie, "and your fish ruined! I'll cook another."

"Don't bother. Milk and a sandwich."

He ate, sitting out on the porch. Not far away Lily's son slept and Jenny watched over him. The undertaker came and went, and Bill sat, his hands between his knees, and Doc Barton and Mat sat beside him.

Ron went upstairs to bed, tiptoeing past the door beyond which Lily's mother mercifully slept. He thought, I've got to get away — as soon as I can without hurting their feelings. I've got to get back to work.

Chapter 3

New York was a furnace. People dragged themselves along the streets, men with their collars open, bareheaded, shirtsleeved, women in limp cotton frocks. There would be an increase in accidents. You couldn't hurry. It was so drippingly hot that you didn't much care if you were run over or not. Tempers were short, days were long. Automobile drivers grew careless and irritable. Youngsters ran screaming under sprays and hoses, splashed in the city playground pools, jumped into fountains while the officers of the law obligingly turned their backs. People slept in the parks or tried to sleep — whole families sprawled out on the baked grass. The beaches were crowded, the subways filled with mothers, crying children, picnic boxes.

Dr. Elwood Allen's Park Avenue offices were air-conditioned. Shades were drawn, they filtered cool green light, an illusion of running water. Fresh flowers, not heavily scented, made little pools of pastel color in the reception room and on Allen's desk. His secretary, Mrs. Petersen, moved about without haste, trim in navy and white, her gray hair cut close to a shapely head. His nurse, Miss Garron, forty-odd and attractive, was crisp as lettuce in her uniform.

Allen sat behind his desk and contemplated Ron Lewis, smiling.

"You're brown," he commented, "and a pound or two heavier."

"Sun," Ron agreed, "and hours spent on the river. As for the weight, that's Mamie's cooking. If I'd stayed much longer I would have become obese."

"I doubt it. Mamie?"

"My stepmother."

"Oh, yes, I remember. Did you find her well?"

"Very, thanks."

"How you could endure to return to work — in this weather?"

Ron said ruefully, "It must be a habit. I hadn't been there three days before I was champing at the bit. I hope I concealed it from my people. They were sufficiently distressed when I left." He looked up, smiling. "At that," he added, "I found myself doing a job . . . busman's holiday."

"What sort of job?"

Ron told him about Lily Treat. Allen's sensitive, clever face grew grave. He said, "Poor girl . . ." He leaned back, fitting the tips of his long, spatulate fingers together. "It's a situation I have encountered too many times. And nine times out of ten the husband refuses to have anything to do with the child."

"I know," said Ron. "When I left, Treat had somewhat adjusted himself. His mother-in-law is remaining to look after the boy . . . healthy kid, by the way, with every right to his chance."

"Of course. It's good to have you back. Your

office is ready for you," said Allen, smiling, "and so am I."

He rose, a short, slender man, with a massive head, too large for his body, and pure-white hair. His face was controlled and ascetic, his dark eyes extraordinarily young and alive. He took Ron into the smaller adjoining room, cool like the others, and well equipped.

Ron said, looking around, "Makes anything I can say inadequate, but you know how I feel, sir."

"You rate your own quarters," said Allen, "and eventually you'll have your own patients." He sat down at the desk, abruptly. He said, "It isn't very common practice for an obstetrician to take on an assistant. But it's either that for me — or give up. Or so Tatum told me. We were classmates at Cornell and Hopkins. I'm forced to take his word."

Tatum was the best heart man in the East. Ron nodded, his face concerned. Allen laughed, tracing pencil circles on the new blotter.

"Don't look like that," he advised, "I'll last . . . thanks to you. Have you found living quarters yet?"

Ron nodded.

"A little flat," he answered, "which isn't much more than around the corner — beyond Lexington. A walk-up, but comfortable enough, big living room, with a bed in the corner, bookshelves, a kitchenette. There's even a fireplace. Used to be a private house."

"Good. By the way, Lydia sent you a message. Will you dine with us tomorrow?"

"I'd like to."

"Lydia," said her father, "is in town only for a few days. Fittings or something. It appears that women order their autumn clothes in the middle of summer. Then she's off again, on a round of visits. The Southampton house is open, of course, and I've been getting down occasional weekends."

He rose.

"Let's go back to my office," he suggested, "and talk things over. I haven't an appointment for half an hour or so."

When Ron left the office it was to make the simple move from his old quarters in the hospital to the new apartment. There wasn't much to move and Bates, the new Resident in Obstetrics, had cheerfully put up with the few things Ron had left there when he went north . . . medical books, and the instruments which over a long period he had bought one at a time, saving to do so, going without. As an intern his salary had been scarcely visible to the naked eye but, as he had not been concerned with outside activities and the expensive courtship of young women, he had not minded. As resident his salary had been substantially increased and he had managed to save for the things he wanted. Of course Lydia came high . . . dinner now and then, flowers, taxis; still, as resident he had been able to afford that.

Now his status was changed. Allen's financial arrangement with him was liberal. He could save, he thought happily, buy the things he needed, and send Mamie money from time to time. The rent of his little flat was not high and his inner man, while it demanded plenty of filling food, did not crave caviar and crêpes Suzette. He would get his own breakfast, and the other meals would be simple, taken on the run wherever he found himself.

It would take time to fit in as Allen's assistant. Many of Allen's patients would resent him, at least at first. That was natural. When you wanted Allen you didn't want a young whippersnapper with no reputation — beyond the delivery room of Lister Memorial — in his place. But, little by little, he could ease himself into the work, the outlines of which were clear enough.

He would assist Allen in the delivery room. He would call on patients after their return home. He would make rounds with Allen and, sometimes, for him, and take over, gradually, much of the clinic work, and the night calls. Many of the night calls were false alarms, induced by too much dinner, a thunderstorm, a fit of nerves. It would be up to him to diagnose, how much was false and how much true, whether the patient was actually in the first stages of labor and ready for hospitalization or, if something untoward threatened, whether Allen should be called.

Not all the women who came to Allen were having babies; some came who wanted them but had not realized their desire. Nor were all the patients in a position to pay large sums for pre-natal care and delivery. Many were professional women in moderate circumstances, or house-wives and office workers subsisting modestly. Allen never refused them. His fee was scaled down to circumstances. A young woman having her first child at Lister, engaging a bed in a two- or three-bed semiprivate room in a ward, who could not afford special nurses but would rely on floor care, was as carefully tended, as sympatheti-cally watched as the woman who came in and engaged a suite and special nurses not only for herself but for the baby. Lydia Allen had more than once been voluble on the subject. She was again, on the following evening when she, her father, her aunt, Mrs. Oland, and Ron dined together in the Allen apartment overlooking the reservoir.

Candles flickered on the table, which was of heavy glass, a strange marine green. The room was filled with the tall, rosy spikes of gladiolus. The manservant moved softly, bringing the cool, delectable courses, iced melon permeated with wine, Vichysoise, smooth, cold and creamy, cold salmon, in a ring of cucumber aspic, squab, soufflé potatoes, green peas, salad and mousse, and coffee.

Lydia wore a linen frock, cut like a sport dress, with a shirtwaist bodice and a full long skirt. It was the pale color of the cucumbers, and emer-alds were green against her small flat ears and on her wrists. She had combed her fair hair up from her neck and it fell in carefully careless curls on top of her small head.

"Am I glad you're back!" she said. "Perhaps Dad will behave himself now."

"In what way," inquired her father, eating little, "have I misbehaved?"

"You know," said Lydia, and her aunt, a large, powdered woman with black eyes like currants in her doughlike face, nodded severely.

"Elwood," she commented, "has always over-worked. There's no reason why at his age he cannot retire."

"I'm here," said her brother mildly, "although the manner in which you discuss me would lead an innocent bystander to believe me miles away. As for retiring . . . nonsense. Not until I have to."

"Which won't be for many years, thank heaven," said Ron.

Allen grinned at him cheerfully.

"Looks as if I had found myself a champion," he said, "and I need one."

But later Lydia drew Ron aside. She said, "Come into my special hideout with me, will you? Aunt Sammy and Dad have things to discuss. She's all upset about the Administration and the vanishing dividend. She seems to think that Dad can do something about it. She's staying in the Southampton dump, this summer, but came up, with me, to see if Dad couldn't write a potent letter to a couple of senators."

Her hideout was a little room off the drawing room proper, between it and the library. It looked high out over the Park and was cool in its summer dress of delicately colored chintz. There were deep chairs before an empty fireplace, a toy of a desk, and a big comfortable couch heaped with pillows.

"First," said Lydia, "the after-dinner shot in the arm."

She rang for service, and obtained it. Ice, glasses, bottles.

"Say when?"

Ron shook his head. "Too hot," he said.

"Nonsense."

"Can't," he said briefly; "sorry."

"You don't look it, you look disapproving."

"I don't mean to, Lydia."

"But you do. You have such an open face!" She splashed Scotch into her glass, a little soda, turned the glass in her thin hand, tinkling the ice. "Light me a cigarette, do," she said, "there at your elbow in the crystal box."

A crystal box engraved *Lydia* . . . a lighter to match. Ron gave her the cigarette and held the lighter for her. He said, "You smoke too much . . . all through dinner I noticed."

"Okay, Gramp," she said, unruffled, "and I suppose I drink too much too?"

"I wish you wouldn't."

"Two cocktails," she said, "wine with dinner — very light sauterne — and now this. I'm abstemious, really."

He said gravely, "You don't need it. You have vitality enough for two."

She said, shrugging, "Maybe you're right. Maybe if I had you around enough, I'd stop. It's just habit and being so dreadfully bored most of the time. Do you know I came up only to see you? — my fittings were an excuse. They have a model of me in the workrooms. But I've missed you, Ron."

He asked gravely, "Have you, Lydia? Or is this just one of your come-on remarks?"

"Come-on?" She widened her eyes at him. "What do you mean?"

"I think you know. A careless sentence thrown out . . . like a straw to a drowning man . . . when he clutches it, it disintegrates and he drowns anyway."

"What a monster you think me." She leaned toward him, her eyes caressing. "You don't know how glad I am to see you. Tell me about your holiday."

He said obediently, "There isn't much . . . I went up to the farm —"

"A real farm?"

"Couldn't be realer . . . debts and all."

"Yours?"

"My stepmother's, for the duration of her life."

"I suppose," said Lydia, "she's a horrible old thing. I've always been leary of stepmothers. My mother died when I was fourteen, I've watched Dad like a hawk ever since. I've often been worried, he's had some pretty narrow escapes.

There was a widow five years ago. Too good-looking. I had a sinking spell or something."

"Sinking spell?"

"Well, I needed attention," she said, laughing; "you know, pale, listless, and couldn't sleep. I went from one doctor to another. I gave Dad plenty to worry about. The widow got tired waiting, went to Europe — and picked herself a title."

He said, "You're a very unpleasant girl, Lydia."

The moment he spoke he was sorry. His face confessed it and Lydia laughed. He thought, I shouldn't have said that, and what's more I didn't mean it. She doesn't mean it either. She thinks of herself as hard-boiled. She seems as brittle as glass. And she's so terribly lonely. After all, her mother died at a time when she needed her most, her father's always been too busy to be with her much, and as for her friends, I wonder if she has any friends really? Under that thin veneer there's a real person, warm and sweet and lonely, he thought with compassion, with an exquisite tenderness — a person you would love forever, once she surrendered to you.

Lydia was speaking. He heard her through his preoccupation. He was thinking not only of her but of the many women he had known, in his professional capacity, women who appeared hard, undefeated, and self-sufficient but who were so terribly helpless and afraid, starved for reassurance and understanding.

"What are you thinking about? You're a million miles away," she was saying.

"No," he told her, "I'm here; thinking of you."

"Of an unpleasant girl?"

"I'm sorry," he said.

"Don't be. It's true," she admitted, "but you like me, don't you? Or don't you?"

"Too damned much," said Ron shortly. "I don't know why. I disapprove of you —"

"That's all right," Lydia said, "I like it that way. I'm fed up with people who approve of me, with yes men . . . who expect me to be a yes woman."

"When my father remarried," said Ron slowly, "I hated it more than I can say. I was just a kid. It didn't take me many years to learn that it was one of the best things that ever happened to him."

"I couldn't feel that way," said Lydia. "I've had my eyes on Miss Garron for ages. She's in love with Dad of course but she doesn't know it, I expect. He doesn't, at any rate. Poor old Petersen's married — and she has an invalid husband — and doesn't constitute much of a menace."

He said carefully, "But you'll marry."

"I suppose so," she said. "What of it?"

"Then why begrudge — ?"

"That's different," said Lydia. She thought, My poor dear, what could lead you to believe that I would ever willingly share my father and his income with any woman? She added, "Go on, tell me about your trip. I suppose you've a girl back home. Never knew a man who didn't.

51

Probably went to school with her, hay rides, ice skating, choir singing, all that sort of thing." She thought, and hedges in the moonlight, hammocks on the porch, only a nice girl wouldn't mention those. Ron shook his head.

"Not even a vestige of a girl," he said.

"Come, come," she said, setting down her glass, "you don't expect me to believe that!"

"Whether you believe it or not, it's true. I hadn't time . . . I was too busy getting an education."

"And I thought," she said, laughing, "that someone was waiting for you under the shade trees complete with cows and a sunbonnet."

He said, slightly irritated, "You were wrong."

"No sentimental pilgrimage, then, to the home of an old love now growing plump, three children, and a husband selling insurance? Ron, you can't tell me that you didn't lay eyes on a female — your stepmother hardly counts — while you were away?"

He said, his momentary annoyance passing, "There was Mrs. Roberts, in the kitchen. She's fat and fifty. Oh, and yes," he said, thinking of Jenny for the first time in several days, "there was a girl —"

"I thought so." She frowned a little. "Pretty?"

"Very."

"Dark or fair?"

"Dark."

He was enjoying himself.

"And?"

"And nothing," he answered. "You are persistent, aren't you? Fine girl, very good nurse. I hope she'll let me get her a job here, in town, someday. She's the granddaughter of our old family doctor — the man to whom I owe as much as I owe any man except my father and now, of course, yours."

"Well," said Lydia, "a nurse . . . well, in my experience they can be pretty damned dangerous."

"They never were to me," said Ron soberly, "and I've known a lot. A finer group of women doesn't exist. Oh, there are the renegades and the cowards, and the shirkers among them, but by and large — my hat's off," he said. "You can't have the remotest idea of the godsend a good nurse can be to a kid fresh out of medical school and not dry behind the ears. I remember my first months at Lister, the ribbing I took and the practical, unobtrusive help I had."

"Sex," said Lydia, "I suppose it didn't rear its ugly head?"

"Now and then," Ron admitted, smiling. "I fell in and out of love, a couple of times. But I hadn't the — élan, let's say, of some of the other interns and little taste for backstairs encounters or for dragging willing gals into empty rooms. I couldn't afford to take 'em out either. And I was always pretty much of a stick, shy and scared." He thought of the little anesthetist with the red hair who hadn't known he existed aside from his routine duties and of the girl in the lab with the amazing violet eyes who *had* known — but he hadn't been able to do anything about her.

"You still are," said Lydia, smiling faintly, "but we'll soon cure you. You don't know how — relieved I am to think you are taking over for Dad."

"I'd hardly call it that."

"He'll rely on you. When are you coming down to the Island?"

He said soberly, "Probably not at all, Lydia, although thanks very much. I hope your father will be able to get away though. Both of us can't."

"I suppose not." She was silent a moment and then said, "Dad makes me tired. Why does he persist in doing all this charity work, and taking these little two-for-a-nickel budget patients? He has enough work to keep him busy without that. A woman who can't afford the best has no right to demand it. It isn't fair. There are hundreds of other doctors."

"That's been argued before," said Ron, "and there's something in it, I expect. But your father doesn't happen to feel that way."

"And you don't either?"

"No," he said, "I don't."

"What a pair." She reached for the ice, withdrew her hand and smiled at him. "You'd rather I wouldn't?" she asked.

"I wish you wouldn't," he said gravely.

"Very well, then, I won't." She rose. "Come along, the big financial talk must be over by now," she said, "and Aunt Sammy —"

"Why Sammy, for heaven's sake?"

"Samuela. It's really her name, can you bear it? She'll want a game of contract. Dad will too, he loves it."

Ron hesitated. He said, "I'm not very good —"

"I'm wonderful. With me as a partner no one will notice your deficiencies and I'll even kick you under the table."

He said uncomfortably, "I can't afford stakes."

"Aunt Sammy," said her niece, "has most of the money in the world and she plays for a tenth of a cent and screams like a wounded doe if she loses a rubber. Come on." She tugged at his arm. "After all," she added, "it's a family game and you're one of the family now."

Chapter 4

Summer dragged along and then it was autumn and Manhattan put on her gayest bib and tucker. The sun was mellow and kind, the wind cool and exhilarating. The shop windows bloomed and people took to walking to work and whistling as they walked.

Ron Lewis had been very busy. He could tell by Mrs. Petersen's attitude and by Miss Garron's that he was fitting in. They had been kind and helpful from the first, yet wary as if they were waiting for him to make a slip. They guarded Allen, he realized, amused, with the savage tenacity of good watchdogs. But so far he had made no error, he had trod carefully and worked hard.

Two of Allen's new patients had been turned over to him, a radio singer, in the first year of her marriage, and the secretary of one of the best-known men in Wall Street. The radio singer, having been sent Allen by one of her more affluent confreres, was patently relieved to put herself in Ron's hands. She said, "Confidentially, I'm terrified of Big Men . . ." and the secretary, while a little annoyed at first, was soon amenable. They were good, cooperative patients. The radio singer was young and nervous, the secretary in her late thirties and nervous because of that. But they liked Ron and he liked them and it looked very much as if, both being healthy and intelligent, there would be no difficulty. Their prenatal care was entirely up to him, but when the time came Dr. Allen would take over . . . unless something unforeseen happened.

Ron made rounds with Allen, and for him during any absence. He had some night calls, the usual type. He had two which were not usual — one woman who showed every evidence of losing her baby and another with a kidney condition as sudden. On each occasion Allen was on Long Island and it was up to Ron to use his own skill and judgment, which he did very successfully.

He was amazed one day toward the end of October to have Mrs. Petersen announce a patient . . . for him . . . a Mrs. Rippen.

"For me?"

"She asked for you."

"You don't know her?"

"I never saw her before. She didn't telephone for an appointment. She said specifically she wanted to see you, not Dr. Allen."

He said, "I have to be at the hospital within an hour. Let her come in, Mrs. Petersen."

She was a tall, well-built young woman in her late twenties. She wore sables carelessly and a tailored suit. She was beautifully made up. She sat down beside the desk and smiled at him.

"I've heard of you, Dr. Lewis."

"That's gratifying," he told her.

She said, "I'm not going to do the customary beating about the bush. I know Dr. Allen wouldn't be interested. He couldn't afford to be. But you are younger, you are his assistant and you might —"

He said, "I haven't my own practice, Mrs. Rippen."

"You misunderstand me. I didn't mean afford in terms of money. Your price doesn't interest me." She added calmly, "I could tell you one of a dozen stories. You'd know I lied. So I'll be perfectly honest with you. I am unmarried. I'm going to have a baby . . . which is careless of me. The baby's father is a well-known man. He can't marry me because his wife won't give him a divorce. We — have been very discreet for about eight years. Even his associates know nothing about me. We don't frequent places where we might be seen. I have a job, because it looks better. My job sends me to Europe, to South America. So does his. We have been happy for a long time, we intend to go on being happy. But it is out of the question for me to have this child."

He said, "I see. I appreciate your circumstances; and I can do nothing for you."

"Aren't you being a little hasty?" she asked. "There must be ways . . . how about an appendix?" She added thoughtfully, "I still have mine, as it happens."

He said shortly, "It is not within my province to remove — appendices."

"I see. Have you forgotten that price is no object? Five thousand dollars is a lot of money, doctor. I'm prepared to —"

He rose. "There is no use prolonging this discussion."

Mrs. Rippen sat perfectly still. She took a platinum and ruby compact from her alligator bag and powdered her nose. She adjusted her sables.

"And you can't advise me?"

"I advise you," he said shortly, "to have your child."

She shrugged.

"I suppose I could," she said serenely, "but I'd rather not. In addition to the problems that would entail, I don't want a child. You," she added, "are pretty inhuman. What sort of chance would such a child have, anyway . . . have you considered that?"

"A chance," he said evenly, "even under existing circumstances, of becoming a decent citizen, of perhaps amounting to something — despite —"

"Its mother and father?"

He said, "Yes."

Mrs. Rippen rose. "I'll have to go elsewhere. As a matter of fact, I have an address or two . . . of competent men, professionally speaking, who aren't idealists." She smiled tautly. "My mistake was an entirely illogical feeling of distaste at going to such a man for help. But it can't be avoided now. Will you tell me your fee for consultation?"

"None," said Ron, and went with her to the door. Once there, he stopped her, a hand on her shoulder. "I wish you'd reconsider. You will run a very real risk, you know."

She shrugged.

"I've been doing that one way or another since I was eighteen," she said indifferently. "Thanks . . . you aren't, after all, wholly inhuman. But I might have sent you a lot of business, not all of it of this sort," she added.

He said, "If you reconsider . . . come back, and we will work out some plan . . . a hospital out of town perhaps . . . I know of one upstate, and a very fine old doctor."

She shook her head. "You can't persuade me," she said, "but it's Christian of you to try."

When she had gone he sat down and wiped his forehead. This wasn't the first time he'd been asked for this sort of help. He preferred the other kind, the girls who trembled, wept and wrung their foolish little hands. Not that he could do what they wanted either . . . but he had been able to persuade one or two . . . had even gone to their parents and done what he could to help.

He wasn't sorry for Mrs. Rippen. She could take care of herself, he supposed, and she'd come out of this all right, given good fortune and a careful man. But —

What a waste, he thought angrily, what a bloody, hideous waste.

Mrs. Rippen was in glorious good health, she was still young, she was, he feared, intelligent. If she had a child it would be a hundred to one that it would be a fine, lusty youngster. But she wouldn't. Yet down in the tenements women

60

were going about their hard, unremitting daily duties, old before their time, carrying a fifth or sixth or even tenth child beneath a filthy apron, while those they had borne were screaming underfoot, undernourished, underprivileged.

Well, there were a lot of women like Mrs. Rippen and most of them didn't have what she believed her excuse. Most of them were respectably, even happily married.

On Christmas Day, Ron dined with the Allens. Allen had had a sharp attack of flu and had been in bed for over two weeks. He had been up and about for a few days but he had lost weight and Ron did not like his color at all. During Allen's illness Ron had delivered three of his cases . . . normal deliveries, but he felt that he was working against odds. One woman had said to him, with a wail, "But I had counted on Dr. Allen!"

Still they would rather have Allen's assistant than put themselves in the hands of anyone else. And things had gone along very well indeed.

Allen gave him a watch. It was under the big tree, waiting for him. Ron, turning over in his hands the thin, costly thing, was deeply touched.

"You shouldn't . . ." he began.

"Indeed I should. Lydia picked it out," he said, smiling, "we hope you like it."

Ron's own offering seemed trivial. A very old medical book in good condition which he had scoured the secondhand bookshops to find in his scant spare time and which would be a modest addition to Allen's really fine collection, and for

Lydia the conventional flowers.

They were alone, after dinner. Allen had gone off, protesting, to take the rest his physician insisted upon, and Aunt Sammy was due at an eggnog party. Ron said, "I have to get to the hospital."

"Just a minute," said Lydia. She stood with him beside the tall and fragrant tree, gay with colored lights and shining ornaments. "I have a present for you."

"But you've already —"

"That was Dad's idea." She went to a table and took a small package, wrapped in red and silver, a sprig of holly thrust through the ribbon. "Here it is."

He opened it, feeling abashed, as always at an evidence of kindness, took a square box from the wrappings, and from the box a folding leather picture frame and opened it.

Lydia's face looked back at him, the eyes grave, the mouth faintly curved. A casual picture, her hair swept back from her face, curling around her ears . . . a revealing, molding sweater.

She said, "The photographer said he was disappointed, that a picture taken of a gal in sweater and skirt was hardly glamorous. But I thought you'd rather . . . pretty-up pictures are stupid."

He said slowly, "I don't know what to say, I would rather have this than anything in the world."

"Anything?"

"Except," he said, on a deep breath, "the original."

Lydia took the picture from his hand and tossed it on the table. She put her slender arms around him and lifted her mouth for his kiss. She said, when as in a dream, his heart racing, he had bent to her lips, "That's more like it. You certainly took your time."

He said humbly, "I didn't dare, Lydia, I was afraid."

"Of what? The worst I could do was say no and I might have changed my mind, I often do," she said laughing. "Come here, sit down. Ron, you're shaking!"

He said, "If you had said no I would never have had the courage to ask again."

"Ask for what?" she demanded. "Must I do all the lovemaking?"

"For your love, darling," he told her.

She leaned her fair head against his shoulder. She said, "I've been in love with you for ever so long. At first I thought, It won't last, it's just one of those chemical things, or whatever you call it. But it did."

He said, "I've so little to offer."

She sat up and looked at him. "That's crazy. Are you out of your mind? You're Father's assistant. One day you'll have his practice."

He said, "I hope it will be many years before that will even be considered. And it isn't on the cards, my dear, that your father's patients would —"

"Nonsense . . . and especially," she said, "now." She added, "I never wanted to marry a doctor, I always swore I wouldn't."

"Why?"

"I hate it, particularly your kind . . . irregular hours, never knowing if you're home for dinner, if you can go to the opera, having you leave in the middle of a play or a party. Oh, I know, I haven't lived with Dad all these years and not realized what I'd be up against. But it can't be helped. Damn!" She put her arms about him and kissed his cheek, her lips cool and curving. "I would have done so much better," she mourned, "with Freddy Netcherfield or Angus —"

"Netcherfield is no good," Ron said.

"How would you know?" she inquired.

"Never mind. And as to Angus — is that the lad with the Adam's apple who was up here one night? You were going out with him, I came in to talk over something with your father."

"In person. He has money," she explained, "and Freddy has looks. You, my lamb, have neither. But I love you. And I don't know why. Maybe," she said with her appalling frankness, "it's because you were so hard to get. I knew you were in love with me but I couldn't — Well, that's all over now."

He said, "I love you, Lydia, and I'll make you happy, I swear it."

She said, "That's odd, you know, because I've never been happy, not really, if by happy you mean peaceful . . . and content . . . and complacent. I've been excited and thrilled and — on the top of the world. But not happy. Maybe that's why I love you — and envy you, Ron. You're happy."

"Yes; I wish I could tell you how deeply."

"Your work," she said resentfully, "that's what makes you happy. I've no share in that."

"I've you now," he said; "that means twice as much happiness."

She said, "We'll be married in June . . ."

"Lydia . . . you must realize" — he looked around the apartment, his bright blue eyes grave — "I can't afford this sort of thing. Nothing even remotely like it. I —"

She said, "Don't be silly, we'll live here with Dad, of course."

He shook his head.

"We'll have our own home," he told her; "it won't be here. But that's the way it is."

She opened her little mouth, just touched with rosy color, and then closed it again. She said, smiling, "All right, we won't quarrel about it. And when you get back from the hospital we'll tell Dad. Do kiss me, Ron, and hold me — very close. I — feel safe when you hold me."

He held her, stroking her hair back from her forehead. He thought, I'll be good to you, Lydia, all the rest of our days. We'll be happy together, you and I and those who will follow. A family, he thought, stability, something to work for, to cling to, the only insurance against loneliness, the best incentive for work . . . the basis of courage.

He tried to tell Dr. Allen something of this, when after his return from the hospital he came back to the apartment and found him with Lydia in the library. But Allen shook his hand and smiled at him. He said, "You couldn't have given me a finer present."

Later Lydia left them alone for a time and Allen said gravely:

"I've been worried about Lydia." He sighed. "She is all my life, beyond my work. I haven't been able to be with her — much. She's a strange little thing, Ron, all impulse and — then no impulse. Had her mother lived . . . I have been afraid that she would marry the wrong man. I haven't interfered with her friendships, it hasn't seemed wise, and now she's twenty-seven . . . no longer a child. But if she had married the wrong man it would have wrecked her. Now I am not only happy, I'm very much relieved. You have been like a son to me these last months . . . I'm very proud of you."

Ron said, "I'll try to deserve that, sir."

"What are your plans?"

"Lydia wishes to be married in June."

"And then? We'll give you time for a honeymoon," promised Allen, smiling, "but after —"

"I thought, a little place near by. Lydia suggested," said Ron, feeling hot under the collar, "that we live here but —"

"I'd like nothing better," said Lydia's father, "but I understand your feeling. And it's best so, your own place, your own life . . . and I won't be lonely. I'll see Lydia every day, and you and I are working together."

Ron wrote to Mamie that night. He said, "It hasn't been announced, and won't be until spring, Lydia doesn't like official long engagements. So don't say anything to anyone but Mat and Doc, will you? I may not get up before I'm married but of course I expect you and Mat to come down to the wedding. I'm walking on air, Mamie, the happiest living man."

Mamie wrote in return, her good, loving heart bared to him on paper. At the end she said, "I'm sorry to have to tell you that I can't give Dr. Barton your good news. He had a stroke last night. Jenny's taking care of him. He's pretty sick, Ron, but we have hope."

Dr. Barton died less than a week later and Ron was unable to go up state for the funeral. He wrote Jenny and wired flowers but he could not get away. Allen was not yet well enough to take over entirely even for a few days. Ron tried to explain this to Mamie, telephoning her, rather than writing. She would, he knew, expect him to come. He said, "Mamie, if there was *any* possible way, you know I would, don't you?"

"Yes, of course," said Mamie. "Jenny understands too, she said so. But it seems queer without you, Ron. You were like a son to him, in a way."

"I know. But he'd be the first to understand," said Ron sadly, "I'm sure he would."

In March the letter came from Jenny. She said,

"I remember what you told me, that day last summer. I can't stay here, Dr. Lewis. Mother's gone to Cooperstown to live with her sister, who has become a chronic invalid, there was nothing else she could do. I have plenty of work here of course, but I feel I'd like to get away. It was one of the last things Grandfather said to me, as it happens. He said, 'Jenny, get out of this little town and try your luck in the city . . . Ron will help you. . . .' "

Ron could help her. It wasn't hard, with Dr. Allen's influence at Lister. Allen, listening to the story, said, "Well, we'll see what we can do. A floor job — on obstetrics, how would that be? If she works in, there might be a supervisor's position later. And after that, who knows? They're short handed now. Lister graduates are preferred of course, but in this case — I'll look into it tomorrow, Ron. She sounds like the type of girl we need, and of course you owe it to your old friend to do what you can for her."

In April, Jenny Barton came to New York. She couldn't sleep as the train rattled through the spring night. She thought, Lister Memorial.

The private pavilion floor nurses at Lister were graduates. It was an old, a revered, an enormous hospital. She thought, I'll see him every day . . . we'll be working together — again.

I must make good, she thought. I can't let him . . . or Grandfather . . . down.

In the very early morning she left the train, pale with fatigue but walking as if she hadn't lain awake all night . . . walking lightly toward her future . . . a porter trotting beside her. She was to go right to Lister.

But Ron was there at the gates, at that ungodly hour. She saw no one but him for a moment, the long lean man with the bright eyes and the friendly smile, so did not at first notice the young woman beside him, very blond, very lovely in the sort of simple suit that comes high in the best workrooms, an impossible bird perched on her fair hair, dark, sleek furs about her shoulders.

"But, Lydia," Ron had protested, "the train gets in before you're even awake."

"I'm meeting her just the same, with you. And taking my car. I'm curious about her and taking no chances," Lydia had said firmly. "Besides, this is part of my job, isn't it?"

"Jenny," said Ron, and went forward to take her hands. "What sort of a trip did you have?" He turned to include Lydia. "Lydia," he said, and Jenny's heart quickened with — astonishment? apprehension? — "Miss Allen," he said, "Miss Barton."

"I've heard so much about you," Lydia was saying mendaciously.

Allen? Dr. Allen's daughter?

Lydia's left hand was bare. Ron's ring on her finger. She did not wear it as a rule as the engagement had not yet been made public. Today she wore it. "It's pretty little," he had said, "but someday I'll replace it, dearest."

"Ron," said Lydia and put her arm through

his possessively, "don't keep poor Miss Barton standing here . . . let's take her out to the car, darling."

So that was that. He said, piloting Jenny toward the car, "I've imagined you've guessed and Lydia doesn't mind your knowing. Doc was to know first of all, but he was taken ill just about that time . . . so —"

Jenny found herself saying the conventional things. Why shouldn't she? He was nothing to her, except a friend. She looked from the car windows to the thronged streets. Her future lay here, in this city, in the hospital. Ron Lewis had no place in that future except as a friend, as a doctor whom she admired greatly and with whom she would perhaps work.

But suddenly she was lonely and afraid.

Chapter 5

Jenny Barton fitted into the crowded, rigorous life of Lister Memorial Hospital as a supple hand into the proper-sized glove. She had been trained in an institution almost as large, in another great city, and the atmosphere was familiar to her. She breathed it as one breathes necessary air — how necessary, she had not realized during her time at home. Yet that time had not been wasted. On the contrary, she had gained immeasurably in experience, nursing in homes where things had been made difficult, meeting emergencies and finding that she had to improvise, exercise her professional ingenuity, with none of the equipment, assistance, or direction afforded by a hospital.

In the private pavilion at Lister, graduate nurses far outnumbered the students. In the wards and on semiprivate floors there were more student nurses under graduate charge nurses. Jenny, having satisfied the requirements, was assigned to day duty on the obstetrical floor, in the private pavilion. She would have preferred the ward — a ward offered more life, more color. It teemed with excitement, it was a cross section of humanity, imbued with sharing, sympathy, and curiosity. On the private floors the majority of patients had special nurses for part, or all, of their stay, solicitous families waited in charming reception rooms, the specials went briskly about their duties, famous doctors, accompanied by interns, made pontifical appearances.

Jenny's quarters in the Nurses' Home were comfortable and she liked the girls with whom she came in contact. They were, for the most part, cordial and helpful and in a month's time she felt as if she had always been at Lister.

Her contacts with Ron Lewis were frequent. She saw him when he made his rounds with Dr. Allen or when he came alone. And during her first weeks at Lister, Dr. Allen had two patients on floor care.

Off duty, too, she saw Ron, usually through the insistence of Lydia Allen that she dine with them, and they often took her to the theater; the first time Ron had to leave in the middle of the second act but she and Lydia remained and later returned to the Allen apartment, where Ron joined them for something to eat and afterward, over Jenny's protests, drove her home. Lydia came with them. She said, laughing, "Darling, if you think I'd let you out of my sight with anyone as attractive as Jenny . . . !"

She was charming to Jenny. "You'll let me call you that, won't you?" she asked on their second encounter. And Jenny, who believed in people, and whose cool judgment was subservient and secondary to her naturally warmhearted impulses, found herself wholly enchanted. Lydia seemed so natural and, under her bright glancing sophistication, so young. Younger than I am, thought Jenny; I suppose it's because she's always been so sheltered.

Ron Lewis as a friend, as a man whom she respected and admired, compelled her affection and her loyalty. He had been, he was, so very kind to her. Her grandfather had loved him. Their initial introduction had been dramatic, one you would not easily forget. In a few minutes you made strides in friendship that could not be covered in years in different circumstances. She told herself, ruefully, that she had quite fallen in love with him during that extraordinary few moments in Bill Treat's little cottage. That wasn't unusual. She was given to falling in love with medical genius, outstanding skill. All through her training she had happily and hopelessly adored the Chief in Surgery, a man nearing sixty, happily and very much married, with grown children. In a lesser degree she had worshiped at the shrine of a clever, irascible pediatrician. Ron Lewis was, however, a special case. In the first place, she had heard of him ever since coming to live with her grandfather. Between Dr. Barton and Mamie's stories a clear picture had emerged of a brilliant, hard-working young man and of a lazy and engaging youngster. Jenny had heard of his escapades as well — the Halloweens which had resulted in the sudden disappearance of gates, fence posts, domestic animals . . . and the pushing over of farmhouse privies, a common concomitant of Halloween goings-on in that part of the world. She knew about the time he'd frightened Mamie to death with his calm securing of a large, nonpoisonous, but nevertheless unattractive snake, and his sorrow when Mamie ordered it out of the house. "But I wanted to dissect it," he had mourned. "I think it's a girl and she's going to lay some eggs."

Yes, she had known all about Ron Lewis and was perfectly willing to accept the picture his doting narrators had drawn. When she saw him, she had thought, in that split instant as he rushed into the room and took things in his own hands, almost before she had adjusted herself to the shock of Lily's death, But he's so *attractive.*

She had thought of that attraction, of his eyes, of his hands and his lean, hard body, during the months before she came to New York. She had a right, she told herself stoutly, to idealize him . . . even to fall in love with him, secretly, a little amused by her own emotion. She hadn't known that he was not free, not until she saw him again, in the station with Lydia beside him.

Now, of course, she had no right.

She would no longer think of him "in that way," she told herself vaguely. He belonged to someone else. She was that rare woman, one who respected the no-trespass signs. A man who belonged to someone else was simply not for her, and so she adjusted herself to think of him in an entirely different fashion.

And I can too, she reminded herself. I wasn't *really* in love with him. It was hearing so much about him, meeting him in that way. There are hundreds of other men, free men.

Not that she was determined to meet them, and to imperil their freedom. She was young, her life was all before her, and she had a profession that was paramount to her. She couldn't talk about it — to Lydia, for instance, who wouldn't understand; to Ron, yes, if the occasion ever arose; to her grandfather always, while he lived. But not even to the nurses with whom she came in daily contact, several of whom became her intimates as time went on, could she express the clear, passionate flame which burned steadily within her and which superseded everything else.

Having — as she thought — adapted her relationship with Ron to her satisfaction, she was willing, even eager, to admit Lydia to her small close circle of friends. Lydia was kind and gay, full of fun. Jenny didn't mind some of the things she said. She's crazy, she told herself affectionately, it's just the way people rattle on, down here, they don't mean it. Besides, Lydia had always had everything. She had led a life so entirely dissimilar from Jenny's that it was sheer fascination to sit and listen to her, to acquire brief, dazzling glimpses of that life . . . to enter, vicariously, a world Jenny had known only through fiction.

Lydia was like the kaleidoscope beloved of Jenny's early years. You turned it, it fell into altering, wholly fascinating patterns. Through Lydia, Jenny heard, secondhand, of many things alien to her, perceived the shifting pattern of a life completely alien to her own . . . Lydia talked a lot. Lydia told amusing stories. Sometimes, after she had been with her Jenny went back to the hospital with her head aching with substitutional, imagined excitement. All those places, all those bright, strange people!

Paris and London, the Riviera, the Italian lakes, the Basque country, the Alps, in other days. Chestnut trees, blue water, gambling casinos, white beaches. The California desert, blossoming into the resort rose; the golden sands of Florida; the mountainous green islands of the Caribbean . . . Newport and Bar Harbor, the Hamptons and Aiken, Lydia knew them all, the storied places. She knew Hawaii and the indigo waters, she knew distant mountains and scalloped seashores, hidden New England towns and great cities.

Polo and yachting, tennis matches and golf tournaments . . . the sidewalks of New York, the glamorous places, the night clubs and restaurants, she knew them all.

It amused her to talk of them, and of people of whom Jenny had read in the public prints and to watch Jenny's dark eyes widen with an innocent, breathless wonder.

"I like your Jenny," said Lydia to Ron, "she's so utterly naïve, so — so credulous, poor girl. She listens to me as if I were a living page from Grimm or Andersen. We must take her out more, darling. She works hard, she deserves it."

He caught her to him. When Lydia was kind

she was adorable. Yet more than once he had caught her in a moment of callous cruelty. That crass little woman who had come to dinner one night . . . she was vulgar, she was a snob, and a fool — but Lydia need not have made it so apparent.

Only strong people can help being what they are; only remarkable people select their paths. If Aunt Sammy had asked Mrs. What's-her-name to dine at the Allens' in order to corner a portion of her large, newly acquired bank account for Aunt Sammy's pet charity, if Mrs. What's-her-name had accepted because a dining acquaintance with the Blue Book Mrs. Oland and her brother was infinitely to be desired, well, Lydia should have known better than to make the poor idiot of a woman uncomfortable — not that she had sufficient brains to realize all Lydia was doing, drawing her out, her bright head on one side and her eyes fixed on the plain, too painted face, but even so —

He had spoken to her about it. "You made fun of her," he accused; "it was very cruel."

"Nonsense!" said Lydia briskly. "She didn't know it and, besides, she rated it. What a woman!"

She was merciless with pretentiousness and stupidity. She was impatient with fools. That was one side of her. On the other she was charming to her father, always, tolerant with Aunt Sammy, generous with her friends — if sometimes she tired of them rather quickly, after a sudden, devoted intimacy, and when she tired she washed them up . . . "I can't endure her any more," she'd say, "she's gone all Christian and forbearing, she *bores* me."

Lydia couldn't bear to be bored.

She was marvelous with servants, Ron learned. They adored her, they worked themselves to the bone for her. She demanded a great deal but appreciated what was given.

And with Jenny she was perfection.

She'd say, when Ron was absent, "I wish you'd known him when he was a little boy. But you couldn't of course, at your age. I wish I knew more about him."

Jenny would oblige, with all she had learned through Mamie and Dr. Barton, and slowly built up a credible, two-dimensional picture of young Ron Lewis. Lydia in her heart viewed it with some impatience. Too pat, too storybook. Local boy makes good. Oh, of course, all the fine, unswerving, hard-working qualities. If he hadn't had them he wouldn't be Elwood Allen's assistant. But she thought, I wish he was more plastic, more vulnerable.

Ron would be hard to live up to, Lydia decided. She was a realist. It would take a bit of doing to change him, even a little, to mold him her way . . . but she would manage.

Like all men, she thought, a little scornfully, he was susceptible on his physical side. An offered, unexpected kiss, a spontaneous or spontaneous-seeming caress, a touch, a word of more

78

than affection, moved him, much more deeply than any logical argument or display of sheer reason. Lydia, cool as her eyes, cool as her voice, was faintly disgusted. But men were like that, she assumed, and if not they were more — or less — than men. Women possessed this weapon, and therefore used it even when it was distasteful.

She did not really mind a demonstration of affection. She liked it, it warmed her mind if not her blood, it amused her to call it forth, it satisfied her. But more than affection was not tolerable. Still — that wasn't her fault, was it? Long ago, in her nineteenth year, she had known and greatly admired a famous actress who had summered in the Hamptons. They had become friends.

"You're like me," said the older woman, "you'll have a bad time, often. Me —" she shrugged her celebrated shoulders — "I haven't a spark of honest emotion. I've had three husbands. I used them, all three, I was even very fond of two of them. One taught me to act, one gave me money and leisure, and the third an excellent social position at a time when most stage women rated a place far below the salt and a sort of court jester position in the better type households. Nowhere does a sense of theater, timing, and careful application to every nuance of your role serve a woman of my type in better stead than in the — intimacies. My husbands never had the least complaint about me. When I divorced the first he was desolate, when I divorced the second he was forlorn. *He* settled enough money on me to pay the war debt. The third died reluctantly. It is a curious thing to pretend emotions which you have never felt. Your mind sits in a corner and watches and is alternately horrified, amused, and applauding. But it's wise, my dear. And if things get too unpleasant there are always migraines . . . or a tricky heart . . . or unavoidable fatigue. That's how I played it. That's how you can play it."

"But I'm not an actress," said young Lydia, lying prone on the green grass of the actress's little garden.

"All women are, and you'll be a very good one," prophesied her friend. "You've a good mind, you're selfish as hell, you've the sort of face and body utterly irresistible to most men — that untouched, remote look gets them every time — and you have will power. I'd like to live to see what you'll become. But I won't."

She didn't, dying three years later of cancer, dying with valiance and fortitude. Not that she wanted to — she wanted to scream and rave and curse, but fortitude and valiance were expected of her, her friends, her devoted sister and the man who had been her last lover — not through any emotional compulsion on her part, but because she was a vain woman and had to keep her hand in, so to speak. So those who loved her suffered torments because she suffered them without a whimper, her doctor was beside himself, and her nurses adored her. All her life, publicly and privately, she had played a part and she played it now, her last role, with great brilliance.

Lydia went to see her, most reluctantly. She hated a sickroom. She loathed ill-health. Her own body functioned perfectly, she was never ill. But she went to see her friend.

She had a few minutes with her, alone.

The room was dark, there were flowers. The small waxen face on the pillow, the yellow color of cream, stirred and the brightly painted lips smiled. "I can talk to you," the older woman whispered. "This is unadulterated hell. Someday they'll leave the painkiller too close, but I doubt if I have the courage. No one knows about me, Lydia. They think I'm dying with supreme gallantry. They think that the old idea persists — the show must go on. That's damned silly. Why? But I can't let even a small audience down, can I?"

Lydia escaped, sickened and horrified. Perhaps it took more bravery to pretend you were gallant than if you really were. When later she heard that her friend had eluded her nurses and taken quite half a bottle of quarter grains of morphine, she was glad for her that she had found that much authentic courage out of pretense.

I couldn't, she told herself. I hate pain, I won't suffer, ever. But I'm afraid of death.

That May she had found the little apartment Ron had been looking for, not that he had much time to look. She took Jenny to see it on her hours off. It was near the East River, not too far from the office, and not at all Sutton Place. It stood, a raw, new building, square and uncompromising, in a street filled with noise and children playing in the gutter, brownstone, shabby houses, some of them converted into basement restaurants with garish neon signs . . . Tony's Chop House and Aunt Nelly's Kitchen and the like. There was a grocery store on the corner. You could hear the rumble of the El.

But it was convenient, the rooms were rather large and light, and the price was one Ron felt he could afford. The outside appearance was solidly respectable, and the little entrance lobby clean and well lighted.

The apartment was on the top floor, and if you had a good imagination you could see over to the river. There were two bedrooms.

"Must have," she'd said firmly.

"But why?" Ron gave up. His training informed him that two bedrooms were preferable and hygienic. His integral background and ancestry was convinced that two bedrooms were unnecessary and too damned newfangled. And his heart was desolate. Much has been written, and spoken, of the departure of glamour when a man and woman are forced to live under each other's feet, in cramped quarters. You know the sort of thing they say. No one is at his or her best in the dawnlight. There's a matter of an unshaven jowl, or the last traces of cold cream, or disheveled coiffures, or a cold in the head. But that was surface stuff, sophistry. A man who can't love a woman with a cold in her head has never loved her, a woman who shudders away from the new rough beard isn't a woman at all. The hell with glamour. Marriage isn't glamour. An affair can be, perhaps, in its first stages. But marriage is intimacy, sharing, and the beauty that is in the loyal, the dazzled, the always illusioned eye of the beholder.

Lights out, the open windows, the long talking in the dark, the beloved head on your shoulder, the tenderness and peace which follows passion or replaces it. This is marriage, this is better than glamour.

Lydia said:

"It's extravagant of me, isn't it?" She looked at him as they stood together in the empty apartment, for the agent had tactfully left them alone. "But . . . I can't help it, darling, I've never slept in the room with anybody except on rare occasions when I've had a friend spend the night with me and the house was full and we had to double up. And then I couldn't sleep and I hated it. Besides," she added, and put her arm through his, "I want to look always beautiful — for you."

"You do, you will —"

"That's what you think, but wait till after the first year," she said, smiling. "And I couldn't, not at such close quarters. Angel, you're wonderful, you deal with women all day long and know nothing whatever about them."

Well, this was the right apartment, two bedrooms or none. He said, "All right, Lydia, if that's the way you want it."

He thought, Maybe after a year or two, we will have another use for the other bedroom . . . perhaps by that time she'll feel differently.

She wouldn't take the apartment that day. She said, "We'll look a little further, think things over. Don't worry, it's a new house, it isn't even half rented as yet. I'd like Jenny to see it."

Jenny, standing there, in the bright spring sunlight cried, "It's perfect!"

"Don't be a fool," said Lydia crossly, and at the expression which flashed over Jenny's face was instantly contrite.

"I'm sorry, I didn't mean it, I'm tired, that's all. Of course it's perfect, just what we want," she agreed. "I'll tell Ron tonight that we'll take it."

Chapter 6

Ron looked in that night on his way home. He was very tired. Allen was out of town on a consultation and Ron had delivered one of their clinic cases that morning, a breach presentation, and a difficult one. He had just been back to the hospital to see his patient and had made Allen's rounds on private floor.

He said, as Lydia came out to the hall to meet him, "I'm dead . . . I can't stay a moment."

"Drink?" she asked.

"A short one perhaps, lots of water." He sat down on the divan in her little hideaway. "Lord, it's peaceful here," he remarked. "I saw Jenny for a moment . . . ran into her in the grounds . . . I was talking to Tatum, and we went out for a walk. It's hot tonight, and she was out there . . . said she'd seen the apartment and was —"

"We can't have it," said Lydia tragically.

"Why not? Someone take it? I told you we should have clinched it. . . . Don't look so distressed, darling," he said, himself very disappointed, "we'll find some other place."

"Ron." She moved close, leaned her head against him, wrinkled her nose. "You smell of hospital," she said.

"Sorry," he told her, "I —"

"It's Father," she interrupted; "promise you won't say a word to him, not a word."

"Of course I'll promise but what —"

"He's terribly upset that we aren't living here with him," she said. "Of course he hasn't spoken to me but Aunt Sammy —"

"I don't understand," said Ron; "he told me he agreed perfectly that we should have our own place."

"Because we wanted it. He's unselfish," said Lydia gently, "but it's really disturbing him, Ron. He can't bear to come back here, alone. I've always been with him."

He thought, That's not true, she's been away, times without number, visiting, Europe, here and there. Well, don't quibble . . . she always came back.

"Are you sure of this?" he asked.

"Perfectly. From little things he's started to say — but Aunt Sammy was quite eloquent. She — frightened me. She said she thought we owed it to Dad to give up our own plans, for a while anyway."

Ron frowned. Tatum had talked to him tonight about his prospective father-in-law. "With reasonable care he'll live for years," he said, "but he has to ease off. It would kill him to quit, we both know that, and he'd rather be dead. But eventually he'll have to give up active practice and be available for consultation only. You know that as well as I do, Lewis. Meantime if things go smoothly, if he isn't upset emotionally —"

Remembering that, Ron asked again, "Lydia, are you *sure?*"

"I couldn't be more certain. And I'm frightened. Oh, Ron," she said, her eyes wide and misty, "I know how you have your heart set on being by ourselves . . . and that's what I want too . . . you don't know how *much* I want it. But, if anything happened, we would never forgive ourselves. I'm all he has, dear. And even seeing him every day isn't the same as being here when he comes home. He's been wonderful about everything, but —"

He said, after a moment, "I can't pay our way, Lydia."

"Ron, this isn't the time for pride. Oh, I do respect it in you, I do understand. But just for a while, dear? I —" her voice broke — "I'm afraid it won't be for long."

"Don't say it, don't even think it," he said harshly.

He thought, She's right, and she's being fair. She hasn't once reminded me what I owe him.

He said, "All right —"

She put her arms about him and kissed him, suffered his instant, breath-taking response. It didn't take her breath except physically. She thought, Easy enough, I don't really mind. She thought, And I do love him, I never loved anyone else, even when I thought I did.

Drawing away she found herself thinking, If he didn't give in, would I love him . . . more?

She said:

"Thank you, darling, but there's just one thing. We mustn't let him dream for a moment that it's because of him. We'll just say we've changed our minds. I'll tell him . . . he'll be home so late tonight, I'll tell him tomorrow. And it's all managed easily enough. My bedroom and the big guest room connect, there are two baths. We'll use this room for our own living room . . . put your books in it, get a sensible desk. It will all work out."

"Anything you say," he told her heavily and rose to go. He was more disappointed than he could say. The one thing he hadn't wanted. Any man wants to be on his own. He said slowly, "There will have to be some financial arrangement. I'll contribute as much to the expenses here as I would if I were paying rent and food bills and all the rest in our own home. That has to be understood. It will be very little compared to the upkeep of a place like this — but that's the way it has to be."

"Of course, darling," she said instantly.

When he had gone, she sat quite still, smiling. Then she rang and asked for a highball. Drinking it slowly, feeling relaxed, and pleased, as purringly satisfied as a pussycat, she thought, Well, that's that.

She had hated the little apartment. She belonged here, with space, among the appurtenances of gracious living, in comfort and in luxury. Ron couldn't give her these things yet. The time would come when he would be able to do so, but it was both stupid and unnecessary to go without until then.

A day or so later Jenny saw Ron, in the corridor on her floor. He stopped to speak to her. She asked, smiling:

"Have you taken the apartment?"

"Well, no." A slow flush touched his cheek-bones, "As a matter of fact, we've given up the idea."

"But it was an ideal place," she began.

"I thought so," he said, "but we've decided not to leave Dr. Allen. We'll live with him, for a time at any rate."

"I see," said Jenny slowly. She was conscious of sharp disappointment. She wanted to say, Don't do it, be your own master over your own household. But she had no right. She thought, I suppose it's the easier way and there's a lot to be said for it . . . still —

She said, "Give Lydia my best. I hope I'll see her soon."

He watched her walk away. There had been, briefly, a barrier between them. Jenny's face was very expressive. He thought, She thinks I'm far gone in luxurious living. It hurt him oddly that she would think that. But he couldn't run after her and say, Look here, this isn't what I want or even my idea but Allen has a cardiac condition and we're afraid —

He turned and went to the elevators.

Lydia told her father. She said, "We aren't taking the apartment after all, ducky."

"What was wrong with it?"

"Nothing. It's quite a sweet place really. I

adored it. But Ron . . ." She laughed. "He thought we could find something rather better. He hasn't the slightest idea of values and rents. So last night he suggested that we stay on here until at least we found something more suitable or until he can afford —"

Allen interrupted. "I don't believe a word of that, Lydia," he said mildly.

She made her eyes wide. "Angel," she said reproachfully, "why?"

"Because I know Ron. And you. You want to stay here, don't you, you don't want to leave your life and live his?"

"That's unkind," she said, "I'd follow him to the ends of the earth, I'd live in a hovel —"

"Don't be dramatic," said her father, "you know you wouldn't. Well, if your mind's made up . . ." He sighed. "I'm sorry for the boy, that's all." He looked at her in exasperation. He loved her deeply, bitterly, irrevocably, knew her as thoroughly as it is possible to know another human being. Only parental love can be so clearsighted and so constant.

She said, "Well, what was the *use?* After all, the rooms are here . . . and there just isn't any sense. I do love Ron," she added, her hand on her father's as it lay, open and delicate and strong, on the desk in his small study; "you believe that, don't you?"

"Yes, but I don't know why."

"What does that mean? I do love him, I want him to be happy. But if he can be happy — my way?" She looked at her father pleadingly. "I won't hurt him," she promised.

"Perhaps not. Not yet, at all events," said Dr. Allen, "in a deeper sense than you realize."

"I still don't know what you mean. Anyway, you won't — I mean — if Ron —"

"I won't give you away," he said grimly. "God knows how you talked him into it."

Lydia smiled faintly.

She said, "Why should you? Don't pretend you won't be glad to have us here."

He said gravely, "My dear, of course I'll be glad. I wasn't facing the prospect of loneliness with pleasure."

When, later, Ron talked to him — in the office, as it happened — he was prepared for the careful explanation. Ron said, "It's just that we talked things over and thought that, perhaps, it might be wise after all if we — if you want us — made our home with you."

He was deeply embarrassed, so Allen was quickly helpful. "There's nothing I'd like better," he said, "my dear boy, you must know that."

Ron said, "Of course we did agree, you and I, that it was best for me and for Lydia to have our own place but — well, that can wait. I — naturally," he went on, his jaw stubborn, "there must be some sort of financial arrangement. Not that it would be commensurate . . . but I've set down the figures — what the rent of the apartment would have been and about what I could afford in the way of upkeep and food and —"

"Anything you wish," said the older man, as embarrassed as the younger.

A day or so later Allen had occasion to drop in and see Tatum, the cardiac specialist. It was his habit to do so every so often for a checkup.

"No change," said Tatum, after it was over.

Allen asked carelessly, "Been talking to Ron Lewis lately?"

"As a matter of fact, just the other night . . . we met in the corridor at the hospital and —"

"Say anything to him about me?"

"The usual. Just what I told you. What you can do, what you mustn't do. After all, he's your assistant. It's up to him to spare you where he can."

"I'm not ready to be relegated to the ash pile."

"Of course not. But you must be moderate. You can't undertake the hard jobs, not and live," warned Tatum, his spare face grave. "You can take this, Woody, that's why I've always talked plainly with you. Routine jobs, yes. Consultations, by all means. But no fireworks."

"Skip it," said Allen. "I know all that. Tell him anything else?"

"Him?"

"Ron, of course."

"Oh, the usual, no undue excitement, no emotional upset."

"That's it," said Allen, "that clinched it."

"What's that?"

"My mind wanders," Allen said; "forget it. I was thinking aloud. By the way, Ron's engagement to Lydia will be announced tomorrow."

"Keeping him in the family?" asked Tatum, going to the office door with him. "Well, a sound move. That's a great young man, I like him."

"I do too," said Allen.

Driving back to his office he put two and two together and arrived at a sufficiently round sum. He mustn't be upset. If for a moment Ron thought that Lydia's leaving her father's house would upset him, he would yield to any argument she might offer. "I bet he didn't say a word to her about Tatum," said Allen aloud. "If he did I don't know him as well as I think."

He closed his eyes and lay back against the upholstery of the big smooth-running car. So that's how it was. Don't be too easy with her, Ron, it will be fatal. But I can't tell him, I can't even warn him, not now, he'll have to find out for himself. God help them both.

The wedding was in June, on a clear bright day, and very simple. "I'd rather," said Lydia, "and it's easier on Father." Privately she dreaded the fatigue and preparations of a large wedding, the complications of bridesmaids and parties and goings-on. She concentrated on her trousseau, on changes in the rooms which she and Ron would occupy, and told her friends that because of her father's rather uncertain health the wedding must be a small one.

They were married in the apartment, in the big living room. No bridesmaids, no ushers. Not a great many people, but those who were there counted. As many again came for the reception afterward.

Mamie and Mat had come down, Ron put them up at a Madison Avenue Hotel, and they stayed only two days. Lydia was delighted with them, they were entranced by her. "Although," said Mat thoughtfully to Mamie, "I dunno why but I'm afraid of her."

"Nonsense," said Mamie, "she's sweet . . . she'll make him a wonderful wife. Jenny says so and Jenny knows her pretty well."

"Still," said Mat, "I ain't sure."

Somehow Lydia had arranged it so that Mat and Mamie were in Jenny's hands during the ceremony and reception, and in Aunt Sammy's afterward. Aunt Sammy could be counted upon, as could her father. When one of Lydia's dearest friends, a girl she greatly disliked, said to her, congratulating her on her appearance — and a prettier bride never stood against a bank of flowers and received felicitations, "Are those the in-laws, my sweet?" Lydia grinned and said cheerfully, "Yes, quaint, aren't they?"

"And how do they like the big city?"

"They love it," said Lydia, "and me."

Her friend regarded Ron. She said gently, "For his sake I'd suffer his relatives gladly, especially if they lived a good way off. Lydia, when the honeymoon is over I warn you I might be interested in husband snatching."

"Which won't," said Lydia, "worry me at all — seeing that it's you, Milly darling."

The honeymoon was spent at White Sulphur. Ron had wanted to go north, but Lydia had vetoed it. "Darling, let's be alone," she said. "We wouldn't be, I mean we couldn't turn your people out of the house . . . and besides . . . well, there's lots of time for that. I'm dying to see the place and the very first time you can take a holiday . . . but not now."

White Sulphur was a little steep, Ron thought, when they talked things over. Not so steep as Honolulu. Lydia had held out for Honolulu but he had assured her that he couldn't possibly spare the time. "Ten days," he said, "at the most."

"Ten days for our honeymoon!"

"We'll have all of our lives," he reminded her.

So in the end, White Sulphur . . . and a corner suite, very lovely, very luxurious. Lydia had reserved it.

Looking around, after the bellboys had deposited their bags and gone, Ron whistled. He said, "Lydia, we'll land in jail."

"Silly," she said, "what about our wedding present from Dad?"

It had been a check, very substantial. Ron said, "I thought we decided to put that in the savings bank."

"You're married," said Lydia, "for the first time, only once."

She was small, she was endearing, she smelled like spring and she looked like spring.

Ten days in White Sulphur, and then home again. Ten strange, bewildered days. She had said, "I'm — stupid, Ron . . . I've not even amused myself. I don't like skating on thin ice. So I'm a little frightened . . . but not of you, never of you."

Patience, gentleness, forbearance, sacrifice. He was a physician, he had talked to hundreds of women who had been frightened or brutalized or physically incapable of happy response. He did not believe the latter of Lydia. Time, he thought, patience, and loving each other so much —

A week before their wedding she had told him, "I don't want to have children, Ron. I mean, not at first."

He'd laughed a little. "Sounds odd," he said, "in the plural."

"I'm serious." She had her arms about him. "I want to be with you, just us," she said. "There's plenty of time."

He had said gently that he understood, but that no marriage was complete without children. "We have so much to give a child," he said, "we are young, we love each other."

"I know," she had told him desperately, "but not — not soon. Please . . . promise me, Ron, promise."

She had been even a little hysterical. Well, time would alter that. And she was right, there was no hurry. It would be better for her to adjust herself to marriage, to look forward to a continuance of their honeymoon for a time.

He promised, smoothing her hair back from her forehead, looking into her distended eyes.

"I'm such a coward," she told him.

"I'll never believe that."

Returning to New York, getting back into his work again, watching the ease with which Lydia settled down to her usual life, of friends, amusements, parties — an ease which he could not acquire, a life which he could not wholly share — he thought, It would have been better if I hadn't said we'd do this, if I had insisted on the apartment. This way, there's hardly a break between her old life and the one she leads with me.

But time was his ally, time was the great factor. He would be patient, he knew, he could wait, for his wife, for the woman who would be truly and happily his wife, and who would supplant, gradually, this reluctant bride, he could wait for her and for the woman who would become, with pride and a deep sense of fulfillment, the mother of his children.

He was thinking this when, returning one evening, he found that he had reached home before his wife. He went into his bedroom to shower and change before dinner. Dressing, he sat down on the edge of the bed to tie a shoelace. He was whistling, softly, a little off key. Where was Lydia? He missed her, he hated to return to a house empty of her.

There was a new medical book on his bedside table, and he picked it up and, leaning against the pillows, half dressed, began to read. But it was hard to concentrate. Another book lay there also. Mamie had given it to him while he was in college . . . a copy of Shakespeare's sonnets. He had little time for outside reading but this book had gone with him all through his medical training . . . this, and a tattered copy of *The Brushwood Boy*, and one or two others.

He put aside the medical book and picked up the other. It opened instantly to a familiar page, to the sonnet he liked best and best understood . . .

Let me not to the marriage of true minds
Admit impediments. Love is not love
Which alters when it alteration finds,
Or bends with the remover to remove:
O, no! it is an ever fixéd mark,
That looks on tempests and is never shaken;
It is the star to every wandering bark,
Whose worth's unknown, although his height
  be taken.
Love's not Time's fool, though rosy lips and
  cheeks
Within his bending sickle's compass come;
Love alters not with his brief hours and weeks,
But bears it out even to the edge of doom.
      If this be error and upon me proved,
      I never writ, nor no man ever loved.

He read it slowly, with deep concentration and a fresher, fuller understanding. That was it, he thought, that was how he felt, and as he believed. Shakespeare had written it centuries ago. True then, it was true now.

He heard the doorbell ring, and a moment later Lydia's light voice. He rose putting the book away. She had come home again, his love, more than his love, his child, his future, his happiness. The air was bright with her, and his heart. She was worth waiting for, he thought, worth living for.

He called her and at her answer all his doubts and vague, unformed anxiety fell from him and he went to meet her with open arms and an unclouded heart.

Chapter 7

On the fourth anniversary of his wedding, Ron Lewis drove to Southampton where Lydia had been in residence for two weeks, going down almost directly after her return from Sea Island. He reflected, maintaining a good but legal speed along the broad highways, that he had seen little of his wife in the past year. In his pocket was his anniversary present, the diamond he had not been able to afford at the time of their engagement.

Lydia had been angry with him because he could not promise her the weekend. "I'll move heaven and earth," he told her, "to be there overnight but more than that . . ."

She said, "You might spend a little time with me, Ron."

It had been that way ever since the first year, even earlier. You'd think, he reflected impatiently, that an obstetrician's daughter would know what we're up against. Babies rarely arrived on schedule. Their mothers were susceptible to shocks, emotional upsets, thunderstorms. Their mothers sometimes fell downstairs or were in automobile accidents. Often when you expected everything to go along normally and smoothly you found yourself coping with a totally unexpected, unforeseen difficulty.

Since the first of the year, Ron had been a full partner — no longer merely an assistant. The offices had been changed about, he now rated his own secretary and his own nurse, sisters, the capable Misses Watson. Dr. Allen had gradually retired more and more from active practice and since January was available only for consultations. He was busy because other men called him frequently and all of Ron's cases were under his advisement. It was fortunate that so many of his old patients had returned to the office, willing to let Ron handle their cases. And there were many new ones. Ron was beginning to acquire a reputation of his own.

He had worked hard for the past four years, he had not spared himself. He kept in excellent physical condition — he thrived, he told Jenny, on hard work, little play, and practically no exercise. He had put on ten pounds in weight but it became him and he could well afford it. He was beginning to get gray . . . early, as his father had.

Jenny had worked on the floor for a year, and had then left, registering at the registry and taking a small apartment with two other nurses, in order to do private duty, in the hospital and at home. Ron called her often during that time. Then she had returned to the hospital to take charge of the private obstetrical floor and only two months ago had been offered and accepted the position which, of all positions open to her in Lister, she had most wanted — that of day supervisor of the delivery room.

"I see less of you," he had complained, only

that morning, when after delivering husky twin boys he had showered, changed, and had a moment with her.

"You see me practically every day," she reminded him.

"With, however," he assured her, "no time for idle conversation. When are you off? Let's have dinner — perhaps. I won't depart with the soup as last time."

Working with Jenny was now familiar to him, and a joy which he took for granted.

In September, Jenny would have a brief vacation and Lydia had asked her to spend it in Southampton. She had not yet accepted. She was a little dubious. She felt uncomfortably that she had neither the clothes, manner, nor small talk for Lydia's table.

This morning Ron had reminded her of her half promise.

"Lydia expects you in September," he said.

Jenny hesitated. "I'm not sure —" she began.

He put his hand on her shoulder.

"Don't disappoint us," he told her, "and you need the change. You work like a nailer, Jenny . . . or is it perhaps that you don't want to leave town for personal reasons?"

Jenny flushed.

"That's nonsense," she said shortly.

"One hears rumors. Don't," he added, "be in too much of a hurry. Or is that selfishness on my part?"

Now, driving down to the Island he was remembering the conversation and the rumors. Jenny Barton was far too attractive to attract purely professional attention. Interns almost invariably fell in love with her and welcomed their service on obstetrical with extraordinary fervor. Cubs, thought Ron, not dry behind the ears. Older men too . . . notably the current Resident in Obstetrics, a good, hard-working young man, Ward Alymer. And there was an outsider in the running — curious how you thought of nonmedical men as outsiders, in this instance. What was his name . . . Smith? Jones? . . . No, Brown, wasn't it? Someone remotely related to friends of the Bartons at home, a successful life insurance man in New Jersey.

He thought, If anyone marries her and takes her away from Lister, I'll haunt him . . . he'll have cut off my right hand.

He reached Southampton in ample time to swim, shower, and dress before dinner. Driving down the lane which meandered to his father-in-law's house he breathed deeply of the salt, flower-scented air. The house stood back in a wide stretch of green lawns, old trees, and flower borders. Beyond it the Allen land ran to the ocean, a tangle of beach grass, climbing purple beach pea, and the tiny mauve flower of the sea lavender. The dunes paraded by, humpbacked from the wind, and the ocean was blue and green, breaking in rainbow spray.

Lydia preferred bathing at the club, all umbrellas and cabanas, but Ron in his scant free time liked going out from the house on a mother-of-pearl morning and invading a beach white and lonely, frequented only by gulls and waves, starfish and shells.

He left his car at the door and his father-in-law came up from under the trees to meet him. His bags were borne inside, the car put away.

"Glad you made it," said Allen, "Lydia's been fidgeting. How are things?"

Following Allen into the drawing room which had a marine quality, cool and cavelike, obtained by the use of pale-green walls and seascape hand-blocked draperies and a decorative motif of seashells and sea horses in the various accessories, Ron said, "All right. Believe it or not, Mrs. Everstrom is naming the twins after us."

"What!"

"Certainly. Allen and Lewis. Impressive, I calls it."

"I had no hand in it," said Allen, laughing.

"Strictly speaking, neither had I," replied Ron, grinning, "but she's determined. Nice little girl . . . says she can't stand her husband's given name nor her father's, and hasn't any uncles. Amazing child, all the fortitude in the world . . . when some time ago the X-rays show what we might expect she swore mildly and said, 'From debutante to multiple mother in one easy lesson.' When this morning I informed her that the babies were definitely male she said groggily, 'I would have boys when things look like war . . . double dependents,' and a little later she remarked that anyway she wouldn't worry about marrying them off."

"What did Everstrom say?"

"He fainted. Didn't I tell you when I phoned? Passed out cold on the reception-room floor to the horror of several pacing and prospective fathers." Ron sighed, "Lord," he said, "it's hot."

"Drink?"

"No, thanks. I'll take a swim presently. Too lazy to move from the chair at the moment. June seems to have borrowed some of the worst features of August. Where's Lydia?"

"I haven't seen her since breakfast," said Lydia's father; "she'll be along presently, I expect."

Ron got to his feet. He said, "She won't like it but I have to go back tomorrow . . . can't help it. Mrs. Everstrom's in Alymer's hands and he'll keep in touch. But Mrs. Thomas came in night before last. I don't much like the way things look." He rose reluctantly from the deep chair into which he had cast himself. "I want to talk to you," he said.

"I'll come along," said Dr. Allen, "and watch you get out of those store clothes."

Ron's room in the big square house, with its wide verandas and weather-stained shingles, had recently been done over. It was definitely masculine, cool, restrained, not a frill or an unnecessary object — enormous ash trays, big chairs, excellent reading lights, the coloring the green-blue of the water and the beige-gold of sand. Lydia had permitted herself a touch of whimsey in his bath, the seashell, sea horse, sea gull pattern of the wallpaper and shower curtains.

Ron undressing, talked rapidly. Allen listened, nodded, spoke his professional piece now and then. He thought, surveying his son-in-law's stripped, firm-fleshed body, what a pity it was that Lydia seemed irrevocably opposed to perpetuating the race.

Later, when the discussion of Mrs. Thomas's case had been concluded, Dr. Allen said:

"Lydia has been unusually restless this summer. I made up my mind when you were married that I wouldn't interfere in any way . . . and that I wouldn't discuss — but frankly I worry about her, Ron. She's too thin, too — hair trigger. And I don't like some of her new friends."

"For instance?"

"Well, for instance . . . since the start of the European war we've been acquiring a number of refugees," said Allen slowly.

"I know, I've met 'em."

"With money," Allen said. "Not that I can blame them . . . but I definitely dislike the expatriate Americans, who couldn't endure our lack of culture and whose roots, friendships, affections — if any — were bound up in London or Paris, Nice or Rome. Now they're back . . . running to cover . . . money, foreign cars, jewels, paintings, and in some instances furniture. Have you met Lydia's latest enthusiasm, Amabell Jarvis?"

"No."

"Forty," said Dr. Allen, "and very good look-ing, although I have long since ceased to take anything but an academic interest in women's appearance. Married here, at nineteen, the Jarvis whose father made himself spectacular in steel . . . with two e's, although some say otherwise. She and her husband went abroad for their honeymoon and remained there. He was killed ten years later in some sort of night-club brawl. She didn't remarry. She has lived ever since in Paris and on the Riviera, when she wasn't trav-eling. Now she's back. She has," he added, "a brother . . . Timothy Wilson. Unmarried, at the moment. Has a place here which she's taken over lock, stock, and barrel. He hasn't been here for years until this season. He hunts big game," said Allen, shrugging. "And it seems there isn't much scope for that now."

He's warning me, thought Ron.

He had put on his trunks, a toweling bathrobe, and sandals. He said soberly. "Bigger game afoot now . . . think we're going to get into this?"

"God knows," Allen answered, sighing.

Nineteen-forty; and people beginning to ask, Are we going to get into it? In October the first young men would register for the draft.

He added, "You'll meet them tonight."

"Who?"

"Amabell and Timothy."

"We won't," said Ron briefly, "have much in common."

"Amabell may think so," said Allen, but Ron,

107

opening the door, did not hear him. Allen rose slowly. He made no hasty, ill-considered movement these days. He said wistfully, "I miss swimming more than golf."

They went downstairs together and presently Ron went out alone to the beach. He sat down there, his back against a small rounded dune, and looked out at the Atlantic. Gulls cried, in their melancholy impatient fashion, and their star-shaped footprints were printed on the wet brown sand. A wave rolled in, breaking in spray, and the sea was golden with the late afternoon sunset. It was cold and bracing, he found, plunging in and swimming strongly, diving through the breakers, letting the water wash away the accumulated torpor of fatigue, heat, dried sweat —

He went back reluctantly, and hearing voices on the terrace, skirted round the bathers' way, through a side door, up back stairs and to his room. The sun would set presently and the salty darkness close down, miraculous with stars. He thought how pleasant it would be to sit quietly at home this evening with Lydia and her father, out on the terrace after dinner, and not talk much. Had she come home? he wondered.

While he was dressing, Lydia knocked on the communicating door and came in.

"Darling?"

"Here," he said.

She was ready for dinner, her fair hair piled on top of her little head in a mass of curls, and looked like a child with her hair caught up carelessly before the bath. She wore a cool striped cotton frock, in the green she most loved, tight in the bodice, full in the long smart skirt, and the emeralds. There were green sandals, very high-heeled, on her bare feet and her toenails, perfect as seashells, were painted the bright, provocative red of her fingernails and her mouth.

He put his arms around her. "I thought you'd never come home," he said.

"Careful of lipstick," she warned him. "And hurry, do, Ron, the mob's coming for cocktails early . . . I thought we'd go to the club and dance after —"

He sighed, "How many of us?"

"Only twenty," she said, "just a family party."

"Who's stopping here?" he wanted to know. Absurd that he didn't.

"Aunt Sammy. Evelyn and Tom. No one else."

"Lydia . . ." He went to the bureau, took from the top the little tooled leather box. "For our anniversary," he said.

She opened it, smiled, and slipped the ring on her finger.

"But it's lovely," she said, "lovely. Thank you, angel." She stood on tiptoe to kiss him lightly. "A smudge, after all," she added tragically. "Ron —" she scrubbed his lean cheek with a wisp of lace and linen — "you're staying the weekend?"

"I can't, dear."

She said, "You might have made an effort, but you haven't. It will be like this all summer."

"I'm sorry."

Lydia shrugged. "Skip it," she said briefly, and he drew his breath in relief. No scene, then? Last summer many scenes. The summer before . . .

She said, "I have a present for you too — wait a minute."

He had finished dressing when she returned with the cuff links — and gave them to him.

"There," she said. "Like them?"

"They're beautiful," he said, wondering how Mamie would react to star sapphires.

"I hoped you'd think so. Do hurry," she urged, and vanished.

Cuff links, cigarette case, evening studs. He was acquiring a jewelry wardrobe, he thought. Lydia's father was generous with her.

Tying his tie he stared somberly into the mirror. Portrait of a successful physician. Park Avenue apartment, Long Island country house, a good small car. Your wife has her own. Platinum and star sapphires . . .

I didn't want this, he thought. This isn't what I wanted.

There was no earthly reason why he and Lydia could not have their own perfectly adequate apartment now. Except that she didn't want it. It had taken him four years to learn that. He knew now that his father-in-law would not have minded.

If I had any guts, he told himself, I'd insist.

Of course, as his income increased so had his contributions to the living expenses. But, he suspected, Allen returned that money to Lydia . . .

not that anyone had told him so.

Once when he had said something, she flashed out at him:

"Don't be stuffy. It will all be ours someday — and after all we're all he has."

True, of course. Realistic. He had hated it, it had hit him definitely at the pit of his stomach and sickened him.

Four years. He had been upstate just once, when Mat died. Lydia had been annoyed. She was booked to go south, she had said, "But I can't change all my plans . . . and you promised you'd come, if only for a week."

It was hard to explain to Mamie why Lydia hadn't been with him. Hard, because she seemed to understand and he would so much rather she hadn't.

He had found Mamie lonely. He had thought, If things were different . . . we'd sell the place for what we can get, bring Mamie to New York to live with us. Out of the question; even in altered circumstances Mamie would be utterly lonely and at sea.

Mrs. Roberts was moving in with her, the two of them would live in the old house together. Bill Treat was still in the tenant house. Ron saw him, on that brief trip home, a year and a half ago. He saw the little Treat boy, a sturdy, happy-go-lucky youngster, brown scratched legs and brown determined face. Mamie said, "Bill's thinking of marrying again."

"Do I know her?"

"No. Rose Lambert. New people, they took the old Tilton farm. Bill's mother-in-law is ill. She likes Rose, picked her out for him. Not that he's got over Lily. He's queer about the boy too, Ron. Does everything for him, no one could complain. But there's something wrong, something missing. I can't explain."

"He still holds the resentment?" asked Ron, unastonished. "It sometimes happens. And it's too damned bad."

He'd like to talk to Bill about that; couldn't of course, he had no right. They weren't intimates, weren't even friends. Yet if the opportunity came he might try.

He tried haltingly, sitting in the tenant house parlor the evening after Mat's funeral, after the boy had gone to bed. He said, "Swell kid of yours, Bill."

"Oh, sure," said Bill, "he's all right."

You didn't get anywhere that way. He tried again, searching for the right words. Bill let him search. Looked at him hard, after a time.

"I know what you're trying to get at, doc," he told him. "It's no use. I never look at him that I don't see Lily."

Ron felt a sharp exasperation, and a sharper pity.

He said, "Other men's wives have died, Bill, and their greatest comfort has been in the children they —"

"This was different," interrupted Bill. "She — never knew. She wasn't his mother, not for a

112

minute. She was dead, wasn't she? Sometimes when I look at him it makes me sick." He jerked his head. "Grandma's ailing," he said, "wants I should get married again, afraid she'll die and leave the boy. Maybe I will. There's a girl — I like her all right, she's not too young, and — But we won't have any kids."

That was that. You did what you had to, what was right, ethical and consistant with your beliefs and your professional oath . . . and what happened? A little boy grew up on a farm and his father was sickened by him. . . .

"Ron," said Lydia, and erupted into the room, "in heaven's name what are you doing? The people are beginning to come."

He shook himself, like a dog, and followed her downstairs.

Chapter 8

The anniversary dinner was very gay. Aunt Sammy was stupendous in — of all things on a hot night — black velvet and pearls. The dining room opened on the flagged terrace and the long table was cool with crystal and silver, early roses, all white, in silver bowls, tall candles flickering.

Amabell Jarvis sat at Ron's right. She was a pretty, febrile woman, redheaded, lean as a whip. Her smooth tinted face was twenty-five only and her hands were forty. She wore very little, extremely well. Her back and neck and breast and her long thin arms were copper colored and she had immense, startling brown eyes.

She said, "I've heard about you."

"Good, I hope."

"Not altogether. It is said that you neglect your wife." She regarded him critically. "Which is stupid," she added, "Lydia's not the type — no Penelope, Lydia." She laughed and it sounded like ice tinkling. "Yet, on the other hand . . ."

"What?"

"Never mind. I didn't know," she said, "that you were as good looking . . . I hear you aren't available socially. How does one go about engaging you — professionally?"

He said gently, "I'm an obstetrician."

"It could be managed," she murmured, "but —"

Aunt Sammy on his left spoke to him, and he turned gratefully.

After cocktails on the terrace, champagne. Lydia raised her glass. She was rather like the wine, he thought, dry, heady, golden, sparkling, restless. She said gaily, "I don't often indulge, but as this is our anniversary —"

"Lucky man," said Timothy Wilson, looking down the table at Ron. Wilson was dark and heavy, with a swarthy face under astonishingly white hair and dark eyes beneath black brows. "You don't appreciate your good fortune."

"Timothy," murmured Amabell, "is very smitten. Or don't you heed the gypsy's warning?"

Ron roused himself. This idiotic give-and-take, this senseless type of conversation! He said, "I expect every man to be smitten with my wife."

Dinner. Coffee and liqueurs on the terrace, the exodus, late, to the club. Music and people and lights. It was very late when they reached home and Ron knocked on Lydia's door and went in.

She was at her dressing table, brushing her hair. He stood a moment looking at her . . . nothing lovelier than a woman brushing her hair, someone had said, hadn't they? The pure line from armpit to wrist, the lifted breast, the slow sweep of the brush.

Nothing lovelier? He remembered the Cinalli girl, one of his clinic patients, lying in the ward, as he came in, her head bent, the child at her breast. He thought of the women who came to his office, heavy and distorted, but with that expression in their eyes, that expression you cannot define, hope and patience and a waiting radiance.

"Wasn't it a lovely party?" She swung around on the padded bench and smiled at him, yawned like a kitten. "I'm so sleepy," she complained. "By the way, you made an enormous hit with Amabell. What did you think of her?"

"Very attractive," he said briefly. He sat down beside her and took the brush from her hand.

"I haven't had a moment alone with you," he said.

"Whose fault is it? Had you come earlier —"

"You would have been out."

"No. And if you would stay —"

"Lydia, I can't."

She patted his cheek. "I know, I'm not cross, really — perhaps next weekend. And I'll come up the middle of the week, for the day, we'll dine together . . . if you can promise me you won't be called."

"You'll stay in town?"

"Not in this heat," she said; "you know what it does to me. I can drive down after dinner."

"Lydia . . ."

Four years. He had been all he had hoped to be, he had been patient and gentle and forbearing. And nothing had changed. She said, with her arms around him, that she loved him. Perhaps she did. Over and over she had said it — if less frequently in the last year. But he had never been able to overcome the reluctance, the cool, still remoteness. Lydia surrendered nothing of herself, gave nothing.

Good God, he was a doctor, wasn't he? If she was nothing to him, a strange woman, a patient . . . he could talk to her with wisdom and understanding, he could even say, "Will you ask your husband to come and see me?"

A lunatic situation.

Lydia yawned again. She said, "Kiss me, darling, and run along. I'm dead."

When he left in the morning she was asleep. He had his early swim and then breakfast with his father-in-law . . . the house guests were of the ring-for-your-tray variety. Then he went upstairs and very softly into Lydia's room.

She slept heavily, almost as if drugged. He did not go too near, fearing to waken her. There was a curious faint odor in the room despite the open windows. He sensed it, and it disturbed him vaguely. It was sweet, and clinging — some new perfume, he thought. Lydia liked perfume and collected it.

She wore a little black mask over her eyes to shut out the morning light. The shades were drawn and the salt air fluttered them and crept in underneath. Sunlight danced through. Ron stood at some distance from the bed. Her face in repose was blank under the mask. All individuality had gone from it. Her mouth, still faintly rose with last night's lipstick, looked swollen and her breathing was heavy.

He went nearer, quietly, saw the glass on the

night table and picked it up. After a moment he set it down again . . . and went cautiously away.

All the way back to New York his mind grappled with this new, this utterly horrifying thought.

But Lydia rarely drank. A glass of champagne the night before, that was all. He recalled Amabell congratulating her on her abstemiousness. "No wonder," said Amabell, "that you keep your figure and your skin."

Before they were married, Ron remembered, he had felt that she drank too much. Not that she was ever — No, of course not, merely a little high-keyed, high-pitched, excitable. But because he hadn't liked it she had stopped, she rarely accepted a cocktail, a social highball. Now and then she said, "Ron doesn't like me to."

He had expostulated on several occasions, "But I didn't mean that you should wear the white badge," he said, "I merely thought —"

She shrugged. "You know me," she'd said, "the whole hog or nothing."

A headache perhaps? Aspirin and a small shot of whisky?

Or she hadn't been able to sleep?

If there had ever been anything, surely Allen would have known and spoken of it to him. I'm imagining things, he told himself, just because I go into her room and find her sleeping too heavily, with a glass beside her that has contained Scotch.

Nevertheless, he thought, when she came to

town he would speak to her about it.

When toward the middle of the week she came to town he had forgotten, as Mrs. Thomas, despite his every effort to save her, had died.

Every effort had been made . . . every effort was not enough. Allen had driven up from the Island, at an irrational rate of speed. Afterward Ron remembered most vividly Jenny's eyes . . . and Allen's. They had been alike in their expression of pity and affection, for him.

Much later, having gone through the utterly dreadful ordeal of informing his patient's husband and parents, he sat in his office with Allen across from him and went over and over in every detail his handling of the case.

Allen said finally, "Stop it, Ron, you're wearing yourself out."

"I must have failed somewhere."

"No. This was an utterly unforeseen complication."

He said restlessly, "I didn't like the way things were going . . . I brought her into the hospital where she could be watched."

Allen said, "You'll have to forget it."

"How do you go about that?" asked Ron after a few moments. "I don't forget failures."

Allen said after a minute, "When I was an intern I was sent out on the bus to deliver a child in a tenement. The patient wasn't one of our clinic cases. I'd never seen her before. A neighbor called the hospital, and I was on service. When I got to the place, up the rickety stairs smelling of cabbage and poverty, I found something that not one experienced obstetrician in a thousand finds over a long period of practice. Locked twins. I tried to remember all I knew, in theory. I made an attempt to displace the second child upward, and failed. So I did what I had to do . . . I sacrificed the first child and prepared to deliver the second. I remember even now the sweat and the horror and the suddenly clumsy feel of the forceps in my hand. But the second child was already dead. I went back to the hospital and I swore to myself that when my internship was over I would never deliver another child. I would go in for general medicine . . . I would specialize in nose and throat . . . I would do cancer research. Anything but *that*." He smiled faintly. "Well," he said, "I didn't keep my oath, did I?"

"No; but you haven't forgotten."

Allen rose. He said, "Judging by your calendar you could, with impunity, take a few days off. Come down to the Island."

Ron shook his head. "I'd rather not. I don't fit in, in my present humor. There's enough routine work here to keep me busy."

"Lydia's coming up tomorrow," said his father-in-law. "I suggest you dine out, get tickets for a play."

"All right," Ron said dully.

Lydia blew into his office, fresh as a breeze, fragrant as wind blowing over a rose garden. She waved the competent Misses Watson aside and perched herself on his desk. She asked, "Any time free — for me?"

He looked at her, and looking, remembered the morning after his anniversary. Surely there had been nothing alarming. Her eyes were clear and bright, as she smiled at him.

"Dinner," he suggested, "theater?"

"Wonderful!"

"And you'll stay in?"

"I can't, darling. I've promised Tim and Amabell to golf tomorrow."

"But surely you can break —"

She said, "I love driving down at night, by myself — dark empty roads, and the stars —"

He said, "I don't like it. You drive too fast."

"Silly!"

"No. I worry about you, Lydia."

"One would never dream it. Shall we see if Jenny can go with us?"

"No," he said firmly, "I want you to myself."

"Poor Jenny, she hasn't much fun. I phoned her last night. She's off today and lunching with me. Sure you won't join us?"

He didn't want to see Jenny. She was too closely connected with the weight on his heart, the troubled searching of his mind, going over every detail of the Thomas case trying to find the blind spot —

He shook his head.

"Dinner, then," she said, "somewhere cool and gay . . . Waldorf Roof perhaps? I'll get seats for something."

She slid off the desk, kissed him and was gone. A little later that morning she sat in a city garden gay with umbrellas and green tables facing Jenny.

"I wanted you to dine and see a play with us tonight," she said, "but Ron . . ." She shrugged. "Sorry, my dear."

If she was trying to hurt Jenny — and why should she? — she did not succeed. "I understand," said Jenny quickly.

"Which is more than I do."

"You underestimate your own charms," Jenny told her with her faint, slow smile. "He's tired. He doesn't want to be reminded of Lister on a free evening."

"It's something more, isn't it? Of course he never tells me anything."

"He lost a case."

"Oh, that. Dad said something. But why should — ?"

"He doesn't lose one often," said Jenny, "and when he does he's sunk. This couldn't be avoided. He'd taken every precaution but —"

"Spare me the details," begged Lydia. "Ron's a fool to take things to heart the way he does."

"He can't help that."

"He could help a lot of things. I never see him, really. When I accept an invitation, for us, it's on the understanding that he may not show up at all or may have to leave in the middle of things. It's distracting, Jenny. Ever since we were married he's promised me that if there was ever a lull he'd go away with me . . . turn things over to Jim Foster, if they were out of Dad's present province, but no! He hasn't had a vacation since we were married. A year ago last spring he joined me at the Richards' in Tyron and flew back after two days . . . some silly woman in a panic."

Jenny remembered the case. Not a silly woman and not a panic, but every symptom of toxemia.

She said consolingly:

"He had every reason to return. I know it isn't easy for you."

"You don't know anything about it! Besides, you're on his side. Doctors and nurses stick together. The way those girls watchdog him at the office. Tweedledum and Tweedledee. They regard me with disapproval. Even when I phone, one or the other drips lemonade at me over the wire. 'Yes, of course, Mrs. Lewis. Dr. Lewis is busy just now, shall I have him call you?' It's maddening. Ron should have married a nurse. You, for choice."

"That's crazy," said Jenny calmly.

"Why? You understand him, you think he's gold, you've always doted on him."

"I'm fond of him," said Jenny heatedly, "but —"

"Don't go all stiff and high hat on me," said Lydia, laughing. "You always idealized Ron. If you had to live with him, however . . ."

Jenny's heart skipped a beat. She was exceedingly annoyed with herself. She said, "You're talking nonsense."

Lydia grinned. She said, "Jenny, I've seen you frequently during the past few years. I like you. You don't always approve of me, but you do conceal it nicely. I feel — free with you. I don't have to be on my guard. You rest me. I like you. And I'm not liking you a bit less because I suggest that the reason you aren't marrying Ward Alymer or that nice Brown boy you brought to dinner last winter is because of Ron."

"That," said Jenny, "is ridiculous and entirely uncalled for."

She thought, in sudden, blinding fear, It isn't true, it can't be. She even prayed, childishly. She prayed, God, don't *let* it be true.

"Okay," said Lydia, "I was merely suggesting that Ron married the wrong woman."

"He married," said Jenny, "the woman with whom he was in love."

"He has a curious way of showing it," Lydia said. "And I'm *bored*. What's the use of being married if you rarely see your husband and if, when you do, he's too tired to be even moderately amusing?"

Jenny said hesitantly, "Lydia, if you and Ron had a —"

"Jenny Barton," said Lydia with venom, "if you are going to suggest that I have a child to relieve my boredom, I'll scream. I'll throw things. It's Ron's prescription for whatever is the matter with any woman and for four years now it's been his prescription for me."

"He loves children," said Jenny slowly.

"You've never seen him in the hospital — with the babies, I mean — have you?"

"No, and I'd rather not. My cousin — Aunt Sammy's ewe lamb — came on from Chicago with her two last winter and we went to Aunt Sammy's for dinner and Ron was absolutely besotted. Of course one of them *does* look a little like me — personally I think she's a shade cross-eyed but —"

The captain came over. He asked, "Are you enjoying your luncheon, Mrs. Lewis?"

"Very much — but there was too much salt in the Madrilene."

He was stricken. He said, "I'm sorry." He lingered . . . "a liqueur perhaps with your coffee . . . ? It is too warm for a house special, I presume, I noticed you didn't —"

"House special?" repeated Lydia, lifting her eyebrows. "What's that? A new cocktail?"

The captain looked amazed. He said, "But you always prefer —"

"It sounds interesting," said Lydia. "No, no liqueur, thank you."

He went away feeling as if someone had hit him on the head with a large hammer. Mrs. Lewis often came here alone . . . and he was certain that the bartender had mixed her as many as three house specials before luncheon and that she had put them away without turning a single golden hair.

When he had gone, Lydia said carelessly:

"Obvious, isn't it, the way they try to lead you

125

to drink? Of course that's where these places make their money. Jenny, you haven't forgotten I expect you down for September. Don't look like that, as if you were mustering any old excuse. You know you don't want to go home."

Jenny had no home, not since Dr. Barton had died. She could go to her mother and her aunt in Cooperstown, but she didn't want to. One of the girls had suggested, as their vacations ran concurrently, that they take a cruise together. Pete Brown wanted her to stay in town . . . Ward Alymer too. She said, "Lydia, it's sweet of you —"

"I won't have any excuses! You must come. You work like a fool. You must take a rest. Perhaps you can persuade Ron to take a few days off at the same time. You have more influence with him than I."

A man came up, threading his way between the gay umbrellas and Lydia shrieked, "Tim, what brings you to town?"

"As if you didn't know! May I sit down?" His dark eyes regarded Jenny with interest.

Lydia made them known to each other. Jenny sat back and drank her coffee and listened to their stenographic conversation, which was entirely without meaning for her, until Wilson said:

"I came up on business, very stuffy train. Are you staying in tonight, my sweet?"

"No, I'm driving down after the theater."

"Good," he said. "May I thumb a ride, darling?"

126

She was instantly animated. "I'd love it. Where shall I pick you up?"

"At the club," said Wilson, "about — elevenish? I'll be waiting."

He went off, to his own table, where a couple of men waited for him, and Lydia, meeting Jenny's eye, shrugged.

"Well," she said defiantly, "I have to be amused, don't I? I didn't marry Ron to retire into a corner, with a lace cap and my knitting. It isn't serious," she added, smiling, "his sister's a very good friend of mine. You'll meet her in September."

Jenny thought, Not if I can help it. Of course I won't go — why should I? I'd just be in the way.

Lydia said coaxingly, "Don't look so severe. I want you, Jenny. I get tired of other people but you're always the same. I rely on you."

Good old Jenny, Jenny thought, nice dog Tray . . . I believe she means that. But why, in heaven's name?

It seemed utterly fantastic to her that Ron Lewis's wife should rely on her.

"All right," she said, "I'll come."

Chapter 9

When, chic as tomorrow's fashion show, Amabell Jarvis walked into Ron's office a few days after Lydia's brief excursion to town, Ron was not particularly astonished. After her various opening gambits such a move was both conventional and indicated.

At the club, after the anniversary dinner, he had danced with her several times. He was by no means an inspired dancer, being rather on the earnest and plodding side. Lydia openly despaired of him but Amabell Jarvis appeared hopeful and, he told her, patient. Gyrating solemnly around the crowded floor, endeavoring to keep his mind on his feet, he had observed, with detached amusement, Amabell's method of attack.

It consisted of conversational reconnaissance — the provocative phrase, like a trial balloon — accompanied by a completely expressionless countenance, the dead-pan approach; and of the physical foray of her personal terpsichorean technique, majoring in measured intimacy. This entertained her partner considerably, possibly, as he admitted to himself, because his personal chemistry remained unaffected. Definitely, Amabell was not his type.

He was busy when she arrived at the office and it pleased him to keep her waiting. When she was admitted to the consultation room by a somewhat disapproving Miss Watson, he observed that all her appointments were in order . . . except one. She admitted this at once.

"I didn't telephone for an appointment — as I was perfectly sure you wouldn't give me one."

He said ruefully, "Professional men — doctors, lawyers, ministers — are always available. But I am quite sure that you are in no need of my particular type of service."

"How kind — to give me the benefit of the doubt." Her long, turquoise eyes danced. "I'm really not well at all. Of course, my dreadful experience in France . . ." She shrugged her shoulders and added, "I'm not sleeping, my appetite is poor."

He doubted that, listening.

"I'm jumpy," she went on, "my disposition is dreadful, and I'm bored."

Ron said after a moment, "I could recommend an excellent internist — or perhaps . . ." He regarded her speculatively. Let her have it, he thought, both barrels. He added, "Let me see, you are, I suppose, forty —"

Amabell demonstrated that she was "jumpy." She said reproachfully, "That's not very chivalrous. Thirty-nine."

Forty-two, thought Ron. Aloud he said, "I would suggest one of my colleagues. Gary Williams — he's extremely competent."

Amabell laughed suddenly. She said:

"All right, colonel, I'll come down. There isn't

a thing the matter with me, really. I just wanted to see you again. As you have remarked, doctors have no protection from predatory females. They are always available. Why I came —"

"Indeed," he murmured, "why?"

She said, "You're impossible. Will you take me to lunch . . . or don't you eat?"

He said, with slight regret, "Not today . . . I'm afraid."

"Some other time?" She leaned toward him across the desk. "Why don't you arrange to come down to the Island more often?"

He answered, smiling, "My time is hardly my own . . . as the race isn't reproduced with any consideration of leisurely weekends. Babies aren't interested in overtime, Sundays, or holidays, Mrs. Jarvis."

She said mournfully, "You might manage Amabell, although it's a silly name, isn't it? After all, I am Lydia's best friend."

One of many . . . a bright parade, a succession.

"Amabell," he agreed. He wrote something on a prescription blank, and held it toward her. She took it, and looked, not at it but at him.

"What's this?"

"The doctors I mentioned. Names and addresses . . . just in case."

She said, "You are determined to keep this call on a strictly business basis."

"Naturally."

"You'll even send me a bill?"

"Of course," he said, without smiling, "I assume that Miss Watson has taken your —"

"A complete dossier," she broke in, and regarded him with open pleasure. Attractive, wary, hard to get. She asked, "You don't really expect me to pay it?"

He said gently, "You are taking up my time."

"I should be very angry with you," Amabell said, "but I'm not. I'll pay your bill, and I'll do you a favor in return. Good for evil. If I were you, I'd neglect my profession more and my wife less."

His face hardened and changed. He said, "I believe you advised something similar the other night."

She said complacently, "I got under your skin, didn't I? Touché. That's something. I am fond of Timothy, he is my only close relative, but I have no illusions about him. He usually gets all he wants. It is rarely conventional. At present he is quite desperately in love with Lydia."

"One cannot blame him," Ron remarked evenly.

She said vigorously, "I could slap you. Are you really so civilized — or, perhaps, so indifferent? If indifferent, then of course it doesn't matter. I am wasting my time as well as yours. Timothy's chief interest lies in pretty women — married women, I might add. He has no desire for personal domesticity. More than one deluded husband has permitted his palpitating wife to divorce him in order to marry Timothy but somehow when the term in Reno or Idaho was over Timothy had disappeared . . . he always sends orchids and a regretful note."

Ron pressed a button and spoke into the contrivance on his desk. He inquired of Miss Watson if there were any patients in the reception room and she informed him that there were two.

He said, "I'm sorry, but I have appointments."

Amabell rose. Her black linen suit resisted creases, her black sailor, set far back on her head, revealed a smooth red pompadour and was augmented by impossible turquoise-colored birds. She drew on her gloves and silver and turquoise bracelets clashed on her thin wrists.

"You're stubborn," she said, "and riding, I may add, for a fall. You can't expect a girl like Lydia to sit at home and twiddle her thumbs."

"It's a shocking picture," he agreed, and rose to escort her to the door. He opened it for her and said, "I hope you find your insomnia a temporary inconvenience."

She made a hideous face at him, to the astonishment of an approaching Miss Watson, and left. He said, "Just a minute, Miss Watson. I'll ring."

That means, give me a moment before you send Mrs. Hallam in. He sat down at his desk and was amazed to find that he was sweating. Amabell Jarvis no longer amused him. It would have been a privilege to wring her neck. But why, he wondered, this elaborate warning? Did she really have any feeling for Lydia . . . was she less fond of her brother than she professed or, he inquired without vanity, was she trying to discover the exact extent of his vulnerability?

The door opened and he looked up, frowning. He had not rung. But it was merely Amabell again, with, in the background, the protesting faces of both the Misses Watson, a sort of starched Greek chorus.

She said, "I came back because I forgot to tell you that the other night Lydia picked Tim up at the club and drove him down to the Island."

The door closed and she vanished. Ron's mouth set, a hard firm line. He rang for Miss Watson and she appeared, unusually voluble.

"I'm sorry," she began, "I —"

He said, "That's all right. Send Mrs. Hallam in, will you?"

Mrs. Hallam was twenty. She had been runner-up to the Number One Glamour Girl of her season. She had married and was now engaged in having a baby. She was small, blond, and nervous. Her mother, a formidable and fashionable beauty, usually accompanied her upon her routine visits but on this occasion she was alone. She was obsessed with the idea that she was certain to die, or, if she didn't, the baby might be born maimed or halt . . . in short, a prey to the neurotic imaginings of many young women in her condition.

Ron kept her with him for nearly an hour. He assured her that she was in every way a completely normal young woman and that she had nothing to fear. Everything was going along nicely. There was nothing to do but wait. She had her instructions — diet, prescribed exercise, rest, sleep. Her job was to achieve and maintain the proper mental attitude. This he was certain she would accomplish.

She said earnestly, "You do help me, Dr. Lewis, every time I come. It's Mother. She drives me crazy, fusses over me as if I was made of glass and —"

"It's your job," he told her, "not your mother's." He smiled at her and she smiled back, reluctantly. "You're grown up," he suggested, "and this is your responsibility."

The next patient was less difficult, another routine visit and checkup, but this child would be her third. Dr. Allen had delivered the first two.

"I miss him," she said frankly. "How is he?"

"Very well," said Ron, "if he takes care."

She said, rising to leave, "You mustn't think that I lack confidence in you. I don't. You've been wonderful."

Nothing, he thought, to be wonderful about. Nice sensible woman, good head on her shoulders, obeys orders, takes things as they come. Wish they were all like her.

He had luncheon sent in, a sandwich and a bottle of milk, and then went to the hospital. While he was there an emergency call reached him and he went uptown immediately to find his patient manifesting a sudden, alarming rise in blood pressure. By the time he had her in the hospital it was late afternoon and he returned to the office conscious of an unusual sense of fatigue.

Twenty-four hours would determine things, for if, after rest in bed, a milk diet and other measures, Mrs. Young's blood pressure continued to rise, the suspicion of impending eclampsia would be strengthened. She would be far better off in the hospital under constant observation, he had assured her distracted husband, summoned from the office. It was probable that she would respond to treatment, the blood pressure would subside, and that eventually she could return home and wait, under careful watching, the termination of her pregnancy. He wished he could assure himself as readily. He dreaded these cases.

He went to the apartment, shortly before dinnertime. He might, he thought, look in at the club or perhaps stay at home and read. He'd look in at the hospital before going to bed.

At seven-thirty, just sitting down to dinner cooked and served by the manservant Lydia had engaged to look after him with the departure of the regular staff for Southampton, the telephone rang.

"What is it, Andy?"

Andy, small, stooped, efficient, reported that Miss Barton was on the wire.

"Good Lord," said Ron, horrified, and went to the telephone.

Jenny said, "Ron? I thought I'd better phone . . . did you just get in?"

135

This was the night they were to dine together. She was to have met him at Henri's. He said, stricken:

"My dear child, are you at Henri's? How long have you been waiting?"

"Only half an hour. You've been held up, I suppose."

He said, "I'll be right there."

He went back to the dining room to tell Andy that he must go on out. "No, no dinner," he said, "sorry . . . I forgot an engagement."

Andy, thinking of chops and salad, sighed. But he was by now accustomed to the vagaries of this household.

Arriving at Henri's, Ron found Jenny sitting on the leather bench waiting for him, without the obvious patience which infuriates a man because it reproaches him. He asked, taking her hands, "Can you ever forgive me?"

"Of course." They went into the dining room and had a table against the wall. She said, smiling, "Don't look so abject, Ron. I assumed you'd been held up."

He said contritely, "Jenny, I forgot. That's all there was to it."

Jenny laughed. "All right, so you forgot. But I reminded you, and here we are." She added, "You look terribly tired. Had a hard day?"

"Not really." He smiled at her, in relief. "You're very unlike most women," he said, "and perhaps I paid you a greater compliment by not lying to you."

She said seriously, "I would hate it if you lied to me, Ron."

They had their dinner, talked of the hospital, of Lydia. It was Jenny who spoke of her first. She said, her smooth brows drawn, "I'm worried about her."

"Why?" asked Ron, lighting a cigarette and ordering more coffee.

"She's terribly restless."

"So her father says. What am I to do about it, Jenny?" he asked soberly.

She shook her dark head.

"I wish I knew," she answered.

"I'm at a loss," he told her. "The only advice I have received — and it was quite gratuitous — is to neglect her less. Just how that is to be accomplished," he added, "I haven't the faintest idea."

She said, "If only she could find some interest with which to occupy herself —"

"Good works?" asked Ron wryly. "Civic duties? Fund raising for this and that charity, for war relief? But she does, my dear, sporadically. She works like hell, she has a genius for organization, for driving herself and other people. Of course she overdoes it, wears herself out, her enthusiasm wears out with it, and she drops it until next time. That's Lydia and as far as I can see nothing can be done about it."

Jenny said, "I know." She looked at him with the frank regard of established friendship. "If only she'd have a child."

"She doesn't want children," he said shortly. He laughed, without amusement. "Funny, isn't it," he added, "when you stop to think how my days are spent?"

Jenny said slowly, "She's afraid. Ron, have you ever considered suggesting that you — adopt a child?"

"That's ridiculous," he said strongly, "as there isn't any reason why we shouldn't —"

"I know," she interrupted, "but if she won't? She might consider an adoption . . . and if she became interested in and attached to the baby then perhaps she would come to want one of her own."

"Rather hard on the first one," he asked, "isn't it?"

"I don't think so, not if she became really fond of it," said Jenny. "I haven't any right to talk to you like this, Ron, only I'm so fond of you both."

She believed that.

He said, "Sounds crazy to me. I don't know though — perhaps there's something in it. I'll talk to her," he promised, "or — would you? She listens to what you say."

"This is your job," Jenny told him.

"I suppose so," he said, sighing. "Well, I'll think it over."

The more he thought about it the better he found himself liking it. If Lydia experienced vicarious motherhood, without pain, without danger . . . if she grew devoted to her adopted baby, sufficiently so to care for the child herself . . .

and if through growing intimacy with it she perceived its helplessness, its innocent dependence upon her, might not that lead her, as Jenny had suggested, to the natural longing for a child of her own body?

This was not something you could discuss during one of her hurried, appointment-crowded visits to town. He would wait until he had a few free days and could go down to the Island and talk to her about it.

He thought, his heart warm with gratitude toward Jenny Barton, It might be the solution of everything.

Chapter 10

He was able to get away over the Fourth and to be with Lydia for a long weekend. He found her very busy with a house party, planned festivities at the club and elsewhere. Timothy Wilson and his sister were much in evidence. Ron thought, wearily, that he had scarcely a moment to himself, to be alone, to be with Lydia or his father-in-law. Cocktails at someone's house, luncheon at one place, afternoon somewhere else, more cocktails, evenings taken up with this activity or that. Let's drive to Canoe Place, let's go to Amabell's, let's swim, Timothy has planned a fishing trip, we're riding at four, we're swimming here at six —

It wasn't until his last evening there that he was able to talk with her.

Before dinner . . . and with the usual mob coming in, he said, going into her room, where she was lying on the chaise longue, "Lydia, I'm leaving tomorrow and we've scarcely had a moment together."

She murmured, her eyes hidden from him by the cotton pads soaked with witch hazel, "Your fault — you know how it is over the Fourth."

"All fireworks," he agreed. "But I want so much to talk with you."

She said, "Tomorrow, then."

"Now. I'm leaving early, before you're up. Lydia, I insist —"

It was a tone he rarely used with her. Hardly, he reflected, a tone which would successfully precede the discussion he was determined to begin. Yet it was one to which she usually responded.

She said, "When you speak like that there's no use." She leaned aside to remove the pads and put them to soak in a bowl of ice and lotion. Her face glistened faintly with cream, and her feet were higher than her head, a pillow under her slender hips and her bare feet elevated.

He said, "I've been thinking . . . would you consider the adoption of a child, Lydia?"

Now she sat bolt upright and stared at him. She said, "I never heard of such a crazy idea."

"I know it," he agreed, "it is lunatic. Because there's no earthly reason why you shouldn't have one of your own."

Lydia rearranged herself, and took up the pads. She said, "That again. I haven't changed my mind, Ron, I won't. Not now. Not yet . . . not for a long time."

"Perhaps," he said, "you mean never."

"Perhaps I do," she told him.

He said, "Lydia, when we first discussed this you gave as your reasons for your reluctance that we were young, that there was plenty of time, that you wished to be with me."

"It isn't my fault that I can't be, Ron, and you know it."

Well, there was no use going into that, he thought grimly. He said, aloud. "If, as I think, it

141

is because you are afraid —"

"What if I am?" she demanded. "At least I'm honest about it. I loathe illness and disfigurement, I can't endure pain, I *won't*."

He said gently, "If, then, you adopted a baby, Lydia, you would be neither ill nor disfigured nor in pain."

She was silent for a moment. Then she said, "There's no use, Ron. I can't imagine anything I'd want to do less."

He rose and moved across the room to stand beside her, looking down on the small, flawless figure, wrapped in a single sheath of silk, at the tumbled fair curls and the glowing skin glistening with cold cream, the broad, unlined forehead. Her face was strange to him with the eyes hidden.

She shook her head restlessly under his silent regard and the pads slipped off. She opened her eyes and stared at him. Then she smiled faintly and put out her hand, and he took it in his own. She said:

"I'm no good, Ron, as a wife. I'd make a worse mother. I don't suppose there's any good my telling you that I love you. Because I do, you know, no matter what I do or say or how little I may seem to. I wish I didn't. It would be so much easier."

"What would be easier?" he asked quietly.

"Oh, everything," she said vaguely. "Will you go away and let me rest?"

He stooped and kissed her and for an instant her arms went around him and she held him

142

close. Only for an instant. Releasing him she said, laughing:

"I told Jenny not long ago that you married the wrong woman. You should have married her, or someone like her. One of these noble, sacrificial, understanding females, strong, silent, and efficient. Who'd sit home and wait for you, and have dozens of babies, to inflate your ego —"

"So you think that's why —" he began.

"Of course," she said.

He said, "Possibly you're right. Men aren't born with the paternal instinct, as a rule. It's acquired. Perhaps their pleasure in paternity is a mere extension of the ego. I wouldn't know. But I do believe that in our case I am not being egotistic. I believe that you would be happier, Lydia, and that our marriage would have some meaning."

She said slowly, "Hasn't it now?"

He was silent for a moment. Then he said, "No. But it has taken me four years to realize it."

She watched him walk away, saw the communicating door close. She lay very still, thinking.

He hadn't given her what she had wanted of him . . . his full time, his complete attention. Her father had warned her before her marriage. He had said, "Never forget you are marrying a man whose profession must come first — if he's worth his salt, Lydia." But she had counted upon herself . . . and herself had failed her.

Why in God's name was she still in love with

him? she wondered angrily. Was it because she could not possess him? His surface surrender to her demands — the apartment, for instance, as a case in point — both pleased and irritated her. Pleased her because she had her own way, irritated her because he was easy to manage. Yet there were other surrenders which she had not forced, could never force.

She remembered something Amabell had said to her once.

"Women like us interest men and infuriate them," Amabell had said, "drive them a little crazy — but we don't hold them, Lydia, not the ones we'd like to hold. We're not the type."

"What type does?"

"As a rule," said Amabell, "the maternal. You're not, and I'm not. Of course," she went on thoughtfully, "I've one string to my bow which — apparently — you lack."

"And that is — ?"

But Amabell laughed. She said, "Think it over."

Amabell, so legend ran, had had half a dozen lovers.

Lydia could recall how smug she had felt, how complacent, how cool and untouched. She loved that vision of herself . . . woman in marble, eternally virginal and remote. She worshiped it. It made her feel immensely superior to the women she knew who lost their heads, who sacrificed their integrity, who permitted and gloried in their abasement. Women blatantly in love —

that sort of love — with their husbands, women like Amabell always pursuing some man, not just for the excitement and danger and pleasure of it — but in order to relinquish their own common sense, their weapons, their freedom.

Timothy, driving down to the Island with her, had suggested that she had never really been in love.

"And what about Ron?"

He had dismissed Ron, laughed a little.

"You're very much mistaken," she assured him.

"You thought you loved him," he explained, "perhaps you still think so. But it would take a very different type of man . . ."

"I suppose you mean your type?"

"Perhaps."

"What is it, exactly?" she had inquired, driving a little too fast and loving it.

He had cautioned her, "Slow down, will you? I enjoy life. What type? Oh, brutal, ruthless —"

"You sound like a movie."

"It holds, just the same. No regard for delicate sensibilities, shocking a woman into awareness . . . and response . . . shaking her out of her vain, shallow little self."

"You think I'm vain and shallow?"

"Of course."

"Then why — ?"

He said cheerfully, "You interest me, you attract me very much. Because obvious and ready women don't. That's my curse. Silly, isn't it? I like them difficult, always believing — credulous creatures — that they are armored. No woman is, you know. Not really."

He had added carelessly that someday Ron — "a very average person" — might tire of being married to a dragonfly.

"Dragonfly?"

"Oh, you know, bright and skittering over surfaces," he had said, "darting and bloodless, beauty constantly in flight."

She remembered how she had laughed at that. She had asked, "You — like dragonflies?"

He had replied, evenly, that they fascinated him.

A few days ago he had sent her the Flato pin, the dragonfly . . . jeweled and quivering, slender and bright. It was locked away in her jewel case.

Timothy was excitement, he drove away her boredom, he amused her. She liked the sensation — to continue his absurd analogy — of being "constantly in flight," darting close, darting away. He could not fashion the net to capture her . . . his were not the hands.

Ron's, she had believed, were. But she had been mistaken. During the first year of their marriage she had come as close to praying as she had ever come in all her life that the miracle would occur, the enchantment descend upon her, the spell be woven. For she had been in love with him, she told herself, and still was . . . No other man had come so close to stirring her.

So she had prayed, with her heart, but had

fought with her nerves and her flesh and her blood. Incredible combat, but there it was — it was not her fault, there was nothing she could do about it.

She rose and went to her clothes closet. Her frocks hung there in orderly rows, scented, on fragrant padded hangers, and encased in cellophane bags. Her hats sat on their shelves, protected and fragile, her shoes, encased in transparent silk, slanted on their shelves. In one far deep end of the closet there was a little safe for her jewelry.

She selected her dress, and closed the door, rang for a maid. Later, while the water ran foaming and fragrant in the tub, she walked restlessly about the room. In the other end of the closet there was a small wooden chest . . . it was locked. She had the key.

She thought, her nerves jangled and jarring, *No one would know* . . .

Ron might . . .

But always after she went to bed, no one. When Ron was here, there was always fatigue, a headache, anything, any excuse. If not, she was doubly safe.

"Isn't Mrs. Lewis wonderful?" someone said to someone else that evening. "She's twice as vivacious as any woman in the room and she never takes a drink."

At night, after the party was over, after you were alone behind locked doors, you could produce the key, unlock the wooden chest, and measure out the exact amount of your release.

She had such long, curious thoughts, important and revealing, when, in the cool darkness, she lay quiet and alone, her nerves no longer tense, her body glowing faintly with the comfort of utter relaxation. Sometimes she wished she could tell them to Ron, perhaps he would understand then. How you could love someone yet not love him. How intolerable the realities were. How magnificently you would fashion the world and life were they in your hands.

They were like dreams, these thoughts. They were freighted with gravity. You could solve all mankind's unhappy problems while you thought them. You could, for instance, define the perfect marriage. . . .

An ivory tower, an invulnerable fortress. Laughter, music, entertainment, and an endless and ceremonious courtship. No realities. No pain, no revulsion, no sorrow, no intrusions. No quarreling, no rancor. But always the lovely expectation which left you free, the tiptoe quality of waiting, endlessly, without termination, through the years. . . .

In the morning, waking late and slowly, her head aching, her nerves taut again, bitterness in her mouth, she would forget almost all she had thought — or was it dreamed? But she would not forget the comfort and the peace. Then there was the day to be managed, she could get through it somehow. Golf and swim, dance and ride, see a thousand people, listen to gossip, dart away from Timothy, dart back again, amused, because there was no real danger.

Day was a burden and night an escape.

But you couldn't manage wholly. Timothy had warned her — Amabell — even her father, in his quiet way. She was losing Ron . . . and Ron himself had said so. But she couldn't lose him, she must not, she had never wholly possessed him, yet all she had she must keep. He belonged to her, at least as much as she would permit him to belong.

He had said that their marriage had no meaning.

What he asked of her she would not, she could not give. But there might be a compromise. He had suggested it, had he not? She thought, Perhaps if I give in that much . . . ?

In late July, having come to a conclusion, she went to town and stopped in at the office. She waited — as usual, she thought impatiently and when she entered found Ron busy on the telephone. Hanging up, he turned and smiled at her. He said, "I didn't expect you, Lydia."

"I know. One of those spur-of-the-moment things. I haven't seen you for a week, do you realize that?"

"Too well," he said.

She sat down and said, "Amabell tells me she kidnapped you the other day and you had lunch together."

"It amounted to just that," he agreed.

"She's a persistent woman," said Lydia. "But

I'm not very worried."

"You needn't be."

She knew that. Amabell had said, "I barged into your husband's office and demanded lunch. This time he gave in. The last time he threw me out and sent me a bill. But he'd really too attractive to be let loose in town all summer. You should be glad I'm taking him in hand and not someone else . . . or am I being too optimistic?"

"Did you have fun?" she asked.

"She's very entertaining," he admitted, "although my schoolboy French is not quite up to her sudden excursions into that language. Next time she makes me take her to lunch I'll bring along a phrase book."

She said, smiling, "Can you take me . . . today . . . now? Or aren't you free?"

"Quite free, as it happens, if you'll go at once. I've a consultation at two."

They lunched near by in a quiet, cool restaurant, where the service was as excellent as the food and there was no distracting music. After they ordered Lydia said, leaning toward him:

"Ron, I've been thinking things over. I was selfish perhaps, and hasty . . . but I've changed my mind."

"About what?" he asked blankly.

"Adopting a child. I've been making inquiries. We can take an English refugee."

She had that all thought out, by now, and the picture it presented was not unbecoming. A nice child, with good manners. A picturesque little boy perhaps, or a small girl, all dimples, fair hair, straight legs and accent. Several of Lydia's friends had taken English children for the duration. It was not only one's duty, it was also very smart, exceedingly in the mode.

"Of course we'd have to wait . . . but I'm sure that eventually —"

He said, startled, "I didn't mean that kind of adoption, Lydia."

"But," she began, "if a suitable —"

He said gently, "My dear, that isn't the point. In the first place, you can't adopt these unfortunate youngsters. They have parents. They have homes. When the emergency is over, they will be sent back where they belong. My idea of adopting a child is not taking a refugee and then sending it home again. My idea is to take a baby, as, young as possible, adopt it legally, bring it up as our own."

She said, "But that's foolish . . . the risk and everything."

"What risk?" he demanded.

She said, "Don't be stupid, Ron . . . there's such a thing as heredity."

Ron shook his head. He said, "Look here, suppose Bob and Myra Patisen died tomorrow in an automobile accident."

"But —"

He went on, "Would you consider there'd be any great risk in adopting that attractive tow-headed boy of theirs?"

151

"Of course not," she said, "but what has this to do — ?"

He said, "Myra's father was notoriously unfaithful to her mother, even physically abusive. Also he drank heavily. Bob's own record, as far as drinking is concerned, isn't particularly good. And his aunt is confined in an asylum for mental diseases. Now do you see what I mean?"

She saw. She said, hesitantly, "But — a *little* baby, Ron?" She shook her head. "No," she said, "I couldn't."

"I suppose not." He said after a minute, "If you want to take a refugee I won't, of course, stand in your way. But that isn't what I mean by adoption, Lydia. And you must consider your grave responsibility."

She said, "There wouldn't be as much as if we adopted a child legally."

"More," he said; "your own children, whether natural or adopted, are expected to share in your fortune or misfortune. They must take what comes. Illness, accident, poverty. That's all right. But a child who is loaned to you — that's another matter, Lydia. No refugee child could belong to you, as it already belongs to its parents or parent. The responsibility is that of a trust."

She said disconsolately, "I thought the idea would please you."

He said, "As I said before, you must do as you wish in this matter. But it is not what I want. Here," he broke off, "comes your ubiquitous boy friend."

Lydia looked up as Timothy Wilson came toward them and, with a nod at Ron, sat down at their table.

"Sorry to barge in," he said, "but I called your office, doctor, and found you would be here. I wondered if Lydia wanted to go to a matinee this afternoon . . . or aren't you staying in?" he asked her.

She said, smiling, "I might, if properly persuaded."

"Good," said Wilson heartily. "Would you drive down after?"

"Yes — in time for dinner."

"Take a supercargo?" he asked. "If you don't mind, doctor."

"I don't mind at all," said Ron. But he did mind, very much.

Chapter 11

Mamie wrote that she and Mrs. Roberts were getting along nicely, that Bill Treat had remarried, and "the little boy seems happy." She covered several pages with her delicate, spidery writing, giving Ron all the homely, daily news: the political shake-up in the township; the sudden accidental death of the young doctor, from downstate, who had settled near by and taken over most of Dr. Barton's practice.

"People liked him," she wrote, "and were beginning to trust him . . . you know how it is here, Ron, we change slowly. His wife, poor girl, is distracted. She is leaving to go home to Binghamton. I don't know what we will do. It's a long drive to town and not many of the doctors there are willing to come so far out on night calls. There isn't anyone in the immediate district now . . . we are hoping that someone will come but you know most of the young men want to settle in a town, at least. Simon Raynold's boy graduated from medical school last year and is interning in Syracuse. He doesn't want to return. Not that I blame him . . . there isn't much here for an ambitious young man who wants to earn a lot of money. All a doctor can make here is a living and friends, but Dr. Barton used to say a man who had friends and a roof over his head needed nothing more to make him happy. But there aren't many like him, any more."

She went on to say that the gray mare had foaled, that Bill had disposed of two fresh cows early in the spring, that there hadn't been enough rain, as usual, and that she and Mrs. Roberts had been canning . . . they'd put up berries, tomatoes, watermelon pickles, beets, relishes, and bread and butter pickles, and she was sending some down to Lydia. "I know," she added, "that you can buy anything you want but sometimes home-cooked things taste better." She added wistfully that she would dearly love to see him and Lydia if they could ever get away.

There was no use in asking Lydia again. It had been four years now and as yet she had not fulfilled her promise; nor was she likely to. In summer she was too busy, in autumn she was settling the town apartment, in winter it would be too cold and besides she would be going south for a while, in spring there were a thousand and one things to do and the Island house had to be opened.

Ron thought, I'll manage somehow, I'll run up there and spend a week with her before winter. I owe it to her.

He sent Lydia the letter without comment and she telephoned him that the preserves and pickles had arrived. "All unpacked," she said gaily, "and on the shelves. I've written Mamie, it was sweet of her. . . ."

He had expected that. She'd write; and next time she was in town she would send Mamie something pretty and useless, something Mamie would exhibit to her friends and then put carefully away and never use. Lydia, after her fashion, paid her obligations. She could write a graceful letter, remember birthdays and Christmases, walk into a shop and order something — "charge to me, send to this address," but anything entailing personal sacrifice was alien to her. If he went to her tomorrow and said, "Look here, I have a free five or six days, how about driving upstate, just you and I?" she would have a hundred excuses. She could not break this engagement, she had people coming every weekend, she'd rather not leave her father, and besides she couldn't be expected to go anywhere on a moment's notice, could she? Civilized living was far too involved for that!

If she expected to go anywhere with him at any time, it would have to be on a moment's notice. He thought, half laughing at the absurd idea, that a man in his situation needed a wife who was part housekeeper and part gypsy.

Amabell Jarvis was like a well-dressed mosquito, buzzing into his ear over the wire — dare she interrupt him? Could he take her to cocktails? She was in town on some mysterious mission connected with French refugees, would he have time for lunch, would he dine with her, couldn't he get away and be on the Island over the weekend, she was throwing a party?

She called so frequently that the Misses Watson began to wear a curious look of restrained reproach. They were not twins, these nice, hard-working thirtyish young women but they might as well have been.

However, it wasn't hard to evade Amabell. You needn't feel so virtuous about it, Ron told himself, on one occasion. Temptation is easily routed if you don't happen to be tempted.

He did not quite dare ask himself how virtuous he would deserve to feel if Amabell hadn't been Amabell but some delightful, attractive — attractive to him, that is — woman who was just as accessible.

He loved Lydia. He was no longer in love with her, he was often impatient with her in his thoughts, frequently hurt by or angry at her. He admitted to himself that after four years there were great gaps in the pattern of his understanding of her. He admitted further that he had married the wrong woman . . . or that Lydia had married the wrong man. A subtle difference. It depended upon who was regarding the problem, which attitude you assumed. But he knew that his senses were still involved by her direct appeal, and that over and above that factor he still felt for her, still experienced, basically, a deep and unhappy tenderness.

As for other women —

Physicians are assumed to be more tempted than most men but it happened that his specialty brought him in contact with women in whom his interest could only be professional. The pregnant woman is scarcely equipped to scatter glamour along her path. His patients were married — save for a few unfortunate girls who came to the clinics. The majority of them were, as far as he knew, happily married. Those who were not were, nevertheless, still bestowing hostages to fortune. He was not in the position of specialists in other fields.

Those who came to him without the customary greeting, "I think I'm going to have a baby," did so with the announcement, "I *want* to have a baby."

To be sure, most of them, after their delivery, during their convalescence, dressed for him . . . the pretty bedjacket, the touch of rouge and lipstick, the charming nightgown — but that is a merely normal reaction from months of heaviness and burden. They titivated for doctors, interns, resident nurses, family, friends . . . and primarily, as a rule, for their husbands. Perhaps those resigned females returning to the hospital for the third or fourth time were not thinking quite so much of their lords and masters when they demanded pink bows, lilac toilet water, and an atomizer, possibly their eyes brightened a little when Ron walked in to ask, "How are we today?" or something equally inane and routine . . . but he was quite aware that he was merely a symbol.

They were grateful to him, they often, in their own phrase, adored him. "My dear, it's worth having a baby just to have Ron Lewis take care of you," they would tell their best friends over the teacup or cocktail glass; "he's marvellous . . .

and so attractive." But a symbol he remained. After months of discomfort, illness perhaps, awkwardness, surely you're free again, young and light, and gay. You're prettier than ever, you have your baby, its doting father, and your admiring friends. You brim with love for the world and everyone in it and so your doctor comes in for a generous portion.

Others, diagnosticians, surgeons, gynecologists — well, theirs might be a different story.

So, said Ron vulgarly to himself, nuts to the temptations current in my profession. I haven't met a good temptation for years! But here was Amabell popping up like a jack-in-the-box, startling, amusing, and wholly unwanted. Which, he sometimes thought, was just as well.

Fidelity is made up of a number of things; it is an attitude of the heart, a discipline of the flesh, a chastity of the loyalties. It can also be a matter of personal fastidiousness, and good luck. Sometimes it is all of these.

Since Ron's marriage no woman had interested him emotionally unless he excepted Sarah Cutler.

Sarah was an obstetrician, and a successful one. She was interning during Ron's residency. She was completely the career woman. He had once told her that she was all high C's . . . career, cleverness, competency . . . and colleague.

They had been friends, in a way, during that early period but he was by then in love with Lydia and his heart was single tracked. Then after completing her internship Sarah had become resident at another, smaller hospital, with which she was still associated. But she was on the courtesy staff of Lister as well and Ron came in occasional contact with her there. Also, she called him in consultation.

Another high C!

She had been, he remembered, or thought he remembered, a big serious girl, careless of her appearance. Yet he recalled that one of the staff men had once remarked that Cutler had the finest bones he had ever seen. He was an X-ray man, so his passion for bones appeared appropriate. "Look," he would cry, "at the modeling of her face, she'll be beautiful when she's ninety."

Latterly Sarah had blossomed out, or perhaps it was because Ron was really seeing her for the first time. She had put on weight which became her and which was properly, even alluringly, distributed. Her face was lovely . . . wide, gray eyes under curiously level dark brows, and hair the color of ripe wheat. She had a beautiful mouth and nose and a slow, grave smile.

Jenny Barton knew her rather well. They had met in the hospital and had become friends. Now and then Jenny dined with her, and liked her enormously. For some time Sarah had been trying to persuade her to leave Lister and take over Sarah's growing, busy office.

He wasn't in love with Sarah Cutler, but she attracted him, and the fact that he was sufficiently vulnerable to become even mildly attracted disturbed him somewhat. He was thinking of this when, in early September, he went to the hospital and as he parked his car saw Sarah driving out of the circle. She waved to him, called something that he could not catch, and drove away.

This was his last hospital call for, he hoped, two weeks; he hoped he might call his soul his own and stay at Southampton. He was picking Jenny up and driving her down after his hospital call was concluded. All arrangements for his brief vacation had been made.

He was just leaving the hospital when he was called to the telephone. When he came out again, he drove direct to the Nurses' Home and found Jenny ready and waiting in the reception room. He asked, without preliminaries, "Pack any uniforms?"

Jenny laughed, "Everything but. . . . What's the matter?" she asked soberly.

"Run upstairs and get one, two for safety," he said; "we have a job to do, I'll tell you as we drive."

She came back promptly, uniforms over her arm, cap and shoes in her hand. "I didn't stop to find another bag," she said apologetically.

"Good. Stow them in the back seat, your bags are already in the trunk," he said. "We'll have to stop at the office."

On the way downtown he explained.

He had a patient — one of Allen's — who, around October first, expected her second child.

She had arranged to be delivered at home, as she had a horror of hospitals. "Home" was a New York apartment, but at the moment she was in Connecticut, at her summer place. The telephone call which had just reached Ron was from the local doctor who informed him that Mrs. Renton had had an accident, a bad fall, and had been put to bed. There was every likelihood, added Dr. White, that she would go into active labor.

"We'll stop for my bag," said Ron; "you can check it for me while I put in a call to Lydia and then we'll be on our way. You and White can assist — he's a good man, I know him slightly. It seems that the two nurses Mrs. Renton has engaged are on cases. I said you'd stand by till they get someone, which will probably be tomorrow at the latest. I picked up the other things we'll need at the hospital, by the way. I needn't tell you your staff is efficient."

They reached the office — both the Misses Watson were on vacation and while Jenny checked his bag he called Lydia. She was not in but his father-in-law was. Hanging up, he said peremptorily, "Let's go!"

Crosstown to the causeway, over the Henry Hudson, the Sawmill, the Cross Country, the Hutchinson, and the Merritt. Jenny sat quietly beside him, her dark eyes remote, her hands folded in her lap. They didn't talk much until they were out of the heavier traffic and on the Merritt. Then he said, drawing a long sigh, "This

162

is no way to begin your vacation, Jenny."

"Why not? I like it," she said, smiling.

"Busman's holiday," he told her. "Well, we'll have to stop on till it's well over, and I'm satisfied about her. Curious thing, I saw her less than a week ago and arranged to have Danvers see her during the two weeks I'd be away."

"Speaking of Dr. Danvers," said Jenny.

"Well?"

"It's just gossip," she told him.

"Shoot," said Ron cheerfully. "I haven't heard any good gossip in years."

"It's not that kind," she said, smiling; "it's just about him and Sarah Cutler."

"Lord," said Ron, startled, "he's ten, fifteen years older, isn't he?"

"Yes, and a widower," she supplemented. "But they're being seen together a good deal. Remember I told you Sarah wanted me to take over an office nurse job with her. I refused, it isn't what I want, and besides we're friends and that's always difficult. She said something however the last time we discussed it which made me wonder; something about changes being considered in her office, but she added, 'I'll need my own nurse.' "

"They'd be a grand pair, working together," said Ron. He felt a slight but definite pang. Dr. Cutler was nothing to him, God knew — but it would be wonderful to love a woman who could work with you, on equal terms. Not that every man felt that way.

He said, "Speaking of people working together, how about you and Ward Alymer?"

She flushed slightly. She said, "Nothing in it, Ron — honestly. If there was, I'd tell you first of all."

"He's a swell guy," Ron commented, "and he's going places."

"But not with me," said Jenny. She added, "I like him very much but —"

"It's a good basis," said Ron, "for marriage."

She looked at him, startled.

"Surely," she asked, "not the best?"

"Liking," he explained slowly, "often becomes love. But sometimes you can love someone without liking them very much and that's not so good, Jenny."

She thought, He means Lydia. She thought further, But I couldn't love Ward, not ever. She knew that now without a shadow of a doubt. At first she had been pleased to find that she attracted him, he was such fun, so clever, and such an amiable companion. Several times in recent months she wondered if something was lacking in her because she could not become in the least emotional over Ward. Girlish, she called it to herself, feeling so much older than she was. The last time they had been out together they had talked long and gravely over dinner and afterward had driven up into Westchester and danced at a little out-of-the-way place, a sort of log-cabin roadhouse with good music, good food, and dim lights. He had drawn her out on the wide side porch and taken her in his arms and kissed her. No one had seen or if so no one had cared. Then for a moment she had responded to his embrace, being young and lonely and ardent. But only for a moment. Afterward she knew.

She thought, as Ron didn't speak again, stealing a look at him, his intent face, his hands on the wheel, I was a little in love with you once, and now I like you better than any man I know. So much that you spoil me for anyone else. And she resented briefly and bitterly that, because she liked him, because she remembered their first meeting and her foolish, idle dreams thereafter, he had spoiled things for her.

He inquired, smiling, "What are you scowling about, Jenny?"

"I didn't know I was . . . the sun maybe."

"You should wear dark glasses driving."

She said, "I can't get enough of the sun, shut up all day as I am. You don't know how I bless daylight saving."

He said, as if he hadn't heard her, "Lydia is going to have our necks for this venture. But it can't be helped."

"Why our necks?"

"I suppose she's planned something for tonight," he said carelessly, "she's always planning something."

There was a short silence. Then Jenny asked, "How's Dr. Allen?"

"All right. He tires easily. The trick is to keep him from doing too much or from any real disturbance. He's started writing his memoirs. I've been after him, you know, for some time to do that. It occupies him and he enjoys it. Mrs. Petersen is with him on the Island — she retired when he did, you know, I imagine on a pension. Garron took another job, right away, one he found for her. But now that he's doing the book he needs a secretary and so good old Petersen is back again. I imagine she hated her retirement as much as he did his. The office handles his work; of course, it's limited now to consultations."

Jenny said, "You've been fortunate in him, haven't you?" and wondered afterward if she had put the tonal emphasis on the pronoun . . . it had been a mental one, of course. Perhaps she had underscored it, not meaning to, for he looked at her quickly, inquiringly, and then away. His voice when he replied was even.

"Very," he said; "he's the finest man I've ever known." His tone was shaken, suddenly, as if with fear. He said quickly, "Well, here's where we turn off the Parkway. We'll soon be there."

Chapter 12

The Renton place proved to be near Ridgefield and was very charming, an old white house, lawns, and great trees. Jenny had a glimpse of flower gardens and a swimming pool as she went up the front steps with Ron.

If the abnormally grave, extraordinarily thin manservant who admitted them was affected by the situation within doors he did not show it. He merely murmured that they were expected, and would the doctor be so good as to come right this way, please? And he would take their things.

"Expected," said Ron to Jenny in an undertone, "is a masterpiece of understatement."

Halfway up the noble stairs that led upward from the square front hall they met a little man running down. He said, "Thank the Lord you've come, Dr. Lewis."

This was the local doctor, White. He looked approvingly at Jenny, nodded at Ron's introduction, and explained.

"I've just had an emergency call . . ." He turned, retraced his steps upstairs and stood talking with Ron on the landing. Jenny, waiting on the wide turn, looked down at the paneled hall and the big fireplace, the flowers shining upward from the vases, and drew a deep breath. A lovely place, she told herself, in which to be born.

A three-year-old boy, with a curly blond head,

his hand in his nurse's, went chattering across the polished floor of the hall, his high clear voice like a bird's. "Where's Mummy?" he demanded. "Why can't I see her?"

Dr. White turned, smiled at Jenny, and went running downstairs again. The hall door closed and Jenny caught up with Ron.

"Automobile smashup," said Ron briefly, "an old patient, who is also White's close friend, his wife and child. They're in Danbury hospital. I told him we'd manage. He'll have nurses here by tomorrow."

The emaciated manservant was waiting for them at the top of the stairs, having evidently come through the wall or by a back way. He tiptoed to a door and stood back, with a gesture.

Ron knocked and a woman opened the door, comfortable and apple-cheeked. She was, she said, Mrs. Connent, the housekeeper.

Gertrude Renton was walking about the room. She was a tall woman with bright red hair and a charming freckled face. Her face was white now and the freckles stood out in bold relief. There was sweat on her forehead.

"Hi," she said cheerfully, "am I or am I not a damned fool?"

Ron went forward and took her hand, and presented Jenny. He said, "I was just about to drive Miss Barton to Southampton where she is to visit Lydia. As she's the Miss Barton who supervises the Lister delivery room, you'll be in good hands."

"I do get a good break now and then," said Gertrude, smiling. She had known Lydia for years and Ron since his marriage. Ron had been present, assisting Dr. Allen at the birth of her son. She liked him and trusted him. Now and then she and her husband saw the Lewises non-professionally — dinner occasionally, theater, or cocktails. "Tom should be here any minute now," she said, "he was driving right out." She cocked a courageous eye at Ron. "What an idiot I am," she said, "catching my heel, and flinging myself headlong down those infuriating stairs."

He said mildly, "If you wouldn't wear high heels . . ."

"I didn't. Mules, if you please, and no heels at all, but slippery. Well, that's that and no bones broken. But" — she shrugged — "I'm bruised and battered. Good old White said nothing to worry about when I called him except of course the obvious fact that I'm going to have this baby pretty soon."

She turned to Mrs. Connent, who was waiting quietly.

"Will you show Dr. Lewis his room," she asked, "and put Miss Barton in next door?" Her face changed, and grew for a moment still, almost stern with suffering, as if she was listening intently and without complaint to pain.

She added, after a moment, "I'm so glad you're here, Ron."

Jenny had brought her uniform out of the car with her. She went into the pleasant room which

Mrs. Connent showed her and asked if she might have the little brown bag from the car. It contained her toilet articles. It was not in the trunk but in the back seat. She asked further if Dr. Lewis's bag had been brought in together with the other things he had indicated he would need.

She changed, settled her cap, knocked on Mrs. Renton's door, and Ron said cheerfully, "Well . . . suppose we see how things are going."

He had concluded his examination when Tom Renton came pounding upstairs and burst in without warning. His wife, lying on her high bed, the sheet drawn to her pointed chin, reprimanded him amiably, "Nice boys knock on doors, Tom."

"What the hell," said Tom, and stammered at the sight of Jenny. He looked wildly at Ron and around the room. He cried, "How badly is she hurt?"

"When we arrived," said Ron, "she was walking around putting pieces in a jigsaw puzzle when it occurred to her. She's all right, Tom, but your second son —"

"Daughter," said Gertrude firmly.

"Daughter," repeated Ron obediently, "doesn't like falling downstairs so she's going to make her debut a little sooner than we thought . . . and now suppose you sit down and tell Gertrude how badly the market behaved today while Jenny and I make some plans, caterers, flowers, champagne, and orchestra, for the debutante."

He drew Jenny into the connecting room, which was temporarily his. He said:

"It won't be very long. Normally we'd count on about the average eleven hours for the first stage, as you very well know, so why am I lecturing? But you can't tell . . . and it looks to me as if it would be much less. Suppose we set up shop. . . . There's a very elegant bathroom," he added, "next door, big enough to float a battleship."

The equipment he had picked up at the hospital consisted of the usual delivery-room sterile bundle, sheets, gowns, everything necessary. There were a few things he needed which Mrs. Connent could supply. And Jenny had checked his bag.

He said, "White won't be back — at least I can't count on him. You'll have to give the anesthetic."

Later he went in to talk with his patient, and then downstairs with her extremely nervous husband. "Suppose," said Ron cheerfully, "you give me a cigar — which I hate — and show me your roses, or haven't you any at this time of year? And a drink wouldn't do you any harm at all. Jenny will stay with Gertrude."

Mrs. Renton was still on her feet. When the men had gone she rose and prowled around the big room, with its white curtains and turquoise rugs and general air of light and simplicity, peace and space. She paused by the card table to look at her jigsaw puzzle. "If only I could find that piece," she said, "before Gertrude Jr. makes her appearance."

Jenny walked over to the table and looked down. She asked, "This one?" picked it up and put it where it belonged.

"I could kill you," said Gertrude. She smiled. She added, "You're very pretty. When little Tom was born Dr. Allen brought his own nurse too."

"Miss Garron?" asked Jenny.

"Do you know her? She was wonderful. Of course she departed as soon as he did, and I was left to the tender mercies of two very nice Lister girls."

"I've never met her," said Jenny, "but I've heard about her." She added, "How about walking a little more?"

"Okay, if you say so," said Gertrude, "but bed is beginning to appeal to me — not that it makes it any better." She walked up and down, stopping now and then to take hold of the back of a chair, and then, presently resumed her prowling. She asked, "I take it you and Lydia are friends?"

Jenny explained . . . and Gertrude nodded. She said, "It seems to me I've heard them speak of you. Ron's pretty grand, isn't he?" She added, slightly plaintive, "I wish he was a little more so . . . I mean, so this would be over . . . Young Tom was stubborn as the devil — took hours and hours and hours."

"Gertrude Jr. won't."

"Think so? You're sweet," said Gertrude Sr. "Look, tell me the truth, doctors are such liars, even the best of them — do you think I've done her an injury? I could kick myself," she said, "falling downstairs. As if I didn't know better!"

"Dr. Lewis," Jenny began.

"Ron to us both. Or isn't that proper in an improvised delivery room?"

"Perfectly proper in the circumstances," agreed Jenny, "as this isn't Lister. Anyway, he wouldn't lie to you, Mrs. Renton."

"That's what you think!"

Jenny said, "This is the loveliest place."

"I like it," said Gertrude, "it belonged to my father. It's too big and an increasing expense, but somehow it's right. I wish I could live here all year round but Tom hates commuting."

"I thought," said Jenny softly, "as I came in, what a wonderful place in which to be born — and," she added, "what a wonderful day . . . clear, but with that lovely blue haze over the hills and the leaves still green and roses still in the garden."

Mrs. Connent knocked and entered, with a tray.

"What's that?" asked Gertrude. "Don't tell me it's *food!*"

"Doctor's orders," said Jenny, "toast, broth, and some rice."

"Good Lord," said Gertrude, "must I eat?" She made a face. "I don't in the least feel like it."

"It's a good idea," said Jenny.

"I shall be sick," said Gertrude dramatically, "or is it, I will? In this case it's both — simple future time *and* determination or necessity or whatever you call it."

"I don't think so," said Jenny calmly. "Later we won't make you eat. But try a little now . . . and then another stroll, and a few more pieces in the puzzle?"

When the tray had gone and the walking had been resumed Mrs. Renton said musingly:

"More pieces in the puzzle. This is one of them — isn't it? — a queer piece, with hurting edges . . . you hate it, you're afraid of it, yet you want to fit it in. It's a lonely business, no matter how many people try to help, you have to do it yourself. I don't mean that you haven't assistance but primarily it's up to you . . . another piece in the life pattern."

The dinner hour came and Ron reappeared, and then Tom and finally Mrs. Connent to sit with the patient while Jenny went downstairs to dine by candlelight, although the long golden shadows still lay thick on the lawn. Afterward, when Ron went upstairs again, she walked with Tom and the engaging little boy in the garden and their talk was all of birds and the blue water of the pool and the wind in the trees because of the child. And then as the dusk deepened she went back upstairs again to relieve the house-keeper.

Everything was ready . . . and waiting. And the house seemed to hold its breath. Mrs. Renton was in bed, when the moon rose high on the horizon and the stars danced in the deep dark blue. Tom Jr. had been to say good night to her long ago. She said to Jenny, "He has such a cute little nose — what do you bet it won't be out of joint?"

They had reached the Renton house around five-thirty. At eleven o'clock that night Gertrude Renton had entered the second stage of her labor.

During the latter part of the first stage Jenny had given her ether, through an Allis inhaler. Coming out, between pains, she had spoken groggily, with her undefeated smile. "How about a little more of that," she had inquired, "nice sticky stuff, like drowning in molasses?"

"You've got to help us," said Ron.

"Oh, I know," she told him, "that's all you men ever want . . . help. Okay . . . no matter how much it hurts."

Gertrude Jr. was born a few minutes before midnight. She weighed seven pounds, she was round, rosy, and a darling. She had a quantity of dark hair and a short, solid little body. She yelled like a banshee and Tom, smoking chain fashion next door and frequently consulting the Scotch decanter, let out his breath in a great sigh of relief and triumph and relaxed in his chair. Ron and Jenny were busy . . . they had two patients now. It was Ron who said, startled, "Good Lord," and opened the door between to inform the palpitant father that he had a daughter. But closed it again, laughing, having discovered him fast asleep in his chair.

At eight the next morning one of Dr. White's efficient nurses arrived and took over. Jenny, who had been up all night . . . because as she explained to Tom, once he had wakened literally to the situation, "you don't just deliver a baby and go gaily on your way" . . . was having coffee in her patient's room and Ron was sleeping briefly and soundly across his bed, next door.

Of them all the patient was the most chipper, color in her cheeks and lips, laughter in her eyes. Her baby was safe, she was safe. The rest would be routine and care, convalescence and congratulations.

Ron and Jenny got off that afternoon. He was confident that he could leave his patient. White would look in on Mrs. Renton, the excellent pediatrician in the neighborhood would take over the debutante. He said, "Well, you nearly ruined my vacation, but not quite. I'll drive up to see you in, say, two weeks. And it won't be long before you're coming to see me."

It wasn't until he had been persuaded to a brief swim, in the Renton pool, and had had lunch that he remembered to call Lydia.

"Cripes," he said to Jenny, stricken, "I forgot all about her. I'll phone and tell her we'll make Southampton in time for dinner."

They went, this time by way of Bridgeport and the ferry to Port Jefferson, across to Riverhead and then on to the Hamptons. They reached the house shortly before dinner and Lydia rose from the marine gloom of the living room to greet them. She said, "You're twenty-four hours or more late."

"Having," supplemented Ron, "ushered a new citizen into this more or less ungrateful world." He attempted to kiss her but she turned her cheek away.

She said to Jenny, reproachfully, "You might have done something about it, Jenny."

"I did," said Jenny, "I helped." She thought of the big room, still except for Ron's quiet voice, of the young woman on the bed, the smell of ether, and the feeling of gravity and tension and importance. She thought of Ron's eyes. She thought of his skillful hands which seemed to possess such a separate knowledge. She thought of the first cry, in that still room, and of the sure, swift things they both had to do, and of Gertrude's smile when she woke, still half in her drugged dream of peace and Ron told her, "Well, you have your wish, a daughter, and, if I'm not mistaken, a beauty . . . she'll break as many hearts as you did, Gertrude."

Blood and sweat, and agony and tears and the hard, choked cry of anguish . . . all so very worth while, thought Jenny, so right, so real, so vital. The feel of the solid little body in her hands, strong but helpless, not yet resigned to helplessness, not yet adjusted to living. Then after the baby was cared for, the waiting beside the mother, vigilant and controlled, helping her through the third, the last stage of this miracle. And then relieving Ron, letting him get the rest he needed, doing the necessary things she had been taught, under his instruction. You had to be sure, you had to know, you must be safe.

Lydia said, "I had a party planned last night. Ron knew it."

"Mrs. Renton," said Ron rather sharply, "didn't plan *her* party. She merely fell down the stairs. It was a fortunate thing for us both that Jenny was with me."

"Oh," said Lydia, "I didn't say you'd arranged it." She looked at them and smiled. "I suppose," she added, "you were up all night?"

"Very nearly," said Ron briefly, while Jenny looked from one to the other.

"Just as long as you were *up*," said Lydia. "How about showing Jenny her room, it's time to dress, and oh, yes, Dad came in, he wanted to see you, you'll find him upstairs."

She turned and went through the French doors to the terrace and Ron took Jenny's arm and went upstairs with her. He said, "Look here, she didn't mean it. I —"

"That's all right," said Jenny, "I don't mind. She's cross with us, that's all."

He thought, I could wring her neck. "Just as long as you were *up* . . ."

He stopped at the door of the room that was to be Jenny's and said, with sudden awkwardness, "I hope you'll be comfortable. I'm afraid there isn't time for a swim. Your bags will be along in a moment."

Without going to his own room or stopping to see his father-in-law, he ran downstairs and out on the terrace. Lydia was lying there in a long canvas chair. She had said it was time to dress and she herself was not dressed, he noticed. She wore a foolish, becoming dirndl, full in the skirt, tight in the waist. She was smoking, and looking out over the garden.

He said, "You weren't very cordial to Jenny."

She shrugged. "Why should I be? I don't feel cordial. She's your friend," she reminded him. "Florence Nightingale, complete with lamp, or is it Mary's little lamb?"

"Be quiet," he said harshly. "You've hurt her, I think, very much, she's fond of you, Lydia."

"Why shouldn't she be?" Lydia asked. "I am not the rose. You are, my sweet. It's a sort of wonderful sublimation. She's in love with you, so she's fond of me. Quaint, isn't it? Well, you ruined my party last night, both of you." She stood up and he saw the dragonfly pinned at the curve of her breast. It quivered its bright wings, a slender, malicious thing, living in jewels. He had never seen it before. She added slowly, "I've been a fool a long time. I thought she was too — damned pure and you too stupid."

Chapter 13

Ron's anger left him suddenly. In its place he experienced a sensation of excessive fatigue, a deep, sodden weariness. Anger was the more satisfying emotion, sharp, positive, and clean as a flame. This was negative, an ache of misery.

He took her reluctant hands and held them. It was a warm night but her hands were cool in his own; cool and too thin. He looked at her with searching intimacy, yet not in any one of the innumerable ways in which a man regards his wife . . . a look entirely stripped of desire or hot hostility, impatience or tolerance, tenderness or appeal.

"Stop looking at me like that," she said, trying to free herself, "I'm not a patient!"

He held her hands firmly, his impersonal physician's eyes holding her own.

"What is the matter with you, Lydia?" he asked quietly.

Lydia's mouth shook, the tears ran swiftly down her abruptly altered face. Ron released her hands and put his arms about her. She said, sobbing, her face against his shoulder, "I'm sorry, Ron."

She was too thin. He could feel her little bones, like a bird's. Her hands had been cold but her face was hot, and drenched. She shook in his arms and he could feel her tension, taut as a wire, as if she were strung on it.

He held her, not speaking, for a little while. Presently he said, "You're tired . . . and something's troubling you. I —"

Lydia broke in. She had recovered her control but her voice was uneven and roughened. "You're going to prescribe," she accused him, "rest, fewer cigarettes — cut out the parties."

"Not bad," he agreed, "if you'd do it."

She lifted her head from his shoulder. Her face was quite composed. She shook her head, and drew away.

"Too dull, darling," she said.

He asked, "Lydia, if I can manage, will you go north with me in the autumn?"

"Of course. But you won't manage, you never do. I'm late, the others will be here soon . . . I must dress; you too, Ron."

"What others?"

She turned and walked toward the French doors, and Ron followed, his hand on her shoulder.

"Just Tim and Amabell," she said carelessly, "and Harvey Reid —"

"Who?" asked Ron, opening the door.

"Darling," said Lydia, "don't be so idiotic. I told you about him — the motion-picture actor . . . the new one who's so much the rage. He's visiting Amabell."

"Good God!" said Ron profoundly.

"He's attractive . . . he'll amuse Jenny . . . Amabell's mad about him."

181

He caught her arm, swung her around.

"We haven't finished our conversation. Lydia, don't you feel you owe Jenny an apology?"

She said, irritated, "I told you I'm sorry." Her face changed. She reached up to kiss him lightly. She said, "You *do* look tired."

He released her, and followed her upstairs. Lydia made few admissions. Her broken, "I'm sorry, Ron," a few minutes ago was one of them. This brief caress, another.

Jenny, a little later, was standing by her window looking out over lawn, marsh grass, and sand to the darkening sea. Her thoughts were in utter confusion, seemingly unrelated. She had immersed her fatigue in a steaming bath, she had put on a simple, becoming dinner frock. She had three, and one, without its little jacket, would serve for a more formal occasion. She thought, I shouldn't have come.

She thought, Lydia does everything well. It's easy when you have the money.

The guest room to which she had been assigned was lovely . . . clear colors, muted colors, raspberry and mauve and an unexpected note of tender blue. Deep chairs and good lights, and rugs soft under bare feet. Casement windows, and painted furniture, bowls of flowers. The bathroom offered all the expensive luxuries — oils and scented salts, great crystal bottles topped with atomizers, spraying cool, fragrant cologne . . . creams and sun-tan lotions, talcums and astringents.

Nothing, thought Jenny, like a hot bath . . . that sort of hot bath.

She thought, What am I doing here? I must have been insane.

She turned from the windows and went to the dressing table and, in the fading light, looked earnestly at her reflection. It was very familiar to her, she knew its good points and its bad. Her eyes were nice, she thought, and her skin. My hair's right. I don't like my nose.

Ward Alymer had said, "The first time I laid eyes on you I thought, That's the loveliest girl I've ever seen."

She could not see herself through Ward's eyes.

She thought, I don't want to marry Ward, I want to go on working, I feel alive when I'm working and almost important. I didn't need a vacation . . . I'm not tired, she told herself and yawned, suddenly, half closing her eyes . . . just sleepy.

When she wasn't working she felt insecure . . . at least here, in Lydia's house. Funny, how she thought of it as Lydia's house. Well, it was, wasn't it? It wasn't Ron's, it had nothing to do with him.

Someone knocked and she swung around on the little bench to call "Come in," and Lydia opened the door and smiled at her.

She's so pretty, thought Jenny.

Lydia said, "I'm sorry I was so cross when you and Ron arrived. I've had a crashing headache all day. . . . It's better now," she added hastily,

"I'm all right. But it's been hot here for days on end, and too many parties . . . speaking of parties, Amabell Jarvis — you haven't met her, have you? but you've met Timothy, her brother — Amabell has Harvey Reid visiting her. They'll be here any minute."

"The motion-picture actor?"

"Thank heaven you know. Ron didn't. Ron," commented Lydia, "doesn't know anything. When I drag him to the movies, he sleeps through everything but the news reel or a Donald Duck." She laughed. "Let's go down, if you're ready," she suggested, "and — it's all right, isn't it?"

"About what?"

"This afternoon. I didn't mean anything. I'm a heel," she said, "I never say the things I mean, only the ones I don't."

"I don't remember that you said anything," Jenny told her.

"Good," said Lydia. She added as they walked down the hall together, "I could smack you, angel."

"Why?"

"For not smacking me."

Ron, standing at the foot of the stairs, saw them come down, arm in arm. Lydia's face was bright with triumph, Jenny's serene and unrevealing.

His guests arrived at that moment, and he went out to meet them. His father-in-law was not coming down to dinner, he had not been so well for the past week, during the sudden warm weather. Ron had been talking to him, sitting beside him in the big corner room while he ate his simple dinner from a tray, looking over the pages of completed manuscript. Mrs. Petersen had gone home for a short stay and Dr. Allen was living his even, restricted life. He had listened to Ron's account of Gertrude Renton's accident and delivery, had asked to see Jenny when the opportunity afforded — "Perhaps she'd come up for a moment after dinner, if it isn't too late?" — and had remarked abruptly that the more he saw of Lydia's friends the less he liked them. "Who is this new one," he had inquired with unusual querulousness, "the one who curls his hair?"

Yes, definitely, Mr. Reid had had a fine permanent. He was a tall, slender young man, with blue eyes and dimples. His manners were too impeccable. Jenny observed him at the table, sitting between Lydia and Amabell, and was greatly amused. His accent was pure BBC and his conversation mostly shop. He complained lightly of the terrific pressure of his work, slandered the feminine star whose leading man he had been, in her last picture, offered three separate items of libelous gossip, and informed his audience that his last director drove him *mad*.

His had been a rapid and steady advance, during the last three years ever since the picture in which he had appeared as a superbly uniformed chauffeur with six lines to speak, quite sinister in a beautiful way or vice versa. Now half of Hollywood's stars were fighting for him . . . he was box office, he was becoming to them, he was young and new. His training had been college dramatics and a spot of summer stock; he couldn't act, said the critics, for sour apples, but elderly women in the audiences went home and looked dourly at their hard-working husbands and the younger ones palpitated when he embraced the glamorous heroine of the shadow story, and his fan mail was stupendous. Timothy Wilson said, happily, in Jenny's ear, "He's doing a horse opera next. That should be a masterpiece of bull throwing . . . or, like all women, are you enraptured?"

She said, "It takes a good deal more to enrapture me, Mr. Wilson."

Timothy raised his voice. "Harvey, old man, here's one girl who hasn't succumbed to your inexpressible charm."

"Not really!" said Mr. Reid with animation and looked at Jenny with growing interest. "Something must be done about that."

Amabell suggested a stroll on the sands after dinner.

She was in good spirits tonight. Ron thought, watching her exchange glances with Reid, Well, she won't bother me any more. He wanted very much to laugh, he felt definitely relieved although his natural masculine pride suffered a slight, if not mortal, blow. He was also somewhat revolted.

Amabell was forty-odd and Reid was possibly

twenty-six. He spoke to Amabell as Reid turned to Lydia. He said, "So you no longer need medical advice."

"If that's an opening gambit," replied Amabell, undisturbed, "it comes too late."

"Interested," he pursued, "in the art of the cinema?"

"Terribly," she admitted, smiling.

He said, brutally, "You should constitute a liberal education, Amabell, and —"

She broke in, looking at him with her long, wicked eyes. "If you mention vicarious youth," she said, "I will scream. Timothy's been rather vocal on the subject. I'm having fun," she added, "and I'm hurting no one."

"That's right," he agreed thoughtfully. "I dare say he's invulnerable, except where his vanity is concerned. But how about yourself?"

She murmured, "I don't get hurt any more. Life's terribly short, my dear. That's a cliché, I suppose, but true like most of them. Or hadn't you noticed?"

He said, "I suppose you'll go to Hollywood in the autumn?"

"It's said to be a curious place," she answered thoughtfully, "I'm anxious to see it." She laughed. "Have you ever seen me look better?"

"No," he said truthfully, "I haven't."

"Then," she told him, "à chaque saint sa chandelle!"

"My schoolboy French," he informed her, "is rusty in the joints. But I follow you. Would you refer to Mr. Reid as a saint?"

"That," she said serenely, "is a literal translation. Let it go at, Honor to whom honor is due. Lydia's looking rather too thin, don't you think?"

"She's always too thin," he said shortly.

She asked carelessly, "Did you like the dragonfly gadget Timothy gave her? I think it's quite charming."

Ron was conscious of an immense, rising anger but said equably, "It's a lovely piece of workmanship."

She said, "Timothy has good taste. Do you know what their bet was about? He wouldn't tell me."

"I didn't inquire," said Ron evenly.

"A perfect husband," said Amabell, and added, "Dragonflies don't have horns."

Ron was silent. It was impossible to speak. You don't go around hitting guests at your table, especially women guests. Relax, he told himself, don't be a fool. She's getting even — or trying to — that's all.

Jenny put out her hand to take a cigarette from the crystal swan near her and Mr. Reid's platinum lighter was already flaming. You thought, cigarette, and there was the light. A wonderful specimen, Mr. Reid.

He said, "You'd photograph very well."

"I doubt it," Jenny answered, "as on the few occasions I've faced a camera I look rather like Dracula's daughter."

"I mean it," he said. "You have good features,

and the right kind . . . and you're just tall enough. Of course," he added thoughtfully, "you'd have to take off ten pounds."

She said indignantly, "I'm five five and I weigh a hundred and eighteen."

"Your figure," reported Mr. Reid, smiling at her, all dimples and remarkable teeth — they had worked hard on those teeth . . . in Hollywood, "is perfect . . . except before a camera, which adds poundage. I thought all girls wanted to be in pictures."

"I don't."

"Wouldn't the excitement attract you, and the attention? I don't suppose the money would matter," he added. A simple frock, but then he knew, by now, that the simplest things often cost a great deal of money. He hadn't learned that on the Iowa farm on which he had been born. No jewels. But often when you had a great many it was smart to wear none. She wasn't, of course, very young, that is, for pictures. He wondered who she was and why she hadn't married? Or perhaps she was divorced.

Jenny said, laughing, "I'm already employed, thank you, Mr. Reid."

He said, "Really — what do you do?"

Decorating, society night-club singing, dress designing, or novel writing? he wondered, fitting her neatly into his scattered knowledge of the setting in which he had encountered her.

"I'm a trained nurse," Jenny answered, "with a job at Lister Memorial in New York."

189

"Good Lord!" He regarded her in astonishment. "I suppose all your patients fall in love with you."

"At the moment I'm not a ministering angel at the bedsides of susceptible gentlemen. My job's quite different." She was enjoying this and enjoying, too, Amabell's aroused attention. "You wouldn't know about it," she murmured, "it's quite specialized."

He asked, "I say, did you see me in *Physician Heal Thyself?*"

"I did."

"What did you think of it? Come, give me an expert opinion."

She said, laughing, "Mr. Reid, please don't ask me to tell you what I think of most of the pictures which deal with the medical and nursing professions."

"But I can take it," he insisted. "I had a very good press."

"You look wonderful in white," said Jenny calmly.

Lydia pushed her coffee cup aside and rose. "Contract," she suggested, "if anyone craves it."

Amabell shook her head. "It's too damned hot. Let's sit out on the terrace and talk about our friends and each other," she said.

"Fancy," Reid said to Amabell, "Miss Barton saw *Physician Heal Thyself* and thought it was tripe."

"I didn't say so," Jenny contradicted.

"But that's what you meant."

"It *was* tripe," said Amabell soothingly. "Don't be upset, lamb, I adored it."

She was in love with him, according to her lights. He possessed a certain animal cunning, and had listened to the best gag men. But he was young and quite beautiful.

"Possibly," said Timothy Wilson, stretching out in a long chair beside Lydia, on the terrace, "Miss Barton doesn't like the movies."

"Or," added Ron, "the art of the cinema."

"But I do," said Jenny, "I'm crazy about them."

"About whom?" asked Amabell. She patted Reid's hand. "Don't be annoyed," she continued, "if your name does not lead all the rest."

"Disney," said Jenny, and Reid snorted. She added, "Garbo because I love looking at her, Bette Davis because she's a wonderful actress, Thomas Mitchell, Spencer Tracy, Gary Cooper."

"None," asked Timothy, "of the glamour guys? Hard on you, Harvey, but nice for rough-hewn, strong, and silent guys like myself and Dr. Lewis."

"I'd forgotten he was a doctor," said Reid . . . if he had ever known it. Lydia was charming. Not his type, but charming. He'd asked, "Who is she — is she divorced?" A natural question, it seemed to him, and someone had said, "Oh, no, she has a husband, not that they work at being married. . . ." He turned to speak to Ron, smiling. He inquired, "Mind if I tell you about my sinus?"

"Not at all," said Ron pleasantly, "although that isn't exactly up my alley."

"Too bad," said Amabell with commiseration, "no gratis advice. What a chiseler you are, Harvey!"

The tall candles in their hurricane shades flickered over the terrace and Reid regarded his host with interest, looking from him to Jenny. An old plot, well worn, well regarded. Society doctor and his pretty social wife, society doctor and his pretty nurse. He could even hear the dialogue and hear the director shouting *"Cut!"*

He asked, "What is your specialty, doctor?"

"I," said Ron solemnly, with the surface of his mind, "I am the Stork."

Chapter 14

Sometime after midnight Ron knocked on Lydia's door. It had been an oddly fatiguing evening . . . or else he was more tired than usual. They had sat out on the terrace, they had had highballs, they had talked. Amabell had suggested the club, and it had been vetoed. Timothy had suggested a couple of cars and a roadhouse somewhere. That had been vetoed also. Lydia, unable to sit still very long, had gone into the living room and put a pile of records on the turntable of the phonograph and they had danced, on the terrace. Harvey Reid had danced with Jenny, first of all. She danced very well, he observed, feeling amiable, a little tight, and royally gracious. Give the poor girl a real boost. Let her go back to her horribly antiseptic hospital and tell all the other girls that she had floated, to the music of Guy Lombardo, in the coveted Reid arms. For of course she hadn't meant a word of it. She was covering up. It was a way to attract his attention . . . it had been done before. Indifference, an act.

"What do you do evenings?" he had inquired.

"Sleep."

The next question was obvious, the script, uncensored, called for it but somehow he didn't say it. He said, instead, "You're very attractive, you know."

"Of course." She added, "This isn't a close-up, Mr. Reid," and his arm relaxed slightly. If this was an act she was a little too good. He thought, But of course, she's in love with Lewis.

He danced next with Amabell, who appreciated closeups.

Now they had gone. "Tennis tomorrow, swimming, cocktails with me," said Amabell, "don't fail. You riding with Timothy in the morning, Lydia?"

Ron, in Lydia's room, watched her fussing about the room, picking up things on the dressing table, setting them back again. He said, "So Wilson gave you that dragonfly thing you were wearing this afternoon."

If she was startled, she did not show it.

"Of course. I told you," she said, but her breath tightened in her throat. Who? Never Timothy! Amabell, then? But why? Amabell had always been on her side.

"You didn't tell me, Lydia."

"I tell you a lot of things. You never listen. What does it matter anyway?"

"I'm a reactionary," he told her, "I don't like my wife to accept jewelry from other men."

"It was a gag," she said mildly, "it doesn't mean anything. Don't be silly, Ron."

"What was your bet?"

"Bet?" She asked, "What bet?"

He said heavily, "Amabell said it was a bet."

"Oh, that . . . yes, of course. The tennis matches," she answered. "I said I'd bet him a riding crop against anything he cared to name and —"

He said, "Oh, don't bother to lie, Lydia. It wasn't a bet."

"Okay," she said, "so it wasn't a bet. So what?"

He stood by the dressing table looking down at the glittering array of jars and bottles. He asked, "Are you in love with him?"

"Don't be idiotic," she said sharply. He thought, She isn't; I know when she's telling me the truth.

"All right," he said, "but now you have even less excuse."

She said, "Ron, please . . . it doesn't mean a thing. He — likes me, I suppose. Perhaps he's a little in love with me. That happens, doesn't it? It's fun . . . it's exciting."

"And I'm not?"

She asked, "When do you have time?"

"And you must have excitement?"

She said sullenly, "I have to have *something*."

His voice changed when, after a moment, he spoke. He asked, "What about the English child . . . the refugee?"

"What do you mean?" she said, staring at him.

"The one you were going to take for the duration."

"Oh, that. I changed my mind, as you didn't seem very keen on it, and besides it would tie us down."

"Us?"

"Me, then. Even with a good nurse, Lulu Wayne has had awfully bad luck with hers, you know, all sorts of childish diseases and —"

"Skip it," said Ron, "it was just a straw —"

She said, fear like a small cold hand clutching at her, "Ron, let's not quarrel."

"I wasn't aware that we were."

"You're angry again," she said childishly; "about Timothy this time."

"Not just this time. I haven't much liked your association with him all summer," he said.

"You're jealous!" said Lydia and the fear left her, and her heart was warm again, light and expectant.

"Perhaps," he said slowly, "I don't know. I'm not sure. Not sure of anything."

"You must be," she said urgently. "Of me, and of my love for you. Ron . . ." She came close and put her hands on his arm. "I — it's you, always. I haven't been unfaithful," she said.

"That's a big word," he told her, "it can mean a lot of things."

She said, "Let me talk to you about it. Come back," she suggested, "in twenty minutes and we'll talk."

He shook his head. He said, "I'm tired, Lydia. I was up most of last night."

He bent and kissed her, briefly.

"Good night," he said, and went through the communicating door, into his own room. The door shut. Lydia stood looking at it, and after a moment she shrugged her shoulders and lifting her hands began to take the tiny pins from her shining curls.

Toward morning Ron was conscious that his door, the one to the hall, was opening. He sat up in bed, alert as he had been in the old days of internship. "Who is it?" he asked sharply.

"Jenny."

"Is anything the matter?"

He snapped on the light beside his bed and looked at her. She was flushed from sleep, her eyes brilliant. She wore a straight silk robe over pajamas and her feet were bare.

"What's wrong?" he asked. "Is it Dad Allen . . . or you, are you ill?"

She said, "It's Lydia."

"Lydie!"

He was out of bed, groping for a robe, for his slippers.

She said, rapidly, "I fell asleep as soon as I went to bed and I woke just now. I'm next door to her, Ron, on the other side. I heard a sound in there, like a moan. I listened and it came again and this time I called her, and she didn't answer. I went down the hall and tried her door but it was locked. I thought at first she was talking in her sleep, but I don't like the way it sounded."

He said, "We'll go through this way."

He went to the door between their rooms but it, too, was locked. He said, "It may be nothing. And breaking down doors makes a hell of a noise. Dad Allen's room is too close . . . I —"

He went to the window and unhooked the

screen. Jenny, following him, asked anxiously, "What are you going to do?"

"The sun-porch roof," he said briefly. "Wait here . . . Hand me my penknife will you? It's on the bedside table."

She waited, standing in the center of Ron's room. The light shone with its steady reassurance. She saw the sheet and summer blanket flung aside, the dented pillow, the cigarette butts in the ash tray. She saw the book he had been reading, before, perhaps, he slept. The room smelled faintly of salt and flowers, of tobacco and leather.

She heard a key turn and the communicating door opened. He said briefly, "I cut a hole in her screen and reached through and unhooked it."

Jenny went into Lydia's room, her heart tight with apprehension. Ron had switched on the light by the bed. Lydia had not awakened. She lay quite still, breathing heavily, and making at intervals the choked, alarming sound.

Ron had her hand, his finger on the pulse. He shook her, spoke to her urgently. She moaned and turned a little but did not answer. He lifted her eyelid.

"Ron, what is it?"

He was staring at something on the bedside table. His face was white and drawn. He said, "Nothing. She'll sleep it off."

"But —"

He said harshly, "She's drunk, Jenny."

"Drunk? But Lydia never . . . Oh, no, Ron," she said, "it isn't possible, it can't be . . . you must be mistaken."

He said, "Even a bad doctor —"

He looked down at Lydia in her stupor. His face was sickened and afraid.

"Leave her alone," he said, "and come on out of here."

Incredulous, Jenny followed him back into his room and he closed the door and sat down on the edge of the bed, his hands limp between his knees and stared at her.

"That's that," he said. "I've been a damned fool."

She said, "Lydia said she had a headache — when we came . . . and she's so terribly nervous. I noticed that tonight."

He said, as if he hadn't heard, "This isn't the first time. Earlier in the summer I went into her room one morning . . . I made excuses too . . . no, not the first." He raised his haggard eyes. "It's all very simple. She sleeps late, she has her breakfast on a tray. When I'm here — or in town — I never see her in the morning or if I go in quietly she is asleep. I don't disturb her. We won't see her today until noon."

"But she's riding with Mr. Wilson!"

"At twelve. Luncheon's at two. Can't you see it, Jenny?"

"I can't see it at all. She never drinks," Jenny reminded him, "not even sherry."

"Not openly," he agreed. "But secretly. It's all

very clear to me now. I — I've failed," he added, "a thousand ways."

Jenny said after a moment, "What will you do?"

"I don't know. Dad Allen mustn't know. That's the obstacle, Jenny. He mustn't know."

Suddenly and without warning, even to herself, she was crying, the tears spilling over, running down her cheeks. She was sick with pity, for him, for Lydia.

"Why, Jenny!" he said, startled.

Jenny wasn't vulnerable. Jenny was always the same, serene and sweet and capable, a shoulder to lean upon, a second right hand. But here she was standing there, making no move to wipe the tears away, twisting her hands like a child, looking at him helplessly, with pity and in anguish.

He rose and took her hands and held them. He said, "Don't, my dear, don't."

She said, "I haven't a handkerchief."

There was one in the pocket of his robe. He took it out and gave it to her and she blew her nose and mopped at her eyes. She said, "I'm so sorry, Ron, for everything."

He put his arms around her, held her. "There," he said, "don't, Jenny. If you go to pieces, what happens to me?"

She was where she belonged. No, she thought, I don't belong here, I never have. She tried to draw away, and could not.

She was warm and vibrant in his arms, she was part of him. He knew it, it was like a shock, dividing his mind; one part of his mind was occupied with Lydia, the other with the woman in his arms.

"Caught you," cried Lydia happily, "I knew it."

The door was open, and she stood there, very unsteady on her feet. Her eyes were swollen and her mouth. Her hair was disheveled. She wore a wisp of chiffon and lace and clung to the door, smiling at them. "Think you're so smart," said Lydia. "I heard you in there."

Ron released Jenny, without haste. He went to the door and took Lydia's arm. He said, "You're going back to bed, Lydia."

"I like being up."

He said definitely, "You've been drinking."

"Clever," said Lydia, and made a face at him. A relaxed sodden face. "Think you're so smart. You're a fool. Jenny's not so dumb, not as dumb as she looks. She's been waiting a long time." Her voice was thick and slurred. "Sure I've been drinking," she said. "Why not? It's fun. All day long, luncheon and cocktails and dinner and all that. No, thank you. I never drink. No, thank you, my darling husband doesn't like women who drink. But he's crazy about women who come creeping into his room and —"

"Be still," said Ron, "do you hear me?"

"Jenny's been crying," said Lydia, pleased. "About what? Did he tell you he wouldn't ask me for a divorce? Of course he won't and I wouldn't give it to him . . . 'cause why? 'cause he doesn't want it. I'm Allen's daughter, and I've all the money in the world. Picked him off a plow," said Lydia, "and made him very fashionable." She began to giggle.

Ron picked her up in his arms. She struggled and fought, she bit and scratched. She cried, "You put me down, this is my house."

He carried her across her room and laid her on the bed.

"Suppose you go back to sleep," he said.

Lydia laughed heartily, her mood veering.

"You should be giving me black coffee, shouldn't you? Or doing something . . . you know, sober her up . . . maybe she'll forget. But I don't forget. I'm an el-elfant," she said, "that's it, elfant! Never forgets."

She looked up at him, smiling.

"How about a little drink?" she inquired. "I'm not mad. If you want Jenny you can have her. I don't care . . . just so long as you leave me alone . . . leave me alone, leave me alone . . ."

Her voice trailed off, the words were indistinguishable, and she slept again, heavily, suddenly.

Ron switched out the light and left her there, going back to his room, walking slowly, his shoulders sagging.

Jenny was waiting, standing by the window. She was not crying now. She said, "She won't forget. I'm so sorry, Ron, so terribly sorry . . . I was such a fool. It was just that I couldn't bear to see her like that, couldn't bear to see you —"

I love you so much, she thought, my darling,

I love you utterly. I've denied it all these years, I've fought it and pretended . . . but it's no use, no use at all.

He said, "Don't worry, Jenny. Tomorrow I'll talk to her, I'll tell her exactly what —"

"She won't believe you."

He said, "I don't suppose that matters much, except on your account. My poor dear," he added, "it all falls on you, doesn't it?"

She said, "I could be gone tomorrow before she wakes."

"Flight isn't the answer or," he said, "it's the wrong one. The immediate problem is Lydia. How long has this . . . ? There are good men," he added; "she can be cured — if she wants to be."

"It can't have gone far," cried Jenny in horror, "perhaps a time or two —"

"You heard her . . . and she was speaking the truth. Getting through the day somehow. It must have been torture," he said, slowly, "watching other people drink, knowing release was within the reach of her hand, waiting until night, and then locking herself in with that stuff, as a woman locks herself in with a lover." He shuddered, all over his long lean body, and was silent. "Go to bed, Jenny," he said dully, "and in the morning — later in the morning, we'll talk."

She stood there apart from him. She could not touch him, nor reach him. She said, "I wish I could help you."

"You have."

"No. I rarely cry, Ron, and when I do it seems that it is the wrong time."

He said absently, "I've seen you cry before, Jenny."

"When?"

"In Treat's little cottage."

"That was long ago," said Jenny. She went to the door, opened it and went on down the corridor to her own room, the other side of Lydia's. She washed her face and hands in cold water, and brushed her hair back from her temples. They throbbed, she ached all over as if she had been bruised and beaten. She could not adjust herself to this.

She could not adjust herself to the new picture of Lydia . . . Lydia, little, delicate, fastidious . . . immaculate . . . Lydia, cool and remote and gay, like a woman moving in calculated steps across a lighted stage. This other Lydia, sodden and silly, her fair hair in disorder, her tinted mask distorted, a brown stain on her chiffon nightgown, her swaying, uncertain step and coarsened, slurred voice. It wasn't Lydia, it couldn't be.

Nor could she adjust herself to the memory of Ron's steady arms and his voice and the feel of his hard shoulder under her cheek. She must forget, she thought.

A woman cries and a man who is fond of her takes her in his arms for a moment. That was all.

Crying, she thought, like a schoolgirl, like a baby, at exactly the wrong time.

She sat down in a deep chair by the windows and looked out. There was the sea, gray under a gray sky. She sat there looking out and the sky was no longer gray and the sea was golden, the sea was blue. A little breeze came up and she saw the gulls flying, restless and lovely, and she fancied she could hear their discordant, complaining voices. There was no sound from Lydia's room, no sound from the big hushed house.

Ron isn't sleeping, she thought, he is sitting there as I left him.

She belonged with him, beside him, helping if she could or, if she could not, just sitting there quiet, waiting. But that was insane. He belonged to Lydia . . .

And Lydia to herself . . .

No, no longer to herself, if what Ron thought was true. But it couldn't be true, it was horrible, it was fantastic, incredible.

I could cry now, thought Jenny, for all of us, cry and cry and cry. But I'm alone, and it's the right time. But I haven't any tears.

She thought, What's to become of us all?

Chapter 15

The strengthening sunlight woke her and Jenny opened her eyes, dazzled, and for a moment bewildered. She must have fallen asleep in this chair by the window, but why had she been sitting here, in her pajamas and thin robe? She moved and felt stiff and cramped, and chilly.

Then she remembered and was appalled by her sense of loss, and in the sanity of sunshine, incredulous.

She went across the room and listened for a sound from next door. There was none. Jenny stood there leaning against the wall, but Lydia's room was silent. Only this wall separated them, a barrier of wood and tinted plaster, but you cannot recall the spoken word or the unconsidered gesture, and once knowledge, like a battering ram, has demolished your flimsy illusions you cannot rebuild the defenses and return to cower behind the smooth shelter of your ignorance.

How quiet it was in Lydia's room.

Jenny thought, What exactly has happened?

That's right, don't evade it, put it in words, face them, down to the least small implication.

Lydia drank, in secret. Early this morning Ron had learned this, had opened the hidden door to Lydia's escape with the key Jenny, unwittingly, had put in his hand. And what else? Nothing, she thought, except that I love him and that

Lydia saw us together.

She thought, I'll have to leave.

She bathed, dressed, and then packed her bags, folding her lingerie neatly, putting her shoes in their little bags, straightening her dresses on the hangers. Very tidy, very mechanical. When almost everything was ready she left the bags open, one on her bed, one on the luggage rack, and her little dressing case on the table, and went down to breakfast. Her stomach was a hard, tight knot and she thought of food with distaste. Coffee, fruit juice. She might manage that much. Lydia would not be down, she hoped that Ron would not be. It would be painful in the extreme to tell him that she must go.

Dr. Allen was breakfasting alone in the big dining room, and looked up to welcome her with his faint, gentle smile. He said, "Good morning, Jenny, what kind of time did you have last night?"

In her profession you learn to dissemble. You can tell your patient, "But you *are* going to be well, you must not worry," when all the time you know that the chances are a hundred to one that you are lying.

She said, "Wonderful. Did you know we were honored with Mr. Harvey Reid's presence at dinner?"

"Who's he?" demanded Allen, ringing for fresh coffee.

Jenny told him, smiling, her description of Mr. Reid spiced with a touch of malice unusual to her. Allen listened, greatly entertained. He asked,

"You stayed up until all hours, didn't you?"

"Were we noisy?" she asked, her breath shortened with apprehension.

"Not at all. I went to sleep about eleven, I fancy, and didn't wake until after dawn. But you look tired . . . a little pale, and there are shadows under your eyes. Not that it isn't becoming."

She said, "I'm not used to even the mildest goings-on, Dr. Allen."

"Do you good," he said heartily, "relax a little, have fun, get away from the hospital. You probably need change even more than rest." He laughed. "I wish I had taken that advice years ago," he added.

He liked Jenny Barton. When she first came to New York he had seen her not only in his own house but in the hospital and had called her on his cases, while she had been on the registry. In her present position Ron reported her the perfection of efficiency and his father-in-law could believe it. He thought, She's a good influence on Lydia too.

He asked, "How about eggs?"

Jenny shook her head. "Not this morning, thanks."

"I like to see young women eat," he complained. "Lydia simply pecks at her food. She consumes all her nervous energy in this absurd dashing around, and then hasn't any left over — she's too tired to eat, although she probably doesn't know it. She's losing weight. I've been at her for months to have a thorough going over. Her metabolism is probably very high. . . ." He shrugged. "Funny," he commented, "a considerable number of women have paid me very well for advice, and still do, now and then. But when it comes to my own daughter —"

Jenny asked, as casually as she could, "Where's everyone?"

"Lydia," said her father, "never appears until noon. As for Ron, he went out early. One of his patients who is staying at the Irving House called him . . . probably indigestion. Anyway, according to his report — he put his head in my door about an hour ago and announced his intentions, he's off to allay her fears, if any."

She thought, I can be gone before he gets back, before Lydia wakes. I'll leave a note. I can say I had a telephone call — it doesn't in the least matter that I haven't had or that they can find it out easily enough — and that I have to go to town and get a train to Cooperstown.

After breakfast Allen insisted that she go out on the terrace with him, in the sun. He kept her there for a while, talking, and when presently she escaped it was with a sense that she must hurry. Ron might be back at any minute.

She heard someone in her room as she came down the hall. She thought, The maid, most likely. I'll ask her to find out if there is a train at this time — and if someone can drive me to the station.

She opened the door and Lydia stood there,

by the windows, smoking.

She turned as Jenny came in and gestured toward the open bags. She asked, "You were going away?"

Lydia's eyes were heavy, and her face a little drawn. Otherwise she looked herself, her hair shining and curled, her lipstick bright. She wore a long fitted robe, the color of her eyes, edged in sable. She said, "It's cooler this morning, isn't it?"

Jenny tried to speak. She couldn't. She came in, closing the door carefully, and sat down on the edge of the bed. Lydia stood still regarding her. Then she said gently:

"Don't be silly, Jenny. Unpack your bags. We promised to go to Amabell's today and tomorrow night I'm giving you a party."

Jenny shook her head. There were words, but she could not find them, couldn't force them past her lips.

"Oh," said Lydia, "last night. This morning, rather. Aren't you making rather an issue —" she broke off, and amplified, smiling — "a tempest in a teapot? Only it wasn't a teapot."

"No," said Jenny, discovering her voice, "it wasn't."

Lydia sat down in the chair by the window. She put her hand down idly between cushion and seat and pulled at something white. It was a handkerchief, still damp. She said, "It doesn't take Philo Vance to deduce that this is yours and that you've been crying."

"Oh, Lydia," said Jenny, on a long, broken breath.

"I don't remember much," admitted Lydia thoughtfully. She glanced up, the handkerchief still in her hand, "I was plastered, wasn't I?"

"Yes."

"I heard voices and I went into Ron's room and there you were."

Jenny said steadily, "I thought I heard you . . . I thought you were ill. I couldn't open your door so I went to Ron's and woke him. He got out on the roof and went in a window. He unlocked the door between your rooms and —"

"No details," said Lydia, "please."

Jenny asked, "Why not? It's something we have to discuss, isn't it? When he — found what was wrong he came back into his room and I followed him. Then you —"

"Listen," said Lydia, "I haven't any excuse . . . except that I felt horrible, as if I'd been basted together and someone had pulled out the thread. Last night at dinner I thought I'd scream. I was so tired, so bored, so — I thought, when I couldn't sleep, afterward, I'll take a drink, maybe that will help. I'm afraid of drugs." Her eyes were wide and guileless. "So I got up," she said, "and went downstairs and got a bottle of Scotch and it hit me like a ton of bricks."

If only, thought Jenny, she wouldn't lie. She's trying to say it's the first time.

"I suppose Ron's furious," said Lydia tentatively.

"I don't know," said Jenny; "he was, certainly, very much disturbed."

"There was nothing," Lydia declared, "to be disturbed about."

Jenny thought, Well, I'm going away anyhow. I won't see her again probably. She said sturdily, "You're not fooling anyone, Lydia, not even yourself. It isn't the first time. Ron knows that."

"Ron — knows? He told you?" Lydia's face changed and was wary and still.

"Yes."

"All right," said Lydia, "so it wasn't the first time. What's he going to do about it?"

"I don't know," said Jenny truthfully.

Lydia got up and crossed the room. She sat down on the bed beside Jenny. She said, "He hates me."

Jenny looked at her. She answered after a minute, "Don't be dramatic, Lydia. He doesn't hate you. He loves you, you're his wife."

Lydia was silent. She said, after a moment, "Give me the ash tray, will you?" She stubbed out the cigarette, twisting it, crushing it. She said quickly:

"Before we were married Ron told me I drank too much. Oh, I wasn't — like last night, ever. But I kept going on a cocktail before lunch and two at dinner and highballs after. He didn't like it, so I stopped. At first I didn't miss it. Afterward I did. But by that time I had a reputation. Lydia, the girl wonder . . . who didn't need a drink to make her the life of the party . . . I swear it began

212

gradually, Jenny, I swear it. Only at night I'd be so deathly tired and it was wonderful to escape, to feel my nerves relax, and my bones . . . yes, my bones. It seemed to me that I was conscious of every one of them . . . hard and still and sharp, holding me up. I could feel my skeleton," she said, "like a framework. And I was cold all the time and shaking inside. You wouldn't understand . . . it's just letting go, and warmth and —"

"My dear," said Jenny gently.

"Every day," Lydia told her, "I look in the mirror. I think, What am I doing to myself? I've seen other women . . . your skin goes, and your figure, and your eyes look like . . . But it hasn't happened to me." She bent her head a moment. She added, "There are other things . . . I can't talk about them."

Jenny said quietly, "You can stop if you want, Lydia. Ron will help you. You're so young . . . you've so much to live for. You can't go on like this, you know. You need rest and care, to build up your resistance."

Lydia spoke as if she hadn't heard. She said, "I remember one thing. I went in Ron's room and it was too bright and things were fuzzy but you were there, you two and I —"

Jenny said, "I was crying."

"What about? I don't remember that."

"You," said Jenny. She thought, That's only half true.

"Me? I'm not worth crying about, I don't even cry about myself. Jenny, don't go away. Stay here, with me. I — if you're here I won't be so afraid."

"Of what?"

"Everything . . . Ron, myself . . . daytimes . . . and most of all, nights," Lydia said.

"But what can I do?" Jenny asked her. "This is your problem . . . you have to face it yourself."

"You can help me," said Lydia. She put her face against Jenny's shoulder. She added, "Unless you hate me too, why won't you help me?"

Jenny put her arm about her. Poor little creature, shallow, false, despicable . . . no, not despicable. Who am I, she thought, who is anyone, to judge? I'm not Lydia. I don't know what makes her tick, I don't know what motivates her, what destroys her —

"Promise me you won't go away."

"I promise —"

I haven't any character, she thought, I'm spineless, a jellyfish. I'll stay, I'll tell myself it's because I want to help her. That's only half true too. I'll stay to be near Ron, to help him if I can. But what can I do but stand by and watch him torture himself, and so torture myself twice over?

Lydia raised her head. She said, "Thanks, I won't forget. I — Good Lord," she cried, "I'm riding, at noon!"

"You can break your engagement. Look," said Jenny, "I'll go back to your room with you, put you back to bed. . . ."

"I feel wonderful," said Lydia. "Don't bother about me . . . I want to ride."

She turned at the door. She said, "Don't you see? I can get through the days."

She closed the door and methodically Jenny set about her unpacking.

Ron, coming along the hall, saw Lydia at the door of her own room. He said absurdly, "So you're up —"

"Evidently," Lydia told him. "Good morning, darling."

He was looking at her, looking for betrayal, for ravage. He saw very little. She smiled. She said, "I was just going to dress."

"Wait a minute." He opened the door, stood aside, followed her in, closing the door quietly. He asked, "You're riding this morning with Wilson?"

"Yes, of course."

"Why of course? I'd rather you didn't. Call him, tell him you have changed your mind."

She asked, "Aren't you being a little arbitrary?"

"Perhaps. Will you call him or must I?"

She shrugged.

"Very well," she said and went to the telephone beside her bed. She asked, waiting for the connection, "Light me a cigarette, will you?"

When Timothy's voice came on the wire she was smoking, standing there tapping her foot. She said, "Tim? . . . Yes, Lydia. I can't ride with you this morning. No . . . No . . . Yes, of course I'm sorry." She smiled and looked toward Ron. "No, I'm not alone," she said. "Yes, this afternoon . . . of course, we'll all be there . . . 'Bye. . . ."

She replaced the instrument and threw herself carelessly across the bed, a thin hand, with the cigarette smoldering between the fingers, dangling toward the floor. She said, "Well, that's that, and I needn't hurry after all. Get on with it," she ordered, "we may as well have it over."

Ron sat down beside the bed. "Perfect picture," she murmured, "doctor and patient. May I take your pulse? How long have you been feeling ill? Any symptoms of morning sickness?"

He said sharply, "It's no use, Lydia. How much do you remember about last night?"

"Plenty," she answered. She closed her eyes and went on sleepily, "Enough to hang you. In a court of law, I mean. And then what happened, Mrs. Lewis? And then I went to the door between our rooms and saw my husband with this woman in his arms. Neither was fully dressed . . ."

He said slowly, "You have a rotten mind, Lydia."

"Of course. Jenny, by the way, was all packed this morning ready to desert the sinking ship. I persuaded her to stay. I accepted her explanation . . . in fact," she added, "I begged her to stay."

"Jenny owes you no explanation."

"That's nice," said Lydia; "that makes everything lovely."

He said, "Look at me . . . you don't believe a word you're saying."

She opened her eyes, closed them again. She

said indifferently, "Perhaps not . . . but it gives me an advantage to pretend I do — if I am pretending."

He said, "Suppose we forget that for a moment. How long have you —" He halted. He couldn't say it. Sordid, shameful. "How long have you been drinking, Lydia?" Those were the words. Somehow he managed them.

"It depends on what you mean by drinking," she murmured, her face unchanged.

He said, "One morning earlier in the summer I came into your room and found you . . . I — made excuses. I thought — It doesn't matter what I thought. Now of course I know it wasn't —"

"Oh," she interrupted rapidly, "let's not be too delicate about it. Three years . . . once in a while at first, then more frequently. One advantage of your profession, you leave early in the morning . . . one advantage of mine — if being your wife is a profession — I breakfast late."

He asked after a moment, "Why? If I am to help you, Lydia, I must know why."

She said, "I don't know. A thousand reasons. I'm sick of the way we live. You're all right, you have your job, you love it. You work and feel that you accomplish something. I run around and arrange bazaars or charity dances or collect overcoats. Contract and matinees and silly women. It bores me."

"I've suggested other occupations," he said.

"Naturally. You have a single-track mind. Have a child, adopt a child . . . what for? I don't want one. You can't solve every woman's problem that way, Ron."

He said, "We'll solve yours, some way. First of all —"

Lydia broke in again. She said, "Jenny's already prescribed, thank you . . . rest and food, building up my resistance, and of course a cure. How are you going to explain it to Dad? Or perhaps you intend to tell him?"

He said, white, "I shan't tell him. You know that. It might, quite literally, kill him."

She said, "Or if I divorced you, Ron . . . that would upset him dreadfully."

"Divorced me?"

"I could. Oh, don't look so grim. You're innocent, Jenny's innocent, you're a couple of noble and maligned souls. Well, I wouldn't give either of you the satisfaction."

"You don't know what you're saying!"

"I know perfectly well. And I've forged another link in the chain, haven't I? Your mutual solicitude. Poor Lydia, what can we do to help her?"

He asked quietly, "What can *I* do?"

"Ron . . ." She opened her eyes and looked at him. He had never seen such naked despair. "I don't know."

He said, after a moment, "Don't cry, Lydia." He sat down on the bed, and took her in his arms.

She wept, like a child. "My head aches," she said. "I feel ghastly."

There were things he could do for that . . . the

usual remedies. He said, smoothing her hair back, "You'll be all right, you'll —"

She said, "It's me, Ron, something in me, something mean and vicious. Something that possesses me and something I lack. It began before we'd been married long, in a way. After you were asleep . . . I couldn't sleep. I'd lie there, hating you, despising myself, wanting to scream, to tear the sheets with my teeth and nails. Yet loving you too. That was the horrible part of it."

He felt as if he had been stabbed, as if he was bleeding to death internally.

She said, half whispering, "If you'd stay with me — talk to me, hold me in your arms, and talk and —" She raised her head and spoke soberly, quietly. She said, "I'll try, Ron, I'll try very hard."

"Of course," he told her. "And now I'll get you something to —"

"Don't go," she said drowsily, "don't go."

He was aware a moment later that she slept, her face relaxed, her eyes hidden, looking defenseless and young and innocent . . . as she must have looked when, long ago, she was a child.

Chapter 16

Ron had no opportunity to see Jenny alone during the day. He had stayed with Lydia until she woke and, exclaiming at the hour, rang for a maid and sent him away. There was no time for a swim before luncheon and after luncheon they went to Amabell's and sat around on the broad green lawns and listened to Mr. Reid talk about his forthcoming picture. They swam after that, returning to Amabell's at cocktail time. And Aunt Sammy arrived for the night, a colleague of Dr. Allen's from Easthampton for dinner, and after dinner a dozen people dropped in.

He watched Lydia, marveling at her ability to hide herself from the world, looking for her beyond the tinted mask, and not finding her. Jenny was quiet, she said little, withdrew herself, an unobtrusive spectator. He must talk to her, he thought, yet what was there to say?

Before the household settled down for the night, he had a moment with her on the terrace. Aunt Sammy was scolding Lydia, at the foot of the stairs. Lydia looked dreadful, she was skin and bones, something must be done about it, she said.

"Jenny?"

"Yes?" Jenny turned and saw him standing just behind her, his hands in the pockets of his blue coat.

He said, "I want to talk to you. I've wanted to, all day. But now that we have a moment, there isn't anything to say."

She said, "I was going, Ron . . . I'd packed, and had an excuse ready but Lydia found out . . ."

"And asked you to stay? Yes, I know, she told me."

He thought, I've no reason to report what else she told me. It would serve no good purpose.

She asked, "What are you going to do?"

"I don't know." He laughed shortly. "Odd, how simple it is when you're — just the doctor. You send for the husband. You say this and that must be done. You issue orders, and hope they'll be obeyed. But in this case the doctor is the husband."

"I know." She suggested tentatively, "If she'd go away . . . a sanitarium perhaps . . . for a while?"

"Can you imagine Lydia in —"

"No," said Jenny, "I can't."

He said, "Last night I thought of something . . . it seemed the solution. Someone with her. Someone she trusts. Someone who cares for her . . . who would be there all the time —"

She thought, Don't say it, don't even *think* it.

He went on steadily, "You . . . there's no one else. I realized what I would be asking — I'd be asking you to give up the work you love, because I — we — need you. But who else could watch her, who else could . . . ?" He sighed heavily. "I'll talk to her about the sanitarium, Jenny, I'll have to. I don't know what we can tell her father. If he were anyone else we could say she was ill, that she needed a rest. But he isn't anyone else. He'd insist on knowing how ill . . . he'd insist on consultations, on diagnosticians. Then where would we be?"

She asked slowly, "On the other hand, how would you explain me?"

"I'd thought of that. You found yourself very tired, even going stale. You asked for a leave of absence from the hospital —"

She said, "And if Lydia wouldn't consent?"

"I thought this morning that she —" He broke off. He couldn't say now, I am sure she wouldn't.

Jenny thought, To be with her, every day, and when Ron's in town, every night. To listen to her, to watch her, to spy on her . . . I can't do it, even if she was willing.

She thought further, Anything, Ron, anything but that. I can't do that, not even for you.

Lydia was calling them. "Where in the world have they gone?" she was demanding of Aunt Sammy. "Jenny, where are you? Is Ron out there?"

He said, "Forget it. I was out of my mind. I couldn't ask it of you, Jenny."

She thought, Of course you can, you can ask anything of me.

They went into the house together and Lydia said, lightly, "You two look terribly solemn . . . you have that in-conference look."

"I don't care how they look," said Aunt

Sammy, propelling her stately bulk toward the stairs, "I'm dead . . . I'm going to bed . . . you keep the craziest hours, Lydia. No wonder Elwood excuses himself, early, he has a little sense."

She wheezed a little going up the steps and Jenny followed, her hand under the older woman's arm. "It's my knee," said Aunt Sammy, "no one does anything about it. Damned fools, doctors. Diathermy, X-ray, massage, heat — and it goes on creaking like a rusty hinge."

Voluble and complaining she lumbered upstairs and demanded when she had achieved the landing, "You, Miss Barton, come with me."

Docilely Jenny followed her into her room. Aunt Sammy groaning, shut the door. She said, "I wish you'd look at my knee. I've no faith in doctors. Maybe you'd know something about it."

"I doubt it," said Jenny, and waited patiently for the inevitable unveiling.

Ron, following Lydia down the hall, stopped at his father-in-law's door. It was ajar and a light burned. He knocked and went in and found Allen propped up against his pillows, his lips faintly blue and his color leaden.

"Why didn't you call me?" Ron demanded.

"What for?" asked Allen.

"You've had an attack," Ron accused him.

"Didn't amount to anything . . . I am still sufficiently master of my fate to reach for the usual remedies."

Ron said, "You'll stay in bed tomorrow."

Allen grinned. He said, "I'm getting old . . . I love attention. Maybe Jenny would sit with me for a while — if I'm to be bedridden."

"Of course she will."

"I didn't mean it, it's her vacation, poor girl . . . but the last time I was forced to have a nurse you procured one who looked like a cross between Olive Oil and Mrs. Jiggs . . . Jenny's very pleasant to look at," he said. "I wonder that some determined man hasn't discovered it."

"Several have, I hear," said Ron, his finger on Allen's wrist, "but none is determined enough, from all accounts. Suppose I sleep in your dressing room tonight?"

"Don't be ridiculous," said Allen. "I'm all right now. I'll sleep. Get to bed, will you? I'll ring that ridiculous bell you had rigged up if I need you."

Ron left his father-in-law's room a little later, his face dark with apprehension. During the summer Allen had had several attacks, all, save the first one, mild enough. But they were becoming more frequent.

When he reached his room he found that the door between it and Lydia's stood open. He went in and found her almost ready for bed. She smiled at him. "What took you so long?" she asked. "I thought Aunt Sammy drafted Jenny into her service —"

"I wasn't with Jenny," he said wearily. "Do say what you mean, Lydia, it's so much simpler."

"But I didn't mean anything," she argued reproachfully, "Aren't you just a little on the defensive, Ron?"

He said briefly, "I was with your father. He has had another attack. Oh, nothing alarming, very mild and short, but still the score adds up."

She said quickly, "Does he want to see me? Poor old Dad."

"He's all right," said Ron, "he'll sleep presently, but this only makes it more evident — if I needed evidence — that he must be spared every disturbance, every distress."

She asked evenly, "Well?"

"Lydia, all day I have been trying to think clearly, wondering what is best for you. The obvious course is, naturally, a sanitarium where, with rest and care . . ."

She cried, scarlet, "I won't go to one of those places! You can't make me!"

He asked quietly, "Do you want to be well, Lydia?"

"Of course, but —" She broke off and looked at him, her face pinched and small. "No," she said, "I don't. I'm all right this way, I'm happy."

"I disagree," he told her. "You're not all right and you're not happy. A sanitarium's out, then." He shrugged his shoulders. "You won't go of your own accord and I can't force you without your father's knowledge. Even, perhaps, if you went willingly . . . what explanation could we give him that would not alarm him, perhaps dangerously?"

"None," she said, with definite triumph.

"I can't take the responsibility —" He broke off and looked at her. "You just told me you didn't want to be cured. That means, among other things, that you don't love me."

"Oh, I love you," she said, half angrily, "If I could be cured of that too, I'd go to a dozen sanitariums!"

"Lydia," he said, "if you'll try, if you'll cooperate, you can be cured and we'll work the rest out somehow . . . our marriage, on a fresh, a different basis. There must be some way —"

He went over to her, lifted her in his arms and kissed her. He said, "If only you'd told me, if only you'd confided in me all along, from the very first —"

He released her and went to the door. He said, standing there, "I want you to leave this open . . . tonight."

She did not answer. A little later he saw her light go out and lay there waiting in the darkness. There was no sound from her room and after what seemed a long time he fell asleep.

An hour or so later he woke. He said, sitting up in bed, "Lydia . . . did you call me?"

"Ron —"

He went into the room and found her sitting on the edge of her bed. She said, "I can't sleep . . . I can't."

"Lie down," he said. He lay down beside her and took her in his arms.

She was shuddering painfully, from head to foot. She said, "Let me go — leave me, Ron, please. I'm all right. I won't do anything . . . I promise."

"I'll stay here," he said.

It was like that for a long time. Promises, pledges, appeals, tears, and at the end brutally frank abasement. He got up finally and asked, "Where is it?"

She told him. "Hurry," she said, "hurry."

He found the key and the little chest in the closet and what was in it. He measured a small amount in a glass and brought it back to her. He watched her drink it. He thought, We'll fight this ourselves — tapering off, sedatives, exercise, rest.

But he could not be with her all the time.

She murmured after a while, "I'm sorry, Ron."

He said, "Try to sleep, Lydia, if you can."

"You won't leave me?"

"No, I won't leave you."

"Not ever? No matter what I do, no matter what I say?"

"Never," he told her, "while I live."

She slept presently and he lay beside her listening to her breathing. He thought, *How much has been my fault?*

He slept fitfully and when she finally woke she heard him moving around the room next door. She felt wonderful, she thought, she had slept like a child. She called him and he came to the door.

"How long have you been gone?" she demanded.

"Half an hour."

"I feel marvelous," she said. "Ring for Mary, will you, Ron? I'll have my tray early."

He rang and after the maid had come and gone, Lydia said, "Come here."

He obeyed and stood beside the bed, looking down. She said, "You see — if you'd just stay with me, always . . ."

A lover, who companions you throughout the night, who holds you in his arms, from whom you derive strength and security. But a lover who demands nothing.

He said, "I can't always be with you."

"Why not?" she asked. "You could give up medicine, we'd be together, we could go away, travel . . . there's enough money, Ron, more than enough."

"What," he asked her, "would your father think of that, exactly?"

She answered, after a moment, "I didn't mean *now*."

She means, after he dies — which might be today, tomorrow, next month, next year. After she inherits what he has accumulated, and one complication is removed, he thought. He could feel neither anger nor disgust, only dull astonishment.

She said, "Can't you understand? It's only when I'm with you that I feel safe."

She was asking this of him, she was asking him to give up something which was as necessary to him as breath . . . she was demanding it. He was her husband. He had loved her . . . God knew

228

how much. Now he felt nothing but a sharp, wounding pity, and a heavy responsibility. How much was his fault? he thought again, and knew he would go on asking himself that for the rest of his life.

She said, "If I knew, if I could believe that when — that later, before we are old, you would be with me, Ron, all the time, that you'd put nothing ahead of me."

"And meantime?"

"I'll try," she told him; "as long as I have something to look forward to I'll want to try."

He said, "You mustn't be alone."

"That's what I've been trying to tell you, just that. It's all I've been trying to tell you, Ron. Come here, sit down."

She put her hand in his, closing her thin fingers with astonishing force over his.

"You've never belonged to me," she said.

He thought wearily, There's more to belonging than being together, day in, day out. He had a sudden, dreadful picture of what his life would be without his work. He was a young man. He had perhaps forty years to live, barring accidents, idle, useless . . . forty years of Lydia.

He said, "No one belongs to anyone else, Lydia."

"They must," she said wildly; "my mother and father did, to each other. Never to me. No one to me, ever. Not even you."

"You can't possess people," he told her; "only children believe that."

She was a child, possessive and unsatisfied, with a child's cold, unawakened flesh, shrinking from realities, and a child's mind — no, not a child's mind; a child's mind is clear and imaginative, open to wonder and the beginning of knowledge.

She asked, after a moment, "Do you suppose that Jenny would come stay with me?"

Jenny? His heart leaped and steadied again. He asked, after a moment, "Why?"

"I wouldn't be alone then," she said. "And Jenny — knows."

Jenny knew and Lydia hated her because she knew. She thought, But she'd be with me, where I could see her any hour of the day and night. I could call her and she'd be there. Not in the hospital, seeing Ron. Not running off with him somewhere, and coming back all shining because they'd been working together. Here. Helping me. Waiting on me. Doing things for me — all the little demeaning things . . . And when Ron came I'd be with him and she'd know that, she'd lie just next door and know it.

She said, "If Jenny stays with me I — I won't be afraid. *If* she stays with me . . . and if you promise . . . Ron . . . if you love me you can do this for me . . . ask Jenny to stay until you are free — until we no longer need her, until you can be with me. Will you promise?"

He could not. She was demanding his life . . . she was bidding him throw it away. The hospital and the white light beating down and his own controlled voice speaking to some woman whose body contracted and labored, seeking its release, and the release of life, the breath of life. This, and all the rest. The sense of sureness and power. The knowledge of being needed.

Lydia said, "I need you, Ron, terribly. This hasn't been me, all these years. Someone else, someone who keeps running away. I won't run away any more. I'll get well," she promised, "I'll get well and —" She heard the maid coming down the hall with her tray. She said, "Ron, if you'll promise, I'll do anything you want, I'll even have a child."

Chapter 17

Ron bent down to breakfast, walking slowly, sliding his hand over the polished banisters. The wood was smooth, cool to the touch, and he thought with a remote corner of his mind of the many hands which had worn it to that texture. The rest of his mind was savagely preoccupied, it was like something hunted, seeking an escape, flinging itself blindly at stone walls, digging frantically into earth, tunneling, and finding no way out.

Dr. Allen was remaining in his rooms today. Ron had looked in on him before going down. "Well?" he asked.

"Fine," said his father-in-law. "Stop fussing."

"You'll behave yourself?"

"What else can I do? What's up, Ron?"

"Nothing . . . why?"

"You look worried, under the mask. If it's over me, forget it. I hope it's over me?"

Ron relaxed his face, consciously. He said, "Naturally."

"Then," said Allen, "your worry's superfluous. Go eat your breakfast."

Jenny was alone at the breakfast table, crumbling the thin toast, drinking her coffee black.

"Good morning," said Ron, and smiled at her. It was not altogether the effort he had imagined.

"Hello," she said. She added, "It's a marvellous day." And then, as the, pantry door closed and they were alone, "How's Lydia?"

"She's all right," he said, his face closed again, hard as a fist.

"Coffee? This is fresh."

He nodded.

She poured the coffee, watching the dark amber flow from the silver spout. "Two," she asked, "and cream?"

Sun slanted in, the curtains stirred at the windows, a robin spoke cheerfully outside, flowers bloomed in the big room. They were alone, drawing close without speech, in a mute, explicable intimacy. You could almost pretend that this was your house, your table, and your man at the head of it, drinking his good coffee. Almost, but not quite.

From another room, sufficiently remote to be soothing rather than irritating, they heard the purr of a vacuum cleaner. They were down earlier than usual.

Jenny roused herself. She said, "I forgot to ask you about your patient."

"Who?" he asked, abstracted.

"At the Irving House, wasn't it? I don't know her name."

He said, "She's all right. Too much lobster, coupled with imagination."

They fell silent again, the pantry door opened and closed, they were served, presently a telephone rang and was answered and then there was silence again.

Ron pushed back his plate, lit a cigarette, and rose. He suggested, "Let's go somewhere — I want to talk to you."

She followed him out of the house into the direct sunlight of the terrace. He said, "Sorry —" and offered her his cigarette case but she shook her head. Abruptly, he sat down on the low stone wall which enclosed the flagged space.

"Here," he said, "beside me."

She sat down, and looked at him. He saw how pale she was, a smooth, even pallor, and how dark her eyes by contrast. Her hair had the sheen of silk, her fine hands were folded quietly in her lap. He regarded her absently as one looks at a picture, without thinking much about it, and saw how beautifully her throat rose from the simple neckline of a cotton frock, the color of faded roses.

He said:

"There are things you don't talk about; or shouldn't. Things that belong, particularly, to a man and his wife. But you are in on this, Jenny. You *know* . . . you are not outside. I must tell you . . . you are the only person to whom I can talk. The one most nearly concerned, aside from myself — and Lydia — is Lydia's father. And I can't, to him."

She nodded, without speaking. She was — or seemed — completely serene. Like the ocean out past the marsh grass and dunes, the ocean as it was on this windless September day, deep and quiet, and on the surface, unruffled. She had such qualities, depth, placidity, undercurrents. She was often silent, a lovely silence, warm and kind.

He said, "Last night was a — a sort of skirmish. We won, I think." He described it, briefly. He added, "But it's a delusion to think we'd always win. Jenny, she wants you to stay with her."

"You suggested that?" she asked evenly, but her heart hammered against her side. No, she thought, *no* . . .

"She did. Quite of her own accord. She said, in essence, that she was afraid to be alone . . . and that you knew."

"I see."

He added, "This morning she asked me to promise to give up my practice, in order to be with her."

Jenny's hands moved, tightened. Color rose suddenly in her face with an effect of shock and violence. Her eyes blazed, they were almost black. She said, "But that's insane . . . you can't, you mustn't."

He said wearily, "I didn't promise. But what am I to do?" His mouth was taut. "She's my wife, and she's ill. It *is* an illness."

Jenny asked, "You'd do that — for her?"

He shrugged his shoulders. He answered after a moment, "How much of this situation has been my fault? I tell you, I feel responsible."

She spoke, without thinking. She said, "How much you must love her."

He turned away and she heard his answer without the interpretive expression of eyes or face. His voice was steady. "No," he said, "not now, not for a long time. Not in the way you mean."

The silence was thick between them, golden and hot with sunshine, broken by the blundering passage of a bee, the high silver sounds of a bird singing.

Jenny began again, groping. "Dr. Allen," she said, "he would be appalled. And if you can't tell him *why* —"

Ron made a swift gesture. He said harshly, "That's it. I pointed that out to her. She's given me a reprieve until he dies. Not in so many words, but that is what she implied."

Jenny drew a sharp breath. Still he did not look at her. He could not.

Presently he said, "This morning she made pledges — she said, if I would do this for her, she would . . . be well again, she would have a child . . ." He paused. He added bluntly, "I told her she wasn't fit. I said, 'You're not fit to have a child.' "

"Need you have said that?"

"It's true, isn't it? A woman in her physical and mental state? You're not stupid, Jenny, nor uninformed."

She said slowly, "The easier way would have been to agree to everything, give her an incentive to be cured . . . and then, afterward . . ."

To her astonishment, he laughed, and she

shrank, a little wounded and incredulous. He said finally, "You're a woman too. Devious, cutting corners, thinking around them, preferring compromises."

Jenny rallied and said sturdily, "Are you always honest? Have you been with every patient? You know you haven't. You've told lies, half lies, coaxed, promised, withheld . . ."

"The end justifies the means," he murmured. "But Lydia isn't a patient. She's my wife, my obligation, and responsibility."

"She's ill. You've said so, yourself," Jenny reminded him.

"So I'm to promise," he said, turning at last and looking at her, "and yet know all the time that I don't intend to keep my word? Is that what you want me to do, Jenny?"

She said, "When she's well she'll see things differently. She's not normal now. In her normal condition she'd realize what an impossibility she's asking, she'd consider what your profession means to you."

"I doubt it."

Jenny went on, "And, too, she wouldn't be afraid, she wouldn't be at all as she now is — can't you see that?"

"Pretty specious," he told her. "Lie to the patient. When she recovers — *if* she recovers — she will understand that it was in a good cause and the right remedy."

Jenny said, after a moment, "You can't handle this, Ron, it's too close to you. Could you persuade her to see someone else, someone impersonal . . ." she hesitated and added courageously, "say James Vernon?"

She saw the muscles tighten along his jaw. Vernon was the Chief in Psychiatry at Lister.

He said slowly, "He's a great man, none better. The wrong man would of course be fatal. Or, perhaps, in this case, even the right one."

She thought, You can't bear to have her go to Vernon, you think it's an admission of failure on your part, it hits you where every man lives, in his sex pride.

How human he was, how vulnerable . . . like any other man. Perhaps more so, because during his working hours the physician plays at God, imposes his superior knowledge, deals with life and death. When you saw Theron Lewis work you forgot he was a man, you thought of him as a sort of destiny, calm and foreknowing, impersonal and detached. She thought, My darling, if there was anything I could do . . .

There was one thing she could so.

Aloud she said, "I'll have to give them time at the hospital to replace me . . . and then if Lydia still wants me, Ron, I'll come."

His face was filled with light. He said, "You'd do it? Don't think for a moment I don't know what you're relinquishing."

"That doesn't matter. Perhaps she won't need me long."

Later she was to remember that.

He rose, stood before her and took her hands

in his own. He said, astonished, "Your hands are cold."

They lay quiet in his, and Jenny smiled at him. She said, "It will work out. You didn't finish saying what you think of consulting Vernon."

He retained her hands in his. "I don't know. I'll have to think about it. Perhaps you're right. But how to persuade her? I'd have to see him, of course . . ."

She said, slowly, "Perhaps not. If she went of her own accord . . . without, ostensibly, your knowledge?"

"You mean, you'd persuade her?"

"I could try," said Jenny. "I don't promise results. But your promise, Ron? What are you going to do about that?"

"God," he admitted, "I don't know."

He dropped her hands and turned away. She said, after a moment, "It's your life. It would be only half a life, Ron, as if you'd gone blind."

But he was walking away from her, across the terrace and into the house. She remained, alone, her hands remembering his, her mind cluttered with doubt, dusty with despair, thoughts scurrying through it like mice in a crowded attic.

He mustn't, she told herself, I'll fight, someone has to fight.

Are you thinking of him, something hard and unyielding asked her, or of yourself? You've a little of him now, his friendship, his affection is dependent upon your working partnership. If you

239

lose that, you lose him. Are you thinking of his welfare or of your own? Why are you so ready to sacrifice Lydia, if it is to be a sacrifice?

She shivered, the voice was silent, and the scrabbling mice-thoughts went busily about their futile errands in the disorder of her mind.

Ron was walking about Lydia's room. She had breakfasted, and then dozed off, and now lay wide awake in bed, complaining, half laughing, half fretful. "I'm much too tired to get up."

He said, standing at her dressing table, his back to her, "Jenny says she'll give up her job and come to us, to live."

She could see his face in the mirror. She cried, "That's wonderful — how did you persuade her?"

"It didn't take much persuasion, Lydia. She wants to help."

Lydia's face was brilliant with secret laughter. I'll bet it didn't, she thought. Strategy. Keep your enemy close to you, where you can watch him, disarm him with dependence. *Love* your enemies, thought Lydia happily.

She said softly, "You haven't promised."

Ron came over to the bed. He sat down on the edge of it and when she put her hands out to him in an appealing gesture, he took them in his own. They were not still and cold like Jenny's had been, warming gradually in his grasp, and unstirring. They were hot, they moved restlessly, were reluctant.

He said gravely, "If, after you are well again,

240

you still feel about this as you now do, I promise I will do as you ask."

He hated himself. Why couldn't he be honest, clean cut, surgical? Say, Yes . . . or, say No . . . ? Jenny had infected him, with her woman's reliance upon compromise and half measures. Cowardice had infected him, the faint hope that there might be a way out, that, as Jenny had suggested, Lydia, in full possession of her regained faculties, would not consider imposing the life sentence.

"Oh, darling," she said . . . and her face was bright again with triumph.

When he had gone she lay back against her pillows, too replete with complacency to stir, to ring for Mary. She thought over the day she had planned, the party tonight. She thought, faintly regretful that she must open her hands and let Timothy Wilson go . . . she no longer had any need for him. She had what she wanted: Jenny under her eyes by day; by night . . . Jenny to companion, to guard her. It was really very amusing. They didn't know that it would be she who would watch Jenny, sly, traitorous Jenny. Butter wouldn't melt in Jenny's mouth. Damn her, damn her to hell . . .

She had Ron's promise. He would keep it.

She hated him.

He had said, "You aren't fit to have a child." Well, she was fit. She'd have her child, she would laugh at them all. The upper hand, the last word. Pretty Lydia, weak and docile, tender and pliant . . . do be careful of her, don't cross her, treat her as you'd treat an invalid child, an imbecile child. She wants to get well . . .

Lydia laughed aloud.

Chapter 18

Jenny resigned her position at Lister to the stupefaction of all concerned. She lied steadily, with complete calm, in answer to every argument, every question. She was tired, she was growing stale . . . she must have time to get herself in hand again. "Nonsense," said her superintendent testily to Ron Lewis, "what's wrong with the girl? Best OB supervisor I ever had . . . strong as a horse, not a nerve in her body . . . what's she intend to do now?"

Ron said carefully, "I wouldn't be too sure. She's worked very hard for the last four years . . . I can see her point."

"More than I can . . . sure it isn't some man? If it is, why doesn't she say so, come out with it? Alymer, for choice?"

Ron said, "No, you're wrong there, I think. For the time being she is going to live with us . . . she —" he swallowed and went on — "she and my wife are close friends . . . Lydia has wanted her to come to us for a long time. You know my father-in-law — he won't have a nurse around except of course when he knows it's immediate. But Jenny's like one of the family . . . and so —"

"Oh," said the superintendent, "I see."

He thought he did, anyway. Good girl, he admitted to himself, chucking things because

243

she's needed. Sure, he knew Elwood Allen, ob-stinate, pigheaded. They might put this over on him. Good for them. He felt better about Jenny's resignation. He didn't like to think of her as overworked.

That was that. Ron left the office and the sweat stood on his forehead and the palms of his hands were wet.

Allen was another kettle of fish. An explanation seemed easy. It wasn't.

"Jenny's given up her Lister job, she's pretty tired," Ron had told Allen carelessly, "she thought her vacation would fix her up but it didn't."

"She looks tired," agreed Allen thoughtfully, "and she didn't seem quite as usual . . . not that she's ever very vivacious. I told her, I recall, that a change was better than a rest in most cases. Still, Lydia did make things hum during the time she was here . . . never a dull moment. Perhaps too few. But she didn't look as if she was at the end of her rope. And I'd have sworn she wouldn't quit unless she was."

"She hides things."

"I suppose so. I don't know her well, not as well as I'd like. What's she going to do, go up with her mother, where is it, Binghamton?"

"Cooperstown. No, as a matter of fact, Lydia's asked her to come and stay with us for a while, for as long as she likes. She'd be company for her and —"

"Lydia has plenty of company." Allen chuckled. "Not that it won't be pleasant to have Jenny around." He looked sharply at his son-in-law and his face altered. "See here," he demanded, "this isn't a conspiracy, is it?"

"What do you mean?"

"Don't look so innocent. I'm not one of your patients, grateful and credulous. I mean, you haven't persuaded yourself that I need a nurse, have you, and selected this way to procure one? Garron will have your ears," he warned, "for if I'm ever to be a chronic in need of bedside nursing, she'd slit your throat before she'd let anyone else —"

Ron said, "No, you're barking up the wrong tree, although, frankly, it's a good idea to have Jenny in the house, when I'm out of it, to scold you now and then and make you rest. I've considered that. Beyond that, no ulterior motive, I assure you."

"I believe you," said his father-in-law, "but" — he shook his head — "there is something here which doesn't quite meet the eye. You'd better come clean. I haven't liked the way you've looked for the last few weeks. What is it, Ron?"

"Nothing."

"If you're keeping something from me," said his father-in-law sharply, "you'll regret it." He spoke with the easy irritability of the cardiac case. Ron grinned and smote him on the shoulder.

"Bats," he diagnosed, "in the belfry. Don't be so damned suspicious."

"Better than butterflies in the stomach," said

Allen. "Well, all right. And I don't mind confessing that Jenny will be an addition to the household. Where are you putting her, in town?"

"Next to Lydia."

"Lydia, eh?" Allen's eyes were sharp again. "What's that for?"

"It's the only free room," Ron said gently. "Of course if you want her next to you and are willing to sacrifice your study —"

Allen grinned. "Sorry," he said, "but, mind you, I'm not wholly satisfied in my mind about this."

"Walk carefully," Ron cautioned, Jenny, "he knows something's up . . . but not what."

They moved back to town in October and Jenny settled down in the household. It would be easier, in the city. In Southampton, during the last weeks there when, released from the hospital, she was free to go, Ron had not been down at all. There were nights when she sat in Lydia's room, or lay beside her on the bed, fighting the quiet and desperate battle, talking or reading to her, giving the sedatives Ron had ordered . . . "p.r.n.," he'd said, "it's up to you, use your own judgment." Sometimes she won, sometimes she lost. Sometimes Lydia clung to her, like a child in the dark, "Talk to me, don't leave me, don't let me . . . whatever I say . . ."

Sometimes Lydia cursed her, and sometimes she wept. And when the battle was a losing one, sometimes her tongue would be loosened and she would talk and talk . . . and Jenny would listen,

sick and still with horror. But this was more than
. . . No, it couldn't be. "Now," Lydia said, "I'll
tell you just why you're here and what I think of
you . . ."

Did she think that, was that why? It didn't
matter, thought Jenny, nothing mattered but
helping her, if she could help her.

And in the morning . . .

"Darling, I'm so sorry. It won't happen again
What did I do, what did I say? No, don't tell me.
I swear it won't happen again and whatever I
said I didn't mean it."

In the city it was different. Ron was at home,
most of the time. There were nights, of course,
when he was out, when he was at the hospital.
But for the most part he was there and Lydia
was his responsibility, except on the occasions
when he came quietly to Jenny's room and called
her and she went in to Lydia's room with him
and they both fought.

"It's no use," he said, more than once, "we'll
have to have outside help, a definite course of
treatment."

Yet he couldn't bring himself to that, it would
mean telling Allen — or lying to him. And you
couldn't lie, in this instance. He was her father
and a physician.

During the days Jenny's time was tacitly her
own. She could see those of her friends who were
free, shop, go to a matinee or a movie. She was
drawing a salary. That was the only way Ron
would have it, and Lydia too. "But," said Lydia,

"you can't do anything else, Jenny."

Well, of course, she couldn't. She hadn't saved, she had sent money to her mother all along. She had to have clothes, she must continue helping Mrs. Barton. She couldn't just eat and sleep in the Allen apartment. It was sensible and logical that she consider this period of her life as another job. A job with Ron, for Ron. She turned his first check over in her fingers, and wished that she might destroy it.

Nominally free or, if Lydia wanted her, to come on a shopping expedition with her or to the theater, or to luncheon, she went. That, too, was her job.

On the nights when Ron and Lydia were out together, she read or knitted, listened to the radio, made herself unobtrusively useful to Dr. Allen. His attacks continued, they were frequent if not severe. He was in bed much of the time. He was no longer available for consultations. He said, "Well, we may as well admit that I'm washed up," but there was the fiction in the family that one day he would be able to go on where he had left off. Jenny managed to spend a good deal of time with him. When he felt well enough Mrs. Petersen came and he dictated to her. Other days, he lay quiet in bed, listening to the radio, and snapping it off when the news was too disturbing. Jenny would knock and come in. Sometimes they talked, sometimes she read to him, often they were companionably silent. He said to her once, "You are the most restful person

I have ever met. It's like being pleasantly alone."

"That's not entirely a compliment," she complained, smiling, "as it means I have no personality."

"On the contrary, I have never met anyone with more. But it doesn't shatter a fellow, it has no steam-roller qualities. You take a landscape," he explained thoughtfully, "the view from a mountain, hill and valley, field and stream . . . or from a beach, the ocean, limitless and altering. That has personality, hasn't it?"

"Am I a landscape," she demanded, "with an old red barn in the foreground and a cow near by, her head through the wire fence?"

"Don't willfully misunderstand," he said testily, "I suppose I'm trying to tell you that you're a part of nature."

She saw Ward Alymer, went out with him occasionally. Her insurance salesman had drifted away; an impatient man, he could not wait forever for a girl to change her mind. In December he sold a large annuity to a widow of substance and married her before she could regret the first payment. But Ward remained faithful. He did not like the setup, he told her. What the hell was she doing in the Allen household? As for being tired, that was nonsense as she had never looked better.

October was pure, cool gold and a laughing wind and, if you bothered to look up, a clean and empty sky, flawed sapphire. November was dark, snow fell early, and presently it was Christmas and Lydia began talking of the south. "Jenny and I," she announced. "You won't miss us, Ron, and it would be good for Dad, you said so yourself, the warmer climate . . . if only he'd come."

Ron said, "He isn't strong enough to travel."

"He doesn't think so. You fuss like an old woman. I thought," she said, "of Boca Raton. There's no reason why you can't come if you want to, Ron."

She was terribly nervous. She would, could not be alone a moment. Her engagement book was crowded. Luncheon, contract, a charity board meeting, cocktails — "tomato juice," she'd say, smiling, "you know I don't drink, more's the pity" — dinner, theater. She couldn't sit, or keep her hands, still, and by the first of the year she was managing to secrete keys — Ron had taken the keys of her room but she had others made — and lock herself in again.

Jenny said despairingly, "If it would help to take her south?"

"Her gang's down there," said Ron, "Wilson, Amabell, the whole kit and boodle of them. I don't know how you'd manage."

"And you couldn't come too?"

He couldn't. He was busy, his engagement pad, too, was full. He had cases booked straight through the winter. "War," he said, "is a boon to the obstetrician. Why do more women have babies during war? And don't say, selectees coming home on leave," he remarked one evening.

"I didn't," said Jenny indignantly.

"You thought it. It's something else, it's psychological. Death all around, youth blown out like a candle, life held so lightly. Nineteen-forty-one and the world in flames. Men create death and women combat it by giving new life. I don't know . . . it seems like that to me. Maybe I'm crazy. A provision of Nature who abhors waste, who manages to produce life from death, the grass springing from the disintegrating flesh, the moccasin flower nodding from the rotten log . . ."

Lydia had been listening, smoking continuously. She cried out sharply, "Stop talking like that," she demanded, "it's horrible, it's ugly, I hate it."

Lydia was afraid of death. She could not imagine a world without her. She could not imagine any other world. She was appalled.

She was as irresolute as a swallow, during the first January weeks, her days were like a swallow's flight, veering, circling, restless and uncertain. She made engagements and broke them, she ordered reservations for the south and canceled them. She couldn't leave Ron, she said, or her father. She had always been extravagant, and now her buying was a frenzy of spending. A short sable jacket, a dozen pairs of shoes, and quantities of frocks, hats, lingerie. Sometimes she bought, and the next day returned the purchases . . . she'd been mad, she declared, she looked dreadful in the dress, or hat or whatever it was.

But custom-made things — and most of hers were custom-made — could not be returned. She overdrew and went to Ron for money. He warned, writing her a check for the overdraft:

"Look here, Lydia, you've got to cut down . . . these aren't normal times . . . taxes are very heavy and will become more so. You'll soon be going without, not only because you can't afford it but because you won't be able to get what you want."

"That's nonsense," she argued; "the newspapers are just trying to scare people."

It wasn't nonsense, he told her. He vetoed her desire for a new car. He had his own, she had hers, and a good stolid chauffeur. No, she would have to make hers do; after all, it was less than two years old.

She reminded him, for the first time during their marriage, that she had her own income.

He said mildly, "But you have spent it, until next quarter."

He had never made any objection to Lydia's "own" money or how she spent it. It was a trust from her mother. He knew that, at least, early in their marriage, Dr. Allen had supplemented it. But Allen was no longer practicing. His own original inheritance and investments brought him an excellent return but dividends were cut these days, living cost more, taxes were steeper. However, Allen still insisted on carrying the major burden of the establishment although, as Ron's practice increased, he was able to do a great deal more. When he suggested moving to less expensive living quarters Allen was testy and impatient. He wasn't, he declared, as yet out of the running, he could still afford to keep things going.

Gradually it became Jenny's job to go on Lydia's shopping expeditions, as unobtrusively as possible and to prevent her, whenever she could, from unnecessary, unbridled spending. She said to Ron one blowy wintry night when Lydia was out of the room, "It's like a disease."

He looked at her and then each turned his regard away. But there was something unspoken and frightening between them.

He asked carefully, "Have you suggested Vernon to her?"

"Several times."

"And?"

"It's no use, Ron, she'd never consult him voluntarily. Besides, she knows him."

"Well, yes, she's met him but what has that to do with — ?"

She said unhappily, "She knows his — specialty. She said, 'I suppose you think I'm losing my mind?' "

Ron spoke out of a heavy silence.

He said, "There isn't a man living who'd diagnose —" He broke off, and added, "As far as I can see, it began in childhood. She's always been rather frail. Her father told me once that she was a brilliant scholar but would, or could not retain what she learned, and soon grew impatient of discipline or restriction. She herself has said she was spoiled, because . . . it was easier for them. By them, she meant her parents. She seems to have resented the close bond and understanding between them, and to have felt that she never came first. After her mother's death she did naturally, with her father. Then when she grew up . . ."

He thought, marriage affronted her, it broke into her dream, it was too much reality, too earthy.

Aloud he said, "With her original temperament and then the drinking as a factor —"

Lydia came back into the room and looked from one to the other.

"What are you talking about?" she demanded.

Her eyes narrowed, her mouth was a red line. Jenny answered, smiling, "You."

"I thought so! But I bet you wouldn't tell me what you were saying."

"That you are putting on weight."

It was true, she was rounder, she had gained eight pounds. She said, her suspicions momentarily forgotten, "I eat too much candy, I'll have to stop."

Candy and sodas and twice as much sugar in her tea or coffee as once she had taken. Jenny had watched, saying nothing. The body was putting up its own fight, substituting as best it could.

For several weeks now there had been no difficulty, no appeals, and no locking of the door.

Yet on the next day it happened. Jenny had gone with Lydia to the hairdresser's, and waited the interminable time it took her to have her scalp treatment, her wash and set, her facial, manicure, and pedicure. When Lydia was under the drier she had one of the girls go into the waiting room and call Jenny. Jenny went back to the booth and Lydia said, apologetically, "Darling, I forgot." Her voice was loud and hollow over the noise of the drier. "I promised to pick up the black dinner dress . . . I wanted to be sure I'd have it tonight. Take the car and get it and call back for me, will you? It will save time, and we promised to meet Marjorie at one. She hates it if anyone's late."

Marjorie. Marjorie Davis. A new friend, sleek, polished, and effectively weary. A new enthusiasm. Lydia had met her at one of the relief organizations. She adored her, her background of Virginia, a Paris convent, and three husbands.

Jenny went off. It took time to get the car, there was no parking space and Cullen had had to drive around the block, when at a little after twelve he returned to call for them. They went to the dress shop, and there was a little delay there also. When Jenny got back to the beauty salon Lydia had gone. The girl who had done her nails said blankly, "But she just left, Miss Barton; she said she was meeting you."

Jenny, disturbed, went to the Ritz to keep the luncheon appointment. Surely Lydia would be there. Marjorie was on the stroke of one. She was a curiously punctual woman. One, one-fifteen, one-thirty. Lydia had not appeared.

"I can't understand —"

"Surely she knew she was meeting me . . .

didn't she say so?" asked Marjorie, annoyed. "*You* knew."

Jenny lied. "Not this morning," she said. "Last night . . . Yes, of course. She must have mixed her dates."

"Sounds very fishy," said Marjorie.

Jenny said appealingly, "You mustn't wait for us, Mrs. Davis. I'll go back home and wait for her . . . perhaps she's there now."

"You could phone," suggested Marjorie.

Jenny came back from the telephone booth. "She isn't there," she said, "and there's no message." Marjorie was looking at her very oddly. She said, improvising, "Ron said something at breakfast this morning . . . about luncheon, I mean. That's it. She's forgotten our engagement with you, she's gone to meet him . . ."

"How uxorious — if that's the word and if it is Ron," said Marjorie, "not that I blame her." She thought of Mr. Davis, who was very fat and very rich, and sighed. She added, "Well, I'll forgive her this time . . . but nobody stands me up more than once."

Jenny went back to the apartment. There was nothing else she could do. She dismissed Cullen and said that Mrs. Lewis would telephone when she needed him. She didn't think she would be going out again today, there were people coming for dinner.

She sat with Dr. Allen, spinning her fictional excuses.

No, she been with Lydia except at the hairdresser's. Lydia had gone off to keep an engagement.

He slept, later in the afternoon. Jenny went into the living room and the tea service came in. She drank a cup of tea, crumbled a biscuit. Her pulse was too fast, her hands shook. She was jumpy as a cat.

At five the bell rang and she ran to answer it, brushing aside the astonished butler.

"Lydia!"

Lydia was smiling, her cheeks were flushed and her eyes brilliant. Her hat was crooked, and her lipstick smeared. She said, "Hello, darling, am I late?"

Somehow Jenny got her to her room. She was very unsteady, and almost incoherent. There were things you could do, and Jenny did them. Afterward when she had Lydia in bed she sat beside her watching her sleep.

Then she went out quietly and found the list of people who were to dine with the Lewis's and called them, one by one, and canceled the engagement. She said that Lydia was down, very suddenly, with the flu.

Ron came home early. She met him and told him, briefly. He asked, "Where in God's name was she?"

"I don't know, exactly. Every bar in town — according to her."

"That tears it. Dozens of people may have seen her."

"It can't be helped now."

"Weren't there people coming for dinner?"

"I canceled. Luckily there were only six and dinner wasn't until eight-fifteen."

"What did you tell them?"

"Flu."

"Is she asleep?"

"Yes, finally."

He said wearily, "So it's to do all over again. This time we'll have to have help — Vernon, or someone like him. And if a sanitarium is indicated, well, we'll have to manage, that's all . . . lie, get the consultants to lie — I can't sacrifice her," he said, "even though it might mean sacrificing him. My God, what a choice!"

At seven Dr. Allen rang his bell and asked to see Miss Barton. When she arrived he asked, smiling, "Any social shenanigans tonight?"

"No."

"I thought I heard something about a party."

"It's off. Lydia came home with a slight temperature . . . it's probably a touch of flu. She's in bed, asleep, after the usual remedies. I made her excuses to her guests."

"Bad time of year," he said, frowning. "Have you called Timmons?"

"She wouldn't hear of it. Ron says she'll be all right. If she's no better tomorrow, we'll have him, first thing."

"I," said Lydia's father, "feel like a new man. I slept most of the afternoon. I'll dine with you and Ron if you will permit me the laxity of a dressing gown. The brocade one Lydia gave me for Christmas. I feel, when I wear it, that I am at a masquerade."

That was a dreadful evening, the three of them at the table, the older man in the brocade dressing gown, decrying his diet, speaking hopefully of his improvement, the other two determinedly bright, cheerful, and entertaining. And not very far away Lydia, asleep.

After dinner Jenny slipped away to sit with her, to return before she had been away too long, reporting that the nonexistent temperature was down and that she slept. And presently Allen, yawning, decided that he was tired. "Foolish," he commented, "how a little exertion throws you. But it's been a very pleasant evening."

Standing with Jenny in Lydia's room, "Do you think he suspects — ?" Ron began.

"No, of course not. Ron, you look terribly tired."

He said, "I'll go to bed. Jenny, don't worry so. In the morning we'll decide."

"Perhaps I should stay with her?"

"No. I'll leave my door open, I'll hear her. Good night, my dear."

Jenny went to bed. It was too early, she would never sleep. She picked up a mystery novel and tried to read. But before eleven she switched out the light. Her brain was numb with thinking. She was tired, after all.

Ron slept, and Lydia. And Dr. Allen, putting aside his book, padded quietly down the hall in his slippers. Dark and still. He'd look in on

Lydia. Not that Ron and Jenny wouldn't know. But she was susceptible to colds, as a child she had twice had flu pneumonia.

He went softly into her room. The door leading into Ron's room was open, but Ron's light was out. A night light burned by Lydia's bed. Allen leaned over her, cautiously, put his thin finger on her pulse and stood there, frowning . . .

He touched her face gently. She did not stir. Her face was flushed, swollen, her breathing stertorous. Yet no elevation of temperature was evident.

He bent closer to the life source, to her breath.

Presently he straightened up and stood motionless beside her. He was remembering a great many things which, at the time of their occurrence, had seemed trivial. Her debut, for instance. He had explained tolerantly, "Lydia isn't used to champagne, absurd child." And the other times, when he had found her excited, febrile, and had warned her, "I wish you wouldn't . . . I know your crowd does . . . but —" she'd laughed always, "Angel, you're crazy . . . I had just one, a *little* one."

Since her marriage to Ron things had been different, or so Lydia's father had thought. How grateful he had been to Ron, not that he had been seriously disturbed about Lydia, beyond the normal anxiety any father would experience.

Now all Lydia's secret life was clear to him, with a horrible lucidity. And Ron's.

That was why Jenny was here. They had tried

to keep this from him and had almost succeeded.

Well, face it, Allen, you've always faced things. Tomorrow, talk to Ron. Now you know it will be easier for him, he won't have to pretend any longer.

He returned to his room, as quietly as he had left it. Getting into bed he lay back against his high piled pillows, thinking, planning. After a while he put out his hand for the pad and pencil which lay on the bedside table. Sometimes, when he could not sleep, he entertained himself by making notes for his book.

For a long time he wrote, at first slowly, painfully, and then with increasing rapidity. There was no sound in the room except his breathing and the scratch of the pencil on paper. Suddenly, he was mortally tired. He folded the sheets together, put them in a long envelope and the envelope between the pages of one of the books lying on the bedside table.

He thought, In the morning . . .

The premonitory pang shook him, an excruciating agony, the sensation as of splinters of glass piercing his heart, the merciless pain in the left arm and shoulder. He fought the rising, familiar panic, felt the icy sweat drench him. He reached for the amyl nitrate ampules on the table.

Ring, rouse the house, rouse Ron.

His hand relaxed . . . the little amyl nitrate pearl rolled to the floor.

Chapter 19

Dr. Elwood Allen had died in his sleep . . . and the world, his world, paused briefly in its headlong rush toward destruction to pay him tribute. He had made lasting contributions to science, his papers had been widely read and discussed during the past twenty years, and although he had been in retirement for some time before his death, his loss would be keenly felt by his profession. He had held important offices in various professional associations, he had lectured to thousands of students who attended the medical school of which he was a graduate. It was understood that he had been assembling notes for his autobiography when he died. His colleagues were hopeful that Allen's son-in-law would be able to write the book, from those notes. He had been closer to him during the past four or five years than anyone else.

Tributes were paid him in the public press and in the journals of his profession. A group of his friends suggested a scholarship fund, to be awarded annually in his name. Special memorial services were held, and presently his name would be inscribed upon the bronze plaque in the vast entrance corridor of Lister Memorial.

Here and there a practical-minded younger man remarked to a friend that Ron Lewis had certainly stepped into a comfortably fitting pair of shoes.

Death occurs, and life continues. Death and life are stones flung into the dark pool of eternity, they make their little impact and cause their little stir, the ripples expand into ever-widening circles and gradually disappear, and the pool is as it was before.

The newspapers had their say, the news weeklies added their quota of information in their staccato, inverted English. The funeral was over, the vault doors closed. Hundreds attended the memorial services but only a few close friends were present at the burial, at which Lydia, in heavy black, looking frail and forlorn, leaned upon her husband's arm or clung to Jenny's hand.

Ron had found his father-in-law that morning. Ron had gone to tell Jenny, and together they had told Lydia, rousing her from her drugged sleep. Jenny would not forget that, not ever. The bright, sharp winter sunlight, when the shades were raised, Lydia's swollen eyes and mouth and slow comprehension.

"No," she had cried out, *"no!"* and then burst into hysterical weeping.

During the days which followed she made two related, yet opposed remarks. She reminded Ron, "Now you're free to keep your promise," and she had said to Jenny, "I suppose you think that because my father's no longer here you two can safely cook up some scheme to get rid of me. Well, you won't, I'll see to that."

"Just what did she mean by that?" Ron demanded when Jenny told him.

"Vernon perhaps? I'd mentioned him again, just before Dr. Allen's death."

He said, interrupting, "Thank God he died without knowing."

Jenny nodded. She asked hesitantly, "Had you said anything to her about a sanitarium?"

"Not recently. That must, however, have been in her mind," he answered dully.

His mouth was set in a tight, unhappy line. He said presently, "Now, of course, I can do the things I should have done long ago, without doing any harm."

The course he must follow seemed simple enough. Vernon first of all, and if Vernon believed it advisable — as it seemed likely that he would, the proper surroundings, medical and nursing care. But nothing involving another person's life is as simple as it sounds.

Jenny asked, "And your promise?"

He could only regard her with mute unhappiness.

She said urgently, "Surely you don't mean to keep it? Surely you will do what you can first to see that she is well again? Because when she is, Ron, she will never demand it of you."

After the will had been read Lydia shut herself up in her rooms, would not talk, would not eat. "What in the world is the matter with her?" demanded Aunt Sammy, voluminous in black and more moved by her brother's death than she would have admitted to anyone. She was devoted to him after her fashion although, while he lived, they had been on a basis of armed neutrality.

Ron had excuses ready, the shock, the suddenness, Aunt Sammy must recall that Lydia had been down with an attack of flu at the time of her father's death . . . she wasn't even now wholly recovered. He had urged her not to attend the funeral but she had insisted.

Aunt Sammy had an answer for everything, and took matters into her own hands. She had a cottage at Delray Beach. She would wire the caretaker, have it staffed and ready and take Lydia and Jenny down at once, the sun, the change of climate would put Lydia on her feet again.

Would Lydia go?

She didn't care. She permitted Jenny to look over last summer's wardrobe, to send new things in from the shops. She was listless and quiet, as if she was thinking alone in the dark. And Ron agreed with a sigh of relief, "Perhaps it's best. Get her away, see that she sleeps and eats and has sun and air and long lazy days and after that —"

He added, "You think I'm evading the issue? Perhaps I am. But frankly in her present state of mind she'd do nothing voluntarily, not even take the first step. Vernon can't help her — or us — unless she is willing. Your job is to see that she is willing, even eager. And perhaps a change of scene at this juncture will do the trick . . . that and the fact that before we can persuade her to see things reasonably, her general physical health must be restored."

Jenny said flatly, "She resents her father's will."

Yet the will would have seemed more than fair to anyone but Lydia.

Dr. Allen had left a considerable estate. His parents had been possessed of substantial means, and he had been an only child. He had made money, in the practice of his profession. Even with mounting taxes, inheritance and income, and diminishing dividends, the estate was large, and personal debts inconsiderable. He had owned the apartment in which they lived, the Southampton place was valuable, free and clear, his investments were largely in government bonds, and sound stocks, both common and preferred. And there was a large sum in life insurance which he had carried for many years.

Allen had left annuities to the two women who had served him faithfully in his office, a legacy to his hospital and small legacies to his servants. He had made his son-in-law coexecutor with his bank. He had left Lydia the apartment, the country house, their contents, and an outright sum of money. The residue was in trust, with Lydia as life tenant, the principal going to her issue. If she died without issue and Ron survived her, the principal was his. If he predeceased her, and she remarried, the money went to her issue, and if she died without children, it was to be divided between his medical school, the hospital, and various charities in which he was interested.

After the will had been read Lydia spoke bitterly to Ron . . . and he could not repeat what she said to anyone, not even to Jenny. She said, "Why don't you let me drink myself to death? I'm worth more to you dead."

They were alone in her room and she was lying quiet on her bed, a wet cloth across her strained and aching eyes. Fury mounted in him until every muscle was taut with it, but it passed quickly and he sat down beside her and took her in his arms. He spoke her name brokenly, in the most acute misery he had ever experienced, and found his throat convulsed and his face wet with tears. Sorrow welled up in him, grief for the man he had loved deeply, as he had loved his own father, and to whom he owed so much, grief for Lydia and the situation in which they found themselves.

Startled, she touched his cheek with her hand.

"You're crying. I'm sorry, Ron, terribly sorry. I didn't mean it," she said.

She spoke gently, wonderingly, like a child and he knew then, irrevocably, how much he loved her, not as a man loves his wife, but as he loves his child, wayward, ill, irresponsible.

Someone knocked and he was called to the telephone. He took the message in the library and returning, told Lydia, "I must go out." He bent to kiss her. "You'll be all right?"

She nodded. Jenny was out doing last-minute errands, so would not return for some time.

After Ron had left, Lydia lay there, thinking.

Restlessness grew in her, her nerves jangled, her body twitched. After a time she rose and went prowling around the apartment, looking for distraction . . . a book, a new magazine. The door to her father's room stood open, and after a little hesitation she went in. She had not been in here since his death. The room was clean and quiet, it looked empty and waiting. A horrible emptiness, a waiting which would not be fulfilled.

Lydia stood, looking around her. Tears were thick in her throat, remembering his patience, his unfailing kindness. The old cry rose in her heart, If only *I* had been kinder. She had so much taken him for granted, even his eventual death.

She couldn't stay here, shaking, crying, shattered by loneliness. Where was Ron, why didn't he come back? She snatched blindly at the books on the night table, several of them novels in bright jackets, medical books, fled with them to her own room, threw them on the bed and herself after them, weeping, for her father, for herself.

A long envelope fell from one of the books and lay on the blanket cover. Lydia sat up, pushing the hair from her eyes, and weighed it curiously in her hands.

The envelope was thick, unsealed, unaddressed.

She took out the many sheets, written in pencil in her father's small, unusually clear hand with the Greek e's.

Ron (he had written) I have just been to Lydia's room . . . I was anxious about her, she has always been susceptible to respiratory infections.

Now I know what you and Jenny have kept from me. Standing beside her, everything was very clear . . . ugly as daylight over squalor.

You did what you thought best and I am grateful. Yet you need not have spared me. This is my job. Somewhere I have failed or I would have realized my responsibility long ago.

You can't fight this singlehanded. You can't even fight it with me to help you, with the best backing of advice we can obtain. You would be torn, disseminated. And I cannot allow it.

Lydia is my child and I love her. But she is worthless. *Worthless.* I can't believe I've written that, and thought it before writing. I have been staring at the word for a full minute. It's true, my dear boy.

You are a valuable person, Ron. You have a great deal to give. You are an integrated human being, and a good doctor. Because you are, there will be other good doctors. One day you will teach them, all you know. But in order to grow and to give yourself as wholly as is possible to our profession you must have the single mind and the dedicated heart. These you have, but they will avail you little if your mind is to be distracted and your heart broken by the tragedy of your personal life.

I was very happy because of your marriage.

Now I am miserable. I should have known, I should have seen, I should have counseled and forbidden.

I am writing this to clarify my own thoughts. Tomorrow, I suppose, I will destroy it. Because tomorrow we must talk.

Ron, you must leave Lydia. You must cut her out of your life as a surgeon extirpates cancer, you must do it cleanly and for good. You love her, or, if you do not, you feel responsibility toward her. Love or no love, you must let her go. Because she will hamper you, she will eventually destroy you, your ambition and your usefulness.

To be useful is the highest mission a man can accomplish.

You will argue with me, now that I know, now that you no longer need keep this from me, that she may be cured.

Possibly. It has been done. But I am remembering Lydia, I have known her longer than you have. Even were she cured of her vice, what would be left? Never, I think, a whole woman, the woman for you, Ron.

Let her be my burden. I will take her away, I will work this out. But whatever happens, you must be free. It is not that I love you more — although you have been as a son to me — and not that I love my child less. It is because I owe this to our profession as you owe it.

You are not, I firmly believe, an ordinary man.

If it comes to that symbol of failure, a divorce, very well. But I am not looking far ahead. I am telling you only that with Lydia you will be a cripple.

You and she have no children to consider, thank God. For a long time I have hoped that there would be a child. I have known that Lydia has refused this responsibility. I have spoken to her on several occasions. She has always put me off, there was, she said, plenty of time. Once she told me flatly, she wished no children, she was afraid, she could not bear pain. She spoke with brutality and anger. I realize now that she was honest because she had been drinking.

Well, she was wiser than I, whatever her motive. She has no right to bear children. And thus, too, you would have half a life, incomplete, frustrated in the only immortality of which we can be sure.

Mine too. I cease with Lydia.

Tomorrow we will talk this out. Don't be afraid of me. I am calm, I am in no danger from this shock. Curious, isn't it, when it has been said that a shock would kill a man in my condition? But this recalcitrant heart must be a tougher organ than my colleagues believe or the cardiogram portrays. I can take this, but you are not to take it any longer. If I was dying I would still say this to you, Ron, I would charge you, with my final respiration, to leave my daughter, to abrogate this sacrifice of your

271

complete usefulness, to go your own way —

I am old and stubborn. Because I am stubborn I will see this through. So in another way I, too, will become useful once more. I will save you, my dear boy, despite yourself —

The letter ended there, breaking off without signature.

Lydia sat with the sheets scattered around her. She picked them up one by one and fitted the edges neatly together. She was as a woman stunned. She could not measure or evaluate the complete, crushing ferocity of this blow.

Little by little her thoughts cleared and centered.

Her father, who had loved her, believed her worthless. He had written that in cold, clear intelligence.

Ron was to leave her, her father had said so.

She herself had said, "Leave me. Let me drink myself to death." She had not meant it. She had not believed it. The foundations of her life were fixed in Ron, and in their marriage. Whatever she did, that remained. *He* remained.

She said aloud, in a hoarse, uninflected whisper, "He mustn't see this . . . I'll burn it."

She was silent. A voice screamed in her brain. It said, Your father wrote this and died. *You killed him.*

But she had loved him.

She had used him, yet she had loved him. She had respected him. He and Ron were the only human beings for whom she had ever known respect.

She could not sit here, thinking. She listened intently. No one moved or stirred . . . perhaps even the servants were out.

She went quietly to the dining room. Possibly someone had been careless.

She could not think and live. The very center of her being was numb.

Someone had been careless. She took the bottle back to her room with her, her hand shook, and the bottle rim clattered against the glass. She spilled a good deal on the floor.

Escape, forget, pretend it was never written.

You're worthless, he will leave you. He didn't need this horrible letter to convince him, he will leave you anyway, and then where will you be?

Ron came in and Jenny had not yet returned. He went to Lydia's room and found her on the bed in her blind and hideous stupor and stood looking at her experiencing once more his sense of hopeless failure.

The letter was beside her, the sheets together. He picked them up, wondering. Saw the writing, and his own name, and was transfixed with premonition. He read it, standing there. Once, twice.

She had read it, and had escaped from it. Temporarily there was no escape for him. Out of the muddled welter of his thoughts one fact emerged, clear and plain. She must not know that he, too, had read it.

He spoke to her, as if she could hear. He said to her, with terrible pity, "But I cannot abandon you, my darling."

He found the envelope and put the letter in it. If he destroyed it she would know, waking, and remembering. He put the envelope in a book which lay near by. Waking, and remembering, she would look for it, she would find it, and would destroy it herself.

She destroyed everything. Yet even if she destroyed him, he had pledged his word . . . "in sickness," he had said, "and in health, for better for worse."

He heard Jenny come in and went to tell her that Lydia was — worse.

Two days later Lydia and Jenny left with Aunt Sammy for Delray Beach. Lydia was quiet, very pale and shaken. She said nothing. But she clung to Ron, leaving, with an intensity which frightened him and which he understood. He dared not reassure her.

They were gone three months, during which time he was very busy. Aunt Sammy sent him brisk bulletins. Lydia was brown, she said, but not eating well. Friends came to see her, driving over from Palm Beach, and proved something of a distraction, although they were not the type of whom Aunt Sammy approved. Jenny was fine, a good girl, a wonderful nurse.

Jenny wrote meticulous reports. Lydia was listless, she said. Her general health improved slowly, and she would not swim or do more than sit on the beach. Twice, for all Jenny's vigilance, she eluded her and obtained liquor, and it had not been easy to deceive Aunt Sammy with a diagnosis of migraine or a bilious attack. Once she had packed, saying she must return north at once, and had not been easy to handle, either. Another time Amabell Jarvis and her brother, coming for a third visit, had insisted that Lydia return with them. She had done so despite Aunt Sammy's conventional disapproval, but Jenny had gone with her. It hadn't been very bad.

"She telephoned you from the Jarvis house," Jenny wrote, "and as you must have realized, she had been drinking. Openly, to the amazement of our hostess. But not very much. We'd been to Bradley's, she played and won. The excitement acted as a sort of release. Don't worry too much, Ron."

He thought, She can't have forgotten. She'll remember the letter, every word of it. He had looked for it after she left and it was gone.

Sometimes he talked, with himself, to his father-in-law.

I can't, he told him, you're asking something that is impossible. Perhaps, if you had lived — But you did not, and the responsibility is mine.

Mamie wrote him, and reported that she was obeying her doctor and her blood pressure was down. It was such a hard trip into town, with the snow and bad roads, that it paid her to keep well. Rose, Bill Treat's wife, was a fine person, the boy adored her. Pity she had none of her own, nor any prospects, but Bill wouldn't hear of it though he did seem to take more of an interest in Lily's boy these days. No new medical man had come into the district. There was some talk of a hospital to serve the rural community but nothing had come of it. You don't find that sort of money lying idle, Mamie wrote. She added that she would give almost anything to see him.

But he could not get away. He was busy with patients, with legal matters pertaining to Allen's will. He thought, When Lydia comes back, we will talk. She must have time now to get hold of herself, to recover at least physically from her father's death. And from, he thought, the legacy her father had unwittingly left her.

He had one diversion, a Mrs. Bates, the sister of a new patient, attractive, witty, a divorcée in her early thirties. She lived alone in a tiny house on upper Fifth Avenue. She was childless and glad of it. "I'd make a rotten mother," she said. Her interests were charity, art, golf and, she added frankly, "men."

She had been interested in Ron since her first visit to his office with her sister, Mrs. Rowen. While Mrs. Rowen was in the hospital, for a minor operation, he saw Sally Bates often. He dined with her first with a group. The second time, alone. She asked negligently, "Everyone's south, you don't mind, do you?"

"On the contrary," he told her, smiling.

After dinner, they sat over coffee in the miniature living room and she asked abruptly, "I suppose you know you're a very attractive man?"

"Naturally," he replied gravely, "as I have had innumerable picture offers."

Mrs. Bates smiled. She said, "I *meant* that, you know."

He felt gauche, awkward, and tried to cover it with the usual banality, which she waved aside impatiently. She said, "You're married, I suppose?"

He nodded, and Sally went on, "It's a pity. But usually, when a man has sufficiently matured to be of interest, he's already bespoken." She added, "But I believe we could be friends."

That was all, that evening. Generally when he made hospital rounds she was with her sister, once she was without her car and he drove her home. After Mrs. Rowen was discharged from the hospital and went south, Ron acquired the habit of dropping in on Sally occasionally at the cocktail hour or in the early evening. She had a stimulating mind and was better looking than a clever woman had any right to be. And was devastatingly honest.

One evening she said, "I wouldn't marry again if the man had as much charm as my ex-husband had money. I lead my own life. There's no one to hurt. I have no parents, no children, and the late lamented, now happily married to a more suitable female, doesn't care what I do. There's no alimony involved, so my objection to rematrimony isn't based upon that factor. . . . I believe that relationships between men and women — women of my sort, of course, who are in the minority — should be based on mutual need, and mutual respect for each other's individuality. I'm not promiscuous. I don't say that I always demand a mind," she added, thinking of the last man with whom she had been in love, "but when I encounter one, in the properly interesting wrappings, so much the better. Everything has its tenure, nothing lasts. When a love affair becomes a matter of habit, it was time to end it six months prior. Without recriminations or claims."

He understood perfectly. Sally was very attractive, he had been celibate a long time. But Sally constituted a temptation which he found he could, successfully, resist.

She understood too. She said, when he came in answer to a telephone message, a day or so later, "So now I have to call you and you come, unwillingly?"

He said something about being very busy.

She laughed. "I thought doctors were realists."

"Aren't they?"

"Scotch, at your elbow, if you want it. You're not, at any rate; you are, I fear, an idealist." She shrugged her shoulders. "Too bad," she said thoughtfully, "as my system isn't infallible. It doesn't work with idealists."

He asked, amused, "Why?"

"Most of them are sentimentalists too," she

said promptly, "or, if you prefer, romantics. And they have consciences." She looked at him, smiling. "Well, it's been fun knowing you and you can't condemn a woman for trying, can you?"

He left, a little relieved, conscious that he would miss her for a time, and aware that he would not be likely to encounter her again except casually and by coincidence.

Now and then, thinking of her, he informed himself that he was probably a fool. The majority of his acquaintances would not condemn him for infidelity, had they known his situation. That is, not if any lapse was conducted with discretion and, he fancied, Sally's "system" included discretion brought to a fine art. But a man can't absolve himself. At least, he couldn't. He thought, Of all the people who know me, those who know me best would condemn me least, yet be the most bitterly disappointed.

Mamie for one. As for Jenny, she was an idealist too.

Chapter 20

Toward the middle of April Ron flew to Delray to bring Lydia and Jenny back. Aunt Sammy was remaining for another three weeks, her daughter and grandchildren would join her. Ron allowed himself four days of sun, languor, and bright blue water. He swam, slept, fished, and relaxed, and that much was wonderful. Too, his first glimpse of Lydia gave him heart. She was rounder, so brown that her eyes were startling, and her fair hair bleached to silver gilt. She seemed very glad to see him, flinging herself into his arms at the airport, sitting close to him in the car on the way to the cottage, openly holding his hand. Jenny, observing this, was conscious of a heart grown leaden. Yet had she not worked and prayed for this, Lydia's returning health — for during the past two weeks she had been noticeably better and less nervous — and so, for Ron's returning happiness?

Jenny gave up her room to him, a small one connecting with Lydia's. Aunt Sammy sniffed, showing him his quarters.

"Too small to turn around in," she commented, "but Lydia wants you next door. Jenny's moved out, she has an ocean-front room. Lydia likes it back here, it's quieter." She added simply that there was plenty of room for Ron right in his wife's room, where, in her opinion, he belonged.

That first night Lydia came in while he was undressing. She looked like a brown child, in her thin white nightgown, her hair pinned on top of her head. She asked, "You'll leave the door open?"

"Of course." He took her in his arms and kissed her. "If you knew how grateful I am to Aunt Sammy and Florida —"

She said wistfully, "I wish we could have a cottage here on the beach."

She was thinking, he knew, of his promise. He said gravely, "Lydia, I promised you that after your father's death . . . that I would give up my practice — but —"

"Don't talk about it," she interrupted sharply, "don't let's talk about anything tonight."

She broke from his arms and ran back to her room. Later, when the lights were out, she called him. "Ron?" she said. "Please . . . I'm frightened."

That night she belonged to him again, holding him with an almost savage possessiveness, crying against his shoulder, imploring him in an agony of terror to love her, to hold her, never to let her go. He was startled beyond belief, he had for a brief moment the illusion that she was his, as he had never known her to be. Yet later he lay thinking beside her, in the sea-murmuring darkness. He thought wearily, She's afraid . . .

He asked her gently, "Lydia, will you talk to me now?"

But she replied drowsily, "I'm sleepy. Ron,

don't go, stay with me."

She was a child, believing in the impossible, the static, the budded flower which never comes to full blossom, the story which has no conclusion, the song which is an endless variation on one theme, repetitive, unaccomplishing, like the *Bolero*. Mamie used to say, "He who says A must say B." But Lydia believed you could go on saying A all your life.

There was a silly game you played as a child. You wrote your name on a sheet of paper and that of the girl you liked the best. You crossed out the matching letters and counted off the remaining, friendship, love, indifference, hate, kiss, court, marry.

Lydia could set down kiss and court. But not marry.

The next night the door stayed open, but she did not call him. She lay awake, straining to hear his even breathing. She thought, I have only to speak.

But the conviction was slowly growing in her that that was not the way. She had tried, she had even, for the first time, felt a personal and immediate urgency, straining lips and limbs and hands to hold him. But it was not the way. He had taken her, because he was a man, she thought bitterly, and she had offered. He could not love her. A woman who had killed her father, whom her own father thought worthless. *But he doesn't know that,* she told herself slyly.

He knew it, he wouldn't need Allen's letter to

convince him. Why hadn't she destroyed it? It was locked in her jewel case. It had destroyed her, but she could not consign it to ashes.

Father? she whispered, in the darkness.

She did not call Ron again, and presently they flew back to the northern spring, which had come suddenly, with all the promise of June. And at home Lydia took up the threads again and tried to weave them into the old, unhappy pattern.

She was altered, she would not see people, she was listless and distrait, she would not go out, she stayed home, Unesponsive to any effort to arouse her. Now and then, despite their watching, she drank heavily.

One afternoon at the end of May, Ron sat beside her, and watched her heavy eyes open and, with an effort, focus. Jenny was asleep, exhausted after three days and nights of horror and abasement.

Lydia said, "I feel ghastly."

He spoke, his hands resting quietly on the arms of his chair. "Is it worth it, to feel like this afterward?"

She was ill and racked, her body a network of irritated nerves. She answered sullenly, "How do I know?"

"Lydia, so much can be done. We can help you, all the way, if you want to be helped."

"I won't go to one of those places!" she cried at him. "You can't make me, I'd die first!"

That was it, she thought, quiet again. Die first.

Get out of this morass, this quicksand of terror. Be free . . . leave him free. That was what her father had wanted.

She whispered, "I can't, I'm afraid, I tell you, *afraid*."

He put his hand over hers. He said, sighing, "Poor child . . ." He thought she was afraid of the sanitarium, of the long struggle . . . physically painful, mentally shattering, nervously exhausting.

She said, after a moment, "Oh, go away, leave me alone, I'm sick, I tell you, I can't bear having you near me. Don't touch me . . . don't." Her voice rose, sharp as an arrow. "Get out," she said, *"get out!"*

He could leave her safely enough, so far as her present condition was concerned. He rose, measured something in a glass, poured water from a thermos, "Drink this, Lydia."

Docile, she drank, and then struck the glass from his hand. "Stop treating me as if I were a child!"

Ron went out, closing the door. He walked, stooped as an old man, into his father-in-law's library. Jenny, coming in, found him there, sitting at the desk, turning an ivory paper cutter over in his hands.

She said, "I slept like the dead. How is she?"

"As you'd expect." He added, "Jenny, this can't go on. There's no one to hurt now. She'll have to go away . . . even involuntarily."

"It will be dreadful."

"I know." The paper cutter snapped in his hands.

Jenny asked after a moment, "And your promise?"

"I can't keep it," he said, very white.

Her heart rose in exultation. He went on dully, "Somehow we'll work it out." He looked at her and tried to smile. "Go out," he ordered, "and get some fresh air, before dinner. You look utterly worn, sleep or no sleep. I'll stay here."

After she returned, while they were dining, a telegram came from Jenny's aunt. Her mother was ill, would she come at once?

She left for Cooperstown on the first train and Ron took her to the station. "I'll be back as soon as I can," she said; "from the telephone conversation with Dr. Herold, I'm convinced it isn't serious."

"Don't worry about us," he said, "we'll manage."

He had his work, his office hours, his calls, the hospital. Lydia was up the next day, very pale, starting at the least sound, but quiet. She came in while he was having breakfast and sat down with him, an almost unprecedented gesture. She drank a cup of coffee, black, strong, and went with him to the door when he was leaving. She spoke to him in the words he had used to Jenny. She said, and put her hand on his arm, "Don't worry."

Somehow he believed her, for the first time.

Lydia went back to her room. She removed

her jewel case from the small wall safe in her bedroom and opened it. She took her father's letter and held it in both hands. The paper grew damp under her grasp. She said aloud, "I'll read it again, I must."

She read it painfully, as a child reads, word for word, forming each with her lips.

She locked herself into the bedroom, and would not answer when later they called her for lunch, except to say, "I don't want any, please go away." The servants looked at each other, alarmed. Should they call the doctor? If Miss Jenny was here, she'd know what to do. The servants knew a good deal. Servants always do. They are not easily deceived.

After a while Lydia rose. She thought, There must be something in the house.

Ron kept things locked up, in his own medicine closet, even simple sedatives. She went into her bathroom, her face like a death mask, and took a clean, new razor blade from its wrappings. If you drew it across your wrists, swift, sharp, and deep, you did not feel much, and your life bled away from you painlessly, or so it had been said.

She cut her finger on the blade, a shallow cut and watched the red blood welling up, with a sudden surge of nausea. She felt faint, and ill, and dropped the razor in the wash basin and went unsteadily to her room and lay on the bed, with her handkerchief around the little wound, and presently it stopped bleeding and there was only the evidence on the handkerchief, and a small stain on the beautiful, intricately embroidered counterpane, that had been a wedding present.

"I can't do it," she whispered.

But what was left? Nothing, nothing. Her father gone, hating her. That isn't true, he didn't hate me. Ron, pitying her. She tried to sneer at Ron, dutiful husband, nature's nobleman. Old school tie and all that sort of thing, she said to herself.

She could not, it did not quite come off. He was all she had, he and her father. They hadn't belonged to her wholly, she hated and resented that. But something of them had belonged, a little, and she could not lose that much. She had lost her father, she must not lose Ron.

I'm destroying him.

Herself, him, as she had destroyed her father.

Lie still, will yourself to die, will that your heart stop beating and that your blood grow cold in your delicate veins, that your tangled nerves relax, and you grow still, all over, forever. Will it, demand it, of God. Say, Let me die, now . . .

Quickly, God, without pain.

She could not will it, God did not listen, and she was alive and weeping horribly, slow, dry, retching sobs. She dared not die and she dared not live.

She heard Ron come in, rose quickly and changed her frock with anxious shaking fingers, bathed her face and eyes and hands, and un-locked her door. She called, when he knocked, "I'll be right out."

He had been uneasy, entering the apartment, the very faces of the servants, closed against him, watchful and even pitying, had frightened him. But when he stood at her door he could hear her moving about, and the small sounds of normal living, hairbrush clatter on the glass-topped dressing table, water running, the single silly song of the enamel powder box with the musical insides, which he had bought for her.

Later she joined him in the living room and they dined. She ate practically nothing.

"Lydia, you are losing the weight you gained down south."

She asked, "How else did you expect me to get into my clothes?" She roused herself with an effort. "What happened today?" she asked.

He looked at her, astonished. She took so little interest in his work. He tried to meet her, now, more than halfway, spoke of a new man on the hospital staff, of an interesting clinic case, a Cae-sarean section — twins, and mother and children doing well. . . .

She was not listening, his eagerness sank back into itself, his voice lagged and his heart, and he went on with his dinner mechanically.

Afterward they had coffee in the library. And when she poured he saw her hand.

"What did you do to your thumb?" he asked.

The small wound was in the ball of her thumb.

Lydia set down the coffee pot. They were alone in the room. She looked at her hand, indifferently, as if it were not part of her. She answered, after a minute, "I tried to kill myself."

"Lydia!" His voice was utterly unnatural, his face erased of all expression, by shock. Steady, warned his common sense, she doesn't mean it, she's trying to frighten you.

Lydia raised her eyes. She said, "Well, it's true. Don't stare at me like that. I did try. With a razor blade. I cut myself, taking it out of the wrapper. It made me sick, so I couldn't do it. There must be an easier way, but even the easiest would be too hard."

"Lydia, for God's sake —"

She looked at him somberly. She asked, "What's the use, Ron? You're going to leave me, I know it."

"Leave you? What are you saying?"

"Of course." She said, after a moment, "From the very first. It was all there . . the first time you kissed me, the first time you said you loved me. You believed it, I believed it, and maybe it was true for a little while. Yet all along you were going to leave me, someday. I've known it for months, so have you. You knew it before I did, years ago, you knew it —"

He asked, "You are thinking of my promise?"

She lifted her heavy lids and looked at him. She repeated dully, "What promise?"

"The one you exacted of me . . . to give up practice after your father's death —"

She began to shake uncontrollably. "Why must you torture me?" she demanded. "Go on, say it, I killed him."

His heart steadied, his mind grew clear. The letter. He had almost forgotten it, in the exigencies of everyday living, in anxiety for his wife. He said sharply, "Lydia, don't be absurd, don't even —"

She had herself in hand again. She interrupted, leaning forward, "I'm sorry. Tell me again, Ron, about your promise."

He drew a long breath. "It's no use," he said. "I can't keep it. I don't believe you'd want me to. I'd be only half a man without my profession."

She said, "Wait here."

While he waited, and the coffee grew cold in the porcelain cups, she went into her bedroom, opened the wall safe, took out the jewel case and from it her father's letter. It took a long time, her fingers had grown thick and awkward, she fumbled with the combination of the safe, the lock of the jewel case, she dropped a sheet on the floor taking the letter from the crumpled envelope.

Returning to the library she walked lightly, feeling curiously elated. At the door the elation passed. Go back, put it away again, better still, tear it up, burn it . . . don't show it to him, you're out of your mind.

Why not show it? It can make no difference, his mind's made up, he is just stalling you, Lydia, he means to leave you, he *has* left you, you are forever alone.

She thought, Perhaps this will make it simpler.

The coffee things had been taken away. Ron was standing by the window, smoking. He turned as she came in. She said, holding out the letter, "I want you to read this."

Chapter 21

She tried to move toward him and could not. It was like being in a nightmare, her feet were rooted, she strained, but was motionless. Go, put it in his hands. But I can't, she told herself bewildered. She thought, I won't, I must be going mad, this can't be required of me.

Ron moved, instead. He put his arm around her, half led, half carried her to the couch, and forced her to sit down. He sat there beside her. The letter was in her hand, her fingers clenched on it. He said, "I don't have to read it, Lydia, I *have* read it."

The shock brought her up sharply, sitting upright, her eyes distended. She said faintly, "You've — read it?"

Her fingers relaxed and the sheets of paper fell from them, to the couch.

He sat still and close but not touching her. He said, "Yes."

"But when . . . when?" She began to tremble. "It was locked up," she said childishly, "I even took it with me, I —"

He said, "I thought you had disposed of it. You see, before you went south . . . I came in and found you —" he hesitated and then said it, the ugly word, firmly — "drunk . . . unconscious, on your bed, the letter beside you. So I read it."

She said quickly, almost incoherently, "I didn't

mean to. I found it in a book, by his bed . . . that afternoon. I took it, there wasn't any name on the envelope. I —"

"You don't have to excuse yourself."

A little color came back into her cheeks. She asked defiantly, "Well, what happens now?"

"I think," Ron told her, "that the answer lies with you."

"With me?" She looked at him, as if by looking she could strip him naked, as if she could see through the outer envelope, into the spirit, past the articulated bone and flesh, blood, and nerves and muscles.

"Of course."

After a little while she said, "But you're going to leave me." She picked up a sheet of the paper, struck it with her fingers. "This tells you to."

"I know."

She cried, "You're glad. You've been given permission —"

He took her hands and held them. She could feel the strong steady life in his hands, it penetrated her cold skin, it relaxed the tension of her fingers.

He said, "I am *not* going to leave you, Lydia, not ever. Not even if you beg me to."

The bright tears ran down her cheeks and into her mouth. After a little she whispered, "Why?"

He said wearily, "You don't understand. Your father didn't. If he had lived, then perhaps — I don't know." He was talking almost to himself, thinking aloud. "I can't," he said, "don't you see that? You're my responsibility. I can't abandon you any more than I could a wife who was an invalid, who was insane. I can't abandon you any more than I could a child, my child."

"Let my hands go," she demanded and he did so, his eyes steady and wounded. She said, "Don't look at me like that. I must get this straight. No matter what it does to us both. What did you mean when you said *if* my father had lived?"

"I don't know exactly," he admitted. "But, as nearly as I can see things now, if he had lived, if we had talked this out, why, then I might have left you. You see, my work is very important to me. It means a great deal more than — success or anything material. It is rooted in me, it has been my life. My work, and then you. Had your father survived, I might have persuaded myself to sacrifice you to my work, as he wished. Yet I didn't know, in the last analysis. . . . Also, no matter what else is not clear, we both know that he could not have lived much longer. Had you, during that time, submitted to him, given yourself up to medical treatment, and been restored to yourself, you would have been able to remake your life again. With perhaps another man."

She cried, "You're thinking of Timothy! I was never in love with him, I was never unfaithful to you."

"My dear," he said gently, "I could never for a moment believe that you had been." He touched her hair and she shrank back against the couch. He dropped his hand and said, "Perhaps I would have been" — he searched for the word — "happier? No, not that . . . yet less anxious if you had been. Is that so strange? For then I would have known that, after all, your body made normal demands, demands which I was unable to arouse. Your mind —" he shook his head, looking away from her — "imaginative," he said delicately — "corrupt." He broke off. He added, "No, I never thought you loved Timothy. I have always believed that, as much as you were capable of loving anyone, you loved me."

She asked, very white, "And if Father had lived and I still wasn't — cured?"

She said it like that, sharp, short, and final.

"I could not have left you then," he admitted.

"But I'm worthless," she cried. "He knew it!" She looked at him, almost insane with the attempt to make him understand. "Can't you see what that did to me, knowing what he thought? I was always so *sure* . . ."

"Yes," he said, "I see now. I hadn't, fully, before."

She asked, "Why don't you have me arrested?"

"You are talking," he said gently, "like a child again. If only you would grow up, Lydia."

She said, "I killed him, you can't deny it. Coming in, finding me, like that, writing that letter, it killed him, Ron."

He said, "There's no use asking you to spare yourself. Perhaps you can't now. You may have hastened his death, Lydia, yet it was inevitable."

"That doesn't help."

"No."

"Say something," she implored him, "anything, tell me I didn't, tell me —"

He said, "This is your burden, I can't help you. There is nothing I can say."

She was quiet, briefly. Then she said dully, "There's Jenny. What will you do about her?"

"What do you mean?"

"She's in love with you. She's right for you. You could love her, perhaps you do."

He shook his head.

"I have known no finer woman," he said. "There are three women, Lydia, who seem to me as fine as women can be. One is dead. She was my mother. One is Mamie, whom you have consistently refused to know. And the third is Jenny."

She said, "If you left me . . . you could have her."

Ron said, "You'll understand, will you? I could no more love another woman while you lived than I could become a different man. By loving, I mean as I understand it; wanting her near me, by night, by day. Sharing with her, drawing from her strength, living with her, in the difficult intimacy of marriage. I could perhaps be unfaithful to you," he said evenly, "for the little release that's in it, brief and bright. But I could not *marry*. I could not be happy, Lydia, in my personal life if you were somewhere, reckless and childish, determined to do yourself harm, surrendered to God knows what excesses."

She said, "If I were dead you could be happy. But I'm not. I tried." Her chin quivered. "I couldn't . . . I can't do even that for you."

Suddenly she was weeping, her head against him, and his body was shaken with the violence of her tears.

She said brokenly, "I'll do whatever you say."

"Lydia?"

"Doctors, anything. You can send me away . . . I'll try. I'm *not* worthless," she said. "I can't be, I mustn't. . . .

He held her, in silence. After a moment she spoke again. She asked simply, "Ron, do you love me?"

"I have always loved you."

"You're not in love with me," she said, "not any more . . . I knew it, that night in Delray. You were sorry for me. And then, I was just — any woman."

Astonishment pierced him like a sword. He had not believed her capable of so much insight.

He said, "Yet that night I hoped. . . ."

"You were disappointed. I — I try," she said, "and I love you, yet there's something —" She raised her face, broken with tears. "Perhaps," she said humbly, "I will learn."

He held her in his arms, her face once more hidden. When after a long time he spoke her name, and she did not answer, he found that she slept, falling asleep as a child does after emotion, worn with it, escaping into temporary peace.

He laid her gently on the couch, rose and stretched his cramped arms. Then he bent to pick her up and carry her back to her room. She woke, while he was undressing her and asked, bewildered, "Where am I? Ron, are you there?"

"I'm here," he said, "I'll be here, all night."

All night he lay beside her, not sleeping, watching her sleep, restlessly, stirring often, speaking so low he could not hear. And when she woke he was there and he saw her eyes open, numb with fear that they had altered, that she would have changed again.

She said, and smiled faintly, "Hello."

"Hello, Lydia."

"You stayed, all night."

"Yes."

She put her hand to his face. "You look dreadfully tired. You need a shave," she said, matter of fact, casual.

While he was shaving she came into his bathroom, in her sheer nightgown, a little jacket flung around her shoulders, her feet bare. "Ron?"

"Yes?"

"When Jenny comes back . . . when is she coming back?"

"The wire said tomorrow night."

"You'll tell her," she asked, one foot rubbing against the other.

"Tell her?"

"What — we decided. Could she go away with me?"

He said gently, trying not to betray his desperate hope, "I'm afraid not, dear."

"All right," she said slowly, "perhaps it would be better, with strangers." She leaned there against the door and looked at him soberly, as a grown woman looks. "It's funny about her," she said, "I — I hate being grateful to her, I hate depending on her. I do, you know. I should be fond of her, but I'm not. I hate her, I'm afraid of her, I'm jealous —"

She went away quietly, closing the door. And when later he followed her, she was in bed again. "I rang for my tray," she said.

"I wish I might stay here with you," he told her.

"I'm all right." She stretched her hand toward him. She said, "We don't know how this will end. Ron, don't try to be kind, tell me the truth, do you want to be free?"

He said, deeply moved, "It isn't a question of wanting or not wanting, Lydia. I cannot be free . . . no matter what you do."

He heard her sigh and when he spoke again she did not answer. He left her and went quietly to his own room.

She lay thinking, her eyes closed, a dull pain gnawing at them from her brain. She thought, The only way I can give him his freedom is to free myself from this beastliness. This *necessity*, she thought. Then he'll have his work again, complete, and himself.

She thought of Jenny and a faint glow of satisfaction warmed her. Jenny would never have him now. I'm not that noble, I thought I was. I'm not noble at all. I'm trying to fight. Fight what? Loss, loneliness, fear?

It would be fighting the hard way. She braced herself as if already upon her, that battle, the armies engaged.

Jenny came back the next night. Ron was not there and Lydia met her at the door. "How's your mother," she asked, "is she better?"

"Much; it was a temporary thing."

"It's late," said Lydia, "you've had dinner?"

"Yes, at the station. It was late so I —"

"Ron's out," Lydia said. She followed Jenny to her room and stood watching her take off her hat and coat. She commented, "You look tired."

"Just a little. It isn't anything really."

"I'm going away," Lydia said, after a moment.

"Away?"

"To . . ." She stopped, and swallowed. "Ron's making some arrangements," she went on, "I'm to see Doctor Vernon tomorrow . . . I suppose." She put up her chin, in defiance. "A sanitarium," she admitted, "that's the nice word for it."

Jenny took her hands. "I'm glad," she said, "so terribly glad."

"You are, I believe it," Lydia said. She shook Jenny's hands off. She said with her back to her, "I wonder why I had to be born into association with good people . . . my mother, my father, Ron, you —"

Jenny said, trying to laugh, "I'm not very good,

Lydia; you make us all sound . . ."

"Smug," said Lydia, "impossible. Elsie Dinsmore and Pollyanna. I don't mean that. I mean *good*. People who aren't good," she said, "they're easier to know . . . you can't be impatient with them, or irritable, they can't make you feel ashamed without saying a word." She turned back again. She said slowly, "You've been so kind to me, Jenny. I know it wasn't . . . just for me. But it was kindness all the same. Perhaps it was for me. Father used to say some people had an instinct for healing. They didn't care how dirty the patient was, in what filth he lived or thought. Ron's like that; and you. I'm grateful to you, and I hate being grateful. I'll miss you —"

Jenny asked, "I'm not to be with you?"

"No. Where I'm going they have their own nurses. I suppose it's better, a clean sweep. I'll miss you," she repeated, "you've been like something to lean on. I could loathe it, push it away, but somehow it was always there."

She left the room and Jenny heard her door close. She finished unpacking, methodically, asking herself, Why . . . but I'll be packing again, I suppose, tomorrow or at the most in a few days.

Ron came in and she went out in the hall and found him in the library as he had been the other afternoon, a few days ago. It seemed a long time.

He rose, his face illumined, "Jenny, it's good to see you. How was your mother?"

She told him briefly and then sat down on the

edge of the desk and looked up at him.

"Lydia tells me she's going to Vernon tomorrow."

"Yes."

"Of her own free will?"

"Voluntarily," he agreed.

She told him, as she had told Lydia, "I'm so glad."

"What's the matter," he asked sharply, "do you feel faint?"

"No, I'm tired, that's all." But the betraying blood had left her face. You could imagine it, you could project yourself into a possible future. Tell yourself, Someday they may be happy and will live as other happy men and women do, lie in each other's arms in the darkness, watch their children growing up. But knowing was different. And now she thought, I *know*.

"Jenny, look at me." He moved closer, took her chin roughly in his hand and tilted her face up. He asked slowly, "So that's how it is?"

Lydia had told him time and time again. He had discounted it, for many reasons. One was because he hadn't wished to face it, and its implications.

She said evenly, "That's how it is, Ron. I'm sorry."

"I haven't deserved it," he told her.

"I think you have, not that it matters." She drew a deep breath. "I'll go on the registry again," she said, "as long as Lydia no longer needs me."

302

Chapter 22

The following spring Ron Lewis drove over the winding road to the farm. It was a long time since he had seen spring on the silver and blue river and the little green buds leafing out, fragile as shadows.

Bill Treat had met him and it seemed odd that it was not Mat, beside him, his hands on the wheel. Bill looked well, and reported as they drove along that Mamie was fine and dandy again, that his wife was busy planting her kitchen garden, that the boy had grown a foot. . . .

"I was a fool," he told Ron soberly, "I never even thanked you for him . . . that time. When I think of all I missed, I could kick myself. Well, I'm thanking you now. I'm trying to make it up to the kid, he's only a little tyke after all." He added diffidently, "There'll be another by fall."

"That's fine," said Ron heartily.

"Well, you know how I felt. But last winter he was sick. Flu. We thought we'd lose him. Mrs. Lewis took turns with Rose nursing him, he was about burning up with fever. I thought Rose would go out of her mind. 'He's all we have,' she said; she couldn't be crazier over him if he was her own, and I got to thinking, I ain't being fair to Rose."

"You weren't," Ron agreed.

"I'm scared," said Bill. "But she said to me

the other night, 'Look here, it's my risk and if I want to take it that's my business.' She showed me a piece in a magazine, how it wasn't the risk it used to be and how a case like — like Lily's, for instance, was pretty rare." He added simply, "I'd give anything if you was going to look after her, doc."

"I wish I could."

After a minute Bill said, "I was sorry to hear about your wife. Mamie told me she'd been sick."

"She has been," said Ron, "for a long time, following her father's death. But she's all right now. She's coming up here to join me in a day or two."

"That's fine," said Bill.

Yes, Lydia was all right now. Someday he would forget the months during which she had been shut away from him, the summonses, the consultations, the relapses, in which she turned sullen and defiant, demanding to be set free, crying that she would kill herself in her own time and in her own way, but she wouldn't be pulled to pieces like this, it was slow torture.

She had skill, the best money could buy, and watching. They healed her body, and then her mind, slowly, with infinite patience. She was nursed, she was distracted, she learned to eat simply, to exercise, much against her will. Walks at first and tennis later, and occupational therapy to occupy her hands and her mind. The relapses grew less frequent and Vernon, coming back after a long talk with her, in the green hill country where they had put her, told Ron, "She'll be all right. I don't have to tell you that we can't guarantee that one day she won't backslide deliberately . . . but the compulsion is gone now. She'd have to force herself back. She'll be very sick if she drinks again. If she can conquer the sickness, school herself not to mind it, then we've lost — but I am hoping that will never happen."

Ron was silent. Then he said, "It will be up to me, I think."

He was silent remembering, and Bill was silent too. They were content, and companionable.

Presently they reached the farm and Mamie was waiting for them. She looked well, very gray now, but her little face was brown and firm and her eyes luminous. She kissed him and said, "I'm glad you're here. Breakfast's ready . . . you must be starved. That train gets in at an ungodly hour. Lydia'll hate it!"

"She's driving up," said Ron. "I was against it, but she promised she wouldn't drive fast and would spend a night on the road. She planned to come with me, as you know, but there have been things to attend to — selling the Southampton house and all — and she wouldn't hear of my waiting." He coughed and Mamie looked at him sharply.

"Been sick?" she demanded.

"Just a cold. I'll be fine now that we have a vacation."

"I fixed your rooms for you like you said," she

305

told him. "I hope Lydia will be comfortable. Run up and wash, you're dirty as can be. Hurry."

The table was laid, the best linen, blue dishes, daffodils in a honey jar. In the bay window the canary sang his heart out, the old cat came in from the kitchen and rubbed against Ron's foot, and the spaniel, alert under the table, barked without conviction.

A fly buzzed against the window and Ron heard Bill Treat's little boy laughing.

"Lord," he said, "it's peaceful here."

"Appearances," said Mamie, "are deceptive. Anything but peaceful — if you ask me, something happening every day. Half the farm boys have gone to camp, I don't know what's going to happen. Some have enlisted. There was a murder on the county road not so long ago — people named Velner. They took a young boy to help when their son had been drafted . . . got him out of some home or other. And because they wouldn't let him take the car one night . . ." She shrugged her shoulders. "That's how it is; seems like there's always something. The young people around here are half-witted, most of the time, running to the city to look for work, or giving up steady jobs to go and find some sort of defense job, saying that they might as well make it while they can as everything's going to blow up anyway."

Mrs. Roberts came in from the kitchen with another batch of pancakes and fresh coffee. She was as round and amiable as ever.

"Take some hot," ordered Mamie, "don't eat those cold cakes. You're pretty thin."

"I haven't been sleeping," Ron admitted.

"You will, here," she promised. "How long can you stay?"

"I don't know. A month maybe . . . I shouldn't, of course."

Yet he should. Aunt Sammy, steam-rollering, had called in one of Allen's closest friends, a general man, hard-headed and hard hitting. Over all of Ron's protests, she had insisted upon it. And Dr. Bateson had looked him over and said briefly, "Be at my office tomorrow at eleven . . . and no nonsense."

There wasn't anything organically wrong, that much was certain. Why should there be? He was only thirty-eight, in the best years of his life. But he was tired, clear through, tired of thinking, of remembering.

"You're no good to your patients this way," Bateson had said definitely, "might as well make up your mind. You're burned out. Get away, quit work, eat and sleep and don't think, and you'll be back on your feet again. No one can do it for you, you'll have to do it yourself."

He hadn't done it himself. Lydia had done it. The day he brought her home she had said, in the car, "You look awful, Ron."

"I don't feel it, I've just had a cold, that's all."

She asked, "Could you go away, with me?"

She kept her voice down but he sensed her anxiety. She had put on weight, her eyes were

307

clear, she had never looked so pretty. Her hands were steady, in her lap, and she had lost that driven, ghost-ridden look which had been so appalling.

She said before he could answer, "We could go up to the farm, Ron, I'd like that."

"Would you really?"

"Honestly," she told him.

He had been happier then than in a long time. He roused himself now to hear Mamie repeat a question. "How's Jenny?" she asked.

"Fine. I haven't seen her much. She's doing private duty and was south all winter with an elderly patient. There'll be a place for her in the hospital soon, if she wants one again."

"Wonder if she'd come back here," said Mamie; "there's been a sort of shake-up and she might get that county job. But perhaps she wouldn't want to, being away so long. We need people like her. Ron, what's happening to the world? I get so confused, the way things chop and change. Not so long ago, we were all for France. Now there isn't any France."

"There's Free France," he said, "and the spirit. Someday it will conquer."

"That Hitler," she said. She interpolated, "You smoke too much. First he was going to free his people from communism, then he was friendly as anything with Russia, and now he's fighting her. It's crazy. Ron, what do you think, what will happen to us, to the world?"

"If I could answer that, I'd be a modern Nostradamus," he said.

"Who? Oh, the man who wrote that book centuries ago. I saw a picture about him, on the screen, when I was in the city last week," said Mamie, "made me creep. Well, I know one thing . . ."

"What's that?"

"Whatever comes," said Mamie, "we can take it. We've done it before, and we can again. This is a great country. It still has growing pains. But nothing stands still, Ron, everything's a struggle. We're learning that."

She rose. "You go sit on the porch," she ordered, "while we clear away. I told Herb Andrews you were coming up and he said, 'Tell Ron he'd better come fishing.' Herb's the happiest man I know, he doesn't have a care in the world. Just eats and sleeps and fishes. Hasn't a cent more than he needs and doesn't want it. Too old to be drafted and wouldn't dream of volunteering. Perfectly easy in his mind about everything. Said the other night, when he stopped in and sold me a string of bass, that whatever happened he'd go on fishing. War couldn't stop that, he said. Fish didn't know anything about war, went on biting just the same. Minnows still swam into the net and you could still dig worms. No government on earth would be interested in his boat or his shack. He didn't owe anyone, he got enough to eat, and he slept like a log . . . I don't suppose there's anyone to worry about either, not even himself. I said, 'You make me tired, you're nothing but a vegetable, you're not more than half alive.' "

Ron laughed. "What did he say?"

"Just that there were worse things than being a vegetable, especially if you were the kind that didn't end up in a stew, and as for being half alive, he'd picked the right half . . . the other half was the kind of living that had to fret and worry and scrape and read headlines, but his half just went fishing."

"He's got something there," said Ron, and went out on the porch to sit in an old rocker which fitted the small of his back as if it had been built for it, and finish his cigarette. But until Lydia came he could find no real satisfaction in letting down, in relaxation. In a way, it was a sort of test . . . this brief separation. Not that they hadn't been separated for months but then he knew where she was, with whom, he knew she was cared for, guarded.

She came, driving the big car expertly, telephoning from the town, and he took the old car and went to meet her and bring her out. She was well, she said, a little tired. Everything had been arranged. Aunt Sammy had insisted on buying most of the furniture. She said, tossing her hat on the seat beside her, as she followed Ron into the yard, and sat there while he came to get her and the bags out of the car, "This is lovely."

"I've always said so."

Mamie came running out, shyer than Ron had ever known her. But Lydia kissed her cheek and said, "I'm sorry I was so long in getting here, Mamie," and Mamie understood.

It was late afternoon, and Ron and Lydia were walking about the place when Mamie came to find them. She said, "Ron, it's more work again."

"What's up?"

"Mrs. Sims, half a mile down the road. Her grandson just phoned. They can't get their doctor from town."

"All right." He smiled at Lydia. "Sorry, darling," he said, and then looked anxiously at Mamie, "I'm not a general man," he told her.

"You can't have forgotten everything you learned except bringing babies," said Mamie sharply. "It hasn't been that long."

Ron grinned and loped off toward Lydia's car. Mamie turned to Lydia. She said, "She won't be his only patient, now that folks know he's here."

Grandma Sims had a pain in her middle. It wasn't her appendix as she had had that removed twenty years ago and the memory of her operation was still the high spot of her existence. Ron, after his examination and a conversation with her harried daughter-in-law, correctly concluded that at seventy-six cucumbers and six cups of coffee were not indicated. Mamie had the usual remedies, at home . . . being so far from a drugstore, you kept up your medicine closet . . . and a diet was prescribed. It took him some time to convince Grandma Sims. Her black eyes snapped.

She said, "Young man, I used to change your diapers!"

Ron was no sooner home again than Bill Treat called him. The boy had cut his hand on a scythe and Rose wasn't feeling very good, she had fainted that morning, but hadn't wanted him to say.

"You see!" said Mamie, as they were having supper. "No wonder doctors don't want to drive twenty-five miles for little upsets. Of course," she added, "they didn't get Joey Dillon into the hospital in time. His appendix ruptured. His folks waited for the doctor, instead of taking him right in. His mother said he'd always been colicky since he was little."

"How old was he?" asked Lydia. . . . "Mamie, this is the most marvellous coffee. . . ."

"Fourteen," said Mamie.

"My God," Ron exclaimed, "what a damnable waste."

He was white, he looked older, angry and hostile, as if he hated the world. Lydia said, "Don't look like that." Then she added, "Yet I don't blame you."

They went to bed early. Lydia, Mamie said, would be tired after her long drive.

Wandering into Ron's room, Lydia said, "Mamie gave me the room next door, I bet she thought it was funny."

"She has a nice mind," Ron answered, "she wouldn't think it funny. She knows you've been ill."

"I'm not ill now."

He warned, "Lydia, be sure. This is a new life we are beginning together, and when you came back from the sanitarium . . ."

"I had to adjust myself. It was a little like being born again, a lot like being married again, not for the first time. I was . . . shy. You won't believe that, Ron. Afraid of myself, even a little of you. You've been so good to me . . . so patient." She came close and told him steadily, "I belong to you . . . something you've saved, something you —"

"Oh, hush," he said and took her in his arms.

When he woke in the morning she was not there. He heard her talking to Mamie downstairs and when he joined them they were already at breakfast. "I'm sorry I'm late," he apologized.

"Do you good to sleep," Mamie said.

"Pay no attention to him," said Lydia. "Doesn't he look dreadful? The bearded wonder."

"I didn't stop to shave," he said defensively.

"That's obvious, darling." He hadn't heard her speak and laugh like that for so long. She said, "Mamie, give me some more coffee and go on telling me about the hospital."

"There isn't any," Mamie said, "I mean, that talk died down, and as far as I can see there isn't a doctor young or old who wants to come out here and take over. I suppose it's going to be a case of the survival of the fittest. You have to go back to depending on your neighbors as you did a hundred years ago."

"Some of them are good neighbors," began Lydia. She stopped, and then "Who's this?" she asked.

It was Bill Treat Jr. He marched in, rosy and sturdy, in a clean, faded blue shirt, small brown pants and grown-up suspenders. His feet were bare and he had a bunch of tulips clutched tightly in one hand. He paraded up to Lydia, acknowledging Mamie and Ron's greetings courteously but abstractedly. He said, in his clear birdlike voice, "These is for you. Mommie sent them." He stepped back and surveyed Lydia. He said, "You're *pretty.*"

"Quick," said Ron, "on the uptake. Knows all the answers. Should be on Information, Please. A quiz kid if ever I saw one." He lifted Bill Jr. to his knee. He said, "William, this is my wife . . . and you don't remember me, do you?"

"No. She's pretty," said William loudly.

"So you said before. Yet they never get tired of hearing it. Young man," said Ron, "I brought you into the world and by God I did a good job of it."

"Mustn't swear," said William, and struggled down from Ron's knee. "I have to go," he said importantly. He smiled brilliantly at Lydia. "I'll be seein' you," he pledged, so grown up, so tough and swaggering, that they dissolved into helpless laughter as soon as he was out of hearing.

"What do you mean you brought him into the world?" Lydia asked.

He said, "Don't you remember . . . the time

I came up here, my last holiday, when William's mother died and —"

She said, "Oh!" She looked at him a moment. "Tell me about it," she said, "again. This time I'll listen."

Two weeks later they were walking down the country road, very fresh and green, Lydia picking her way like a cat in the ruts. She complained, "I'm tired. Let's sit down here, on this big stone. Ron, it's been wonderful —"

"It's been more than that."

She touched his hand. She said, "I'm learning. I'm trying . . . Ron, I've been talking to Mamie. She told me little Bill nearly died last year. . . ."

"He nearly dies now," he said, "every time you speak to him. I never saw such a crush . . . if he was twenty years older I'd knock his damned little block off."

She said, "He's a dear little boy. I never knew a child before, not really. Listen, Mamie's been praying that you'd come back here and practice."

"How can I?" he asked slowly.

She said, "We've such a lot of money. We don't need it. We could build a little hospital, Ron, you could run it. We could build ourselves a house, here on your father's land. . . ."

He was so moved he could not speak. Then he said, "Lydia, I — I can't tell you how —"

She said swiftly, "Don't misunderstand me, Ron. It would take me a long time to adjust

315

myself. You would have to be very patient. Yet you will be. I won't even promise you to be — content. But I'll be happy, because we are together."

He said, "You must think it over."

"I have thought, even since I came here. It would be Father's hospital. You'll work it out somehow." Her voice shook, but she added, "Perhaps he will know, perhaps he will believe I am not altogether worthless."

"My dearest," he said brokenly, "my dearest . . ."

He took her in his arms, and sat there holding her. A car rattled by and the driver leaned out and shouted, grinning. But they did not hear him.

She said, after a while, "I'll miss — people. And New York. But it won't matter. I can always go down and have a whirl. When I can trust myself, Ron." She looked at him steadily. "I won't ever be much of a person," she said honestly. "I tire of things, I'm mean and shallow and a little crazy, I think. After I came home from the sanitarium I felt new, made over. I was in a way. I didn't want to drink, it made me sick to think of it. Yet I'm not new, I'm the same person, just cured of a disease. My character is the same . . . flawed and ugly. But I love you, and somehow you love me."

"Always."

She said, with a flash of mischief, "You're even a little in love with me again."

He said, "William's fault. He made me realize I'd better go back to what they call up here my courtin'."

She said, "It will work out. The hospital, I mean. Other men will come. And you'll have a full life. A laboratory maybe someday for research. We won't need much for ourselves. . . . I'm extravagant," she said, "but not as extravagant as I was. That was part of the other thing, an ugly part. Ron, you'll help me?"

He asked, "Lydia, why do you want to do this?"

"You gave up a great deal for me," she said, "you gave up your real freedom because you felt I was your responsibility, your obligation. Well, you're mine. That's the way it is. I have to do something too. I won't be nice about it. I'm not self-sacrificing by nature." She pulled away from him and rose. "Let's go and tell Mamie," she said. "And soon we'll have to go back to New York. There's the apartment to get rid of, and your practice to wind up, and a hundred and one things." She added, "Jenny will be glad. She's big enough."

He took her hand and they walked along the road together. She said after a minute, "You must write Jenny . . ." She stopped and looked at him. "I'll always think she was right for you, Ron."

He said soberly, "How do I know? I did not love her, I loved you. Someday there will be a man who is free to love her and none other, and

317

he will be right for her, much more right than I."

At the gate William came running to meet them, clinging to Lydia's hand, looking at her with his clear worshiping eyes. He said, "Mother wants you should come to supper someday. Maybe tomorrow?" asked William.

On the porch Lydia stopped and looked back at small William running across the space between the houses. She said, "Wait, Ron, before we tell Mamie."

"Well?"

"I want a child," she said, "a little boy . . . rather like William, but more like you." Her face was grave and strained, and her mouth shook pitiably and because he could not bear to see her afraid again he took her and held her so that he could not see her face. She asked, low, "Am I, will I be — fit?"

He said, "Yes; but . . . are you afraid?"

"Terribly. But not as afraid as I will be happy," she told him.

They went into the house to find Mamie. He thought, There's a long road ahead. It would not be easy. But he dared believe in himself and in Lydia. He had delivered Bill Treat's son out of death and Bill Treat's son had brought, with his mother's flowers, the promise of life in both his hands to offer it to Lydia. Tomorrow would be another day, and what it holds no man can foretell, but he would have his work and his wife, and God willing his child. He would try not to fail them, or himself. Lydia would forget, perhaps, all that had brought her step by step to the old farmhouse. She would find things hard, she would sacrifice, it might seem to her a good deal, and what she gained she might not greatly value. He did not know. He could only hope.

"Mamie," Lydia was crying, "Mamie, where are you? We've something to tell you."

Mamie came out of the kitchen smoothing her apron. "What in time," she began, "have you two been up to?"

"You tell her," Ron said. "It's your gift, Lydia, not mine."

And while Lydia told her he stood in the bay window listening, watching them. The spring wind came sweetly through the open windows, a wind of promise, the very breath of life.